indigo slam

AN ELVIS COLE NOVEL

ROBERT CRAIS

An Orion paperback

First published in Great Britain in 1998
by Orion
This paperback edition published in 1999
by Orion Books Ltd,
Orion House, 5 Upper St Martin's Lane,
London WC2H 9EA

An Hachette UK company

Reissued 2012

A CIP catalogue record for this book
is available from the British Library.

Printed and bound in Great Britain by
Clays Ltd, St Ives plc

The Orion Publishing Group's policy is to use papers
that are natural, renewable and recyclable products and
made from wood grown in sustainable forests. The logging
and manufacturing processes are expected to conform to
the environmental regulations of the country of origin.

www.orionbooks.co.uk

Praise for Robert Crais

'[...] [...] fully [...] *Time Out*

'A[...]
re[...]

'T[...] simple [...]
ac[...]

'This is a novel of suspense, and it keeps racking up the tension until the very end. Crais is an old-timer at this kind of thing and *The Watchman* is him at his very best' *Irish Times*

'Robert Crais is shooting for the big time with all guns blazing' *Guardian*

'The story moves along at top speed in typical Crais fashion, with lots of ultraviolence, gallows humour and great writing. A must from first page to last' *Independent*

'Robert Crais is a major crime-writing talent, exciting and thought-provoking' *Sunday Express*

'Crais tells a compelling tale that glints with wit, intelligence and expertise' *Literary Review*

Robert Crais is the author of seventeen novels, including the international bestsellers *The Forgotten Man*, *The Last Detective*, *Demolition Angel* and the Edgar-nominated *L.A. Requiem*. He has two additional Edgar nominations as well as Anthony and Macavity awards for his series of Elvis Cole and Joe Pike crime novels. Crais has also written for acclaimed television shows such as *L.A. Law* and *Hill Street Blues*. *Hostage* has been made into a major motion picture featuring Bruce Willis. He lives in Los Angeles. Visit his website at www.robertcrais.com.

By Robert Crais

The Monkey's Raincoat
Stalking the Angel
Lullaby Town
Free Fall
Voodoo River
Sunset Express
Indigo Slam
L.A. Requiem
Demolition Angel
Hostage
The Last Detective
The Forgotten Man
The Two Minute Rule
The Watchman
Chasing Darkness
The First Rule
The Sentry

Dedicated with love and admiration
to Wayne Warga and Collin Wilcox,
two worthy men, always overhead.

ACKNOWLEDGMENTS

The author appreciates the invaluable help of several people: Howard A. Daniel III of the Southeast Asian Treasury regarding foreign currencies and printing techniques; Kregg P.J. Jorgenson for his insights into Seattle, the U.S. Customs Service, and crime in the Pacific Northwest; and Gerald Petievich for opening many doors at the United States Secret Service, and to the agents there who, requesting anonymity, shared their technology and expertise. Any errors contained herein are the author's sole responsibility.

A novel is a world built by many hands. Thanks to Patricia Crais, Lauren Crais, William Gleason and Andrea Malcolm, Jeffrey Liam Gleason, Carol and Wayne Topping, Aaron Priest, Norman Kurland, Robert Miller, Brian DeFiore, Lisa Kitei, Marcy Goot, Chris Murphy, Kim Dower, Samantha Miller, Jennifer Lang, and, especially, Leslie Wells.

SEATTLE

At two-fourteen in the morning on the night they left one life to begin their next, the rain thundered down in a raging curtain that thrummed against the house and the porch and the plain white Econoline van that the United States Marshals had brought to whisk them away.

Charles said, 'C'mere, Teri, and lookit this.'

Her younger brother, Charles, was framed in the front window of their darkened house. The house was dark because the marshals wanted it that way. No interior lights, they said. Candles and flashlights would be better, they said.

Teresa, whom everyone called Teri, joined her brother at the window, and together they looked at the van parked at the curb. Lightning snapped like a giant flashbulb, illuminating the van and the narrow lane of clapboard houses there in Highland Park on the west side of Seattle, seven and one-half miles south of the Space Needle. The van's side and rear doors were open, and a man was squatting inside, arranging boxes. Two other men finished talking to the van's driver, then came up the walk toward the house. All four men were dressed identically in long black slickers and black hats that they held against the rain. It beat at them as if it wanted to punch right through the coats and the hats and hammer them into the earth. Teri thought that in a few minutes it would be beating at her. Charles said, 'Lookit the size of that truck. That truck's big enough to bring my bike, isn't it? Why can't I bring my bike?'

Teri said, 'That's not a truck, it's a van, and the men said we could only take the boxes.' Charles was nine years old, three years younger than Teri, and didn't want to leave his bike. Teri didn't want to leave her things either, but the men had said they could only take eight boxes. Four people at two boxes a person equals eight boxes. Simple math.

'They got plenty of room.'

'We'll get you another bike. Daddy said.'

Charles scowled. 'I don't want another bike.'

The first man to step in from the rain seemed ten feet tall, and the second seemed even taller. Water dripped from their coats onto the wooden floor, and Teri's first thought was to get a towel before the drips made spots, but, of course, the towels were packed and it wouldn't matter anyway. She would never see this house again. The first man smiled at her and said, 'I'm Peterson. This is Jasper.' They held out little leather wallets with gold and silver badges. The badges sparkled in the candlelight. 'We're just about done. Where's your dad?'

Teri had been helping Winona say good-bye to the room they shared when the men arrived fifteen minutes ago. Winona was six, and the youngest of the three Hewitt children. Teri had had to be with her as Winona went around their room, saying, 'Good-bye, bed. Good-bye, closet. Good-bye, dresser.' Beds and closets and dressers weren't things that you could put in eight boxes. Teri said, 'He's in the bathroom. Would you like me to get him?' Teri's dad, Clark Hewitt, had what he called 'a weak constitution.' That meant he went to the bathroom whenever he was nervous, and tonight he was *very* nervous.

The tall man who was Jasper called, 'Hey, Clark, whip it and flip it, bud! We're ready!'

Peterson smiled at Teri. 'You kids ready?'

Teri thought, of course they were ready, couldn't he see that? She'd had Charles and Winona packed and dressed an hour ago. She said, 'Winona!'

Winona came running into the living room with a pink plastic *Beverly Hills 90210* raincoat and a purple toy suitcase. Winona's straw-colored hair was held back with a bright green scrunchie. Teri knew that there were dolls in the suitcase, because Teri had helped Winona pack. Charles had his blue school backpack and his yellow slicker together on the couch.

Jasper called again, 'C'mon, Clark, let's go! We're drowning out there, buddy!'

The toilet off the kitchen flushed and Teri's dad came into the living room. Clark Hewitt was a thin, nervous man whose eyes never seemed to stay in one place. 'I'm ready.'

'We won't be coming back, Clark. You're not forgetting anything, are you?'

Clark shook his head. 'I don't think so.'

'You got the place locked up?'

Clark frowned as if he couldn't quite remember, and looked at Teri, who told him, 'I locked the back door and the windows and the garage. They're going to turn off the gas and the phones and the electricity tomorrow.' Someone with the marshals had given her father a list of things to do, and Teri had gone down the list. The list had a title: *Steps to an Orderly Evacuation.* 'I just have to blow out the candles and we can go.'

Teri knew that Peterson was staring at her, but she wasn't sure why. Peterson shook his head, then made a little gesture at Jasper. 'I'll take care of the candles, little miss. Jasper, get 'em loaded.'

Clark started to the front door, but Reed Jasper stopped him. 'Your raincoat.'

'Hunh?'

'Earth to Clark. It's raining like a bitch out there.'

Clark said, 'Raincoat? I just had it.' He looked at Teri again.

Teri said, 'I'll get it.'

Teri hurried down the hall past the room that she used to share with Winona and into her father's bedroom. She blew out the candle there, then stood in the darkness and listened to the rain. Her father's raincoat was on the bed where she'd placed it. He'd been standing at the foot of the bed when she'd put it there, but that's the way he was – forgetful, always thinking about something else. Teri picked up the raincoat and held it close, smelling the cheap fabric and the man-smell she knew to be her father's. Maybe he'd been thinking about Salt Lake City, which is where they were going. Teri knew that her father was in trouble with some very bad men who wanted to hurt them. The federal marshals were here to take them to Salt Lake City, where they would change their names. Once they had a Fresh Start, her father had said, he would start a new business and they would all live happily ever after. She didn't know who the bad men were or why they were so mad at her father, but it had something to do with testifying in front of a jury. Her father had tried explaining it to her, but it had come out jumbled and confused, the way most things her father tried to explain came out. Like when her mother died. Teri had been Winona's age, and her father had told her that her momma had gone home to see Jesus and then he'd started blubbering and nothing he'd said after that made sense. It was another four days before she'd learned that her mother, an assistant night manager for the

4

Great Northwest Food Store chain, had died in an auto accident, hit by a drunk driver.

Teri looked around the room. This had been her mother's room, just as this house had been her mother's house, as it had been Teri's for as long as she could remember. There was one closet and two windows looking toward the alley at the back of the house and a queen-size bed and a dresser and a chest. Her mother had slept in this bed and kept her clothes in this chest and looked at herself in that dresser mirror. Her mother had breathed the air in this room, and her warmth had spread through the sheets and made them toasty and perfect for snuggling when Teri was little. Her mother would read to her. Her mother would sing 'Edelweiss.' Teri closed her eyes and tried to feel the warmth, but couldn't. Teri had a hard time remembering her mother as a living being; she remembered a face in pictures, and now they were leaving. Good-bye, Mama.

Teri hugged her father's raincoat tight; just as she turned to leave the room she heard the thump in the backyard. It was a dull, heavy sound against the back wall of the house, distinct against the rain. She looked through the rear window and saw a black shadow move through the rain, and that's when Mr. Peterson stepped silently into the door. 'Teri, I want you to go to the front door, now, please.' His voice was low and urgent.

Teri said, 'I saw something in the yard.'

Peterson pulled her past a third man in a still-dripping raincoat. The man who'd been loading the boxes. He held his right hand straight down along his leg and Teri saw that he had a gun.

Her father and Charles and Winona were standing with Mr. Jasper. Her father's eyes looked wild, as if at any moment they might pop out right onto the floor. Jasper said, 'C'mon, Dan, it's probably nothing.'

5

Her father clutched Jasper's arm. 'I thought you said they didn't know. You said we were safe.'

Jasper pried Clark Hewitt's hand away as Mr. Peterson said, 'I'll check it out while you get 'em in the van.' He looked worried. 'Jerry! Let's move!'

The third man, Jerry, reappeared and picked up Winona. 'C'mon, honey. You're with me.'

Jasper said, 'I'll check it with you.' Jasper was breathing fast.

Mr. Peterson pushed Jasper toward the door. 'Get 'em in the van. Now!'

Jasper said, 'It's probably nothing.'

Charles said, 'What's happening?'

A loud cracking came from the kitchen, as if the back door was being pried open, and then Peterson was pushing them hard through the door, yelling, 'Do it, Jasper! Take 'em!' and her father moaned, a kind of faraway wail that made Winona start crying. Jerry bolted toward the street, carrying Winona in one arm and pulling Teri's father with the other, shouting something that Teri could not understand. Jasper said, 'Oh, holy shit!' and tossed Charles across his shoulder like a laundry bag. He grabbed Teri *hard* by the arm, so hard that she had never felt such pain, and she thought her flesh and bone would surely be crushed into a mealy red pulp like you see in those Freddie Krueger movies, and then Jasper was pulling her out into the rain as, somewhere in the back of the house, she heard Mr. Peterson shout, very clearly, 'Federal Marshals!' and then there were three sharp *BOOMS* that didn't sound anything like thunder, not anything at all.

The rain fell like a heavy cloak across Teri's shoulders and splattered up from the sidewalk to wet her legs as they ran for the van. Charles was kicking his legs, screaming, 'I don't have my raincoat! I left it inside!'

The driver had the window down, oblivious to the rain, eyes darting as Jerry pushed first Winona and then Clark through the side door. The van's engine screamed to life.

Jasper ran to the rear of the van and shoved Teri inside. Clark was holding Winona, huddled together between the boxes and the driver's seat. Winona was still crying, her father bug-eyed and panting. Two more *BOOMS* came from the house, loud and distinct even with the rain hammering in through the open doors and windows. The driver twisted toward them, shouting, 'What the fuck's happening?!'

Jerry yanked a short black shotgun from behind the seat. 'I'm with Peterson! Get 'em outta here!'

Jasper clawed out his gun, trying to scramble back out into the rain, saying, 'I'm coming with you!'

Jerry pushed Jasper back into the van. 'You get these people outta here, goddamnit! You get 'em out *now*!' Jerry slammed the door in Jasper's face and the driver was screaming, 'What happened?! Where's Peterson?'

Jasper seemed torn, but then he screamed back, 'Drive! Get the hell outta here!' He crushed past the cardboard boxes to the van's rear window, cursing over and over, 'Always some shit! Always goddamn bullshit!'

The van slid sideways from the curb as it crabbed for traction. The driver shouted into some kind of radio and Jasper cursed and Teri's father started crying like Winona, and Charles was crying, too. Teri thought that maybe even Federal Marshal Jasper was crying, but she couldn't be sure because he was watching out the van's square rear window.

Teri felt her eyes well with tears, but then, very clearly, she told herself: *You will not cry.* And she didn't. The tears went away, and Teri felt calm. She was soaked under her raincoat, and she realized that the floor was wet from rain that had blown in when the doors were open. The eight cardboard boxes that held the sum total of their lives were wet, too.

Her father said, 'What happened back there? You said we were safe! You said they wouldn't know!'

Jasper glanced back at her father. Jasper looked scared, too. 'I don't know. Somehow they found out.'

Teri's father shouted, 'Well, that's just great! That's wonderful!' His voice was very high. 'Now they're gonna kill us!'

Jasper went back to staring out the window. 'They're not going to kill you.'

'That's what you people said before!' Her father's voice was a shriek.

Jasper turned again and stared at Teri's father for the longest time before he said, 'Peterson is still back there, Mr. Hewitt.'

Teri watched her brother and sister and father, huddled together and crying, and then she knew what she had to do. She crawled across the wet, tumbled boxes and along the van's gritty bed and went to her family. She found a place for herself between Winona and her father, and looked up into her father's frightened eyes. His face was pale and drawn, and the thin wet hair matted across his forehead made him look lost. She said, 'Don't be scared, Daddy.'

Clark Hewitt whimpered, and Teri could feel him shivering. It was July, and the rain was warm, but he wasn't shivering because he was cold. Teri said, 'I won't let anyone hurt us, and I won't let anything happen to you. I promise.'

Clark Hewitt nodded without looking at her. She held him tightly, and felt his shaking ease.

The van careened through the night, hidden by the darkness and rain.

8

Three years later:
Los Angeles

CHAPTER 1

It was plant day in the City of Angels. On plant day I gather the plants that I keep in my office and take them out onto the little balcony I have overlooking West Los Angeles, where I clean and water and feed them, and then spend the remainder of the afternoon wondering why my plants are more yellow than green. A friend who knows plants once told me that I was giving them too much water, so I cut their rations in half. When the plants turned soft as well as yellow, another friend said that I was still drowning them, so I cut their water in half again. The plants died. I bought new plants and stopped asking other people's advice. Yellow plants are my curse.

I was sneering at all the yellow when Lucy Chenier said, 'I don't think I'll be able to get away until much later, Elvis. I'm afraid we've lost the afternoon.'

'Oh?' I was using a new cordless phone to talk to Lucille Chenier from the balcony as I worked on the plants. It was in the low eighties, the air quality was good, and a cool breeze rolled up Santa Monica Boulevard to swirl through the open French doors into my office. Cindy, the woman in the office next to mine, saw me on the balcony and made a little finger wave. Cindy was wearing a bright white dress shirt tied at the belly and a full-length sarong skirt. I was wearing Gap jeans, a silk Tommy Bahama shirt, and a Bianchi shoulder holster replete with Dan Wesson .38-caliber revolver. The shoulder holster was new, so I was wearing it around the office to break in the leather.

Lucy said, 'Tracy wants me to meet the vice president of business affairs, but he's tied up with the sales department until five.' Tracy was Tracy Mannos, the station manager of KROK television. Lucy Chenier was an attorney in Baton Rouge, Louisiana, but she had been offered a job by KROK here in Los Angeles. She had come out for three days to discuss job possibilities and contract particulars, and tonight was her last night. We had planned to spend the afternoon at the Mexican marketplace on Olvera Street in downtown LA. Los Angeles was founded there, and the marketplace is ideal for strolling and holding hands.

'Don't worry about it, Luce. Take all the time you need.' She hadn't yet decided if she would take the job, but I very much wanted it to happen.

'Are you sure?'

'Sure, I'm sure. How about I pick you up at six? We can go for an early dinner at Border Grill, then back to the house to pack.' Border Grill was Lucy's favorite.

'You're a dream, kiddo. Thanks.'

'Or, I could drive over and pull the veep out of his meeting at gunpoint. That might work.'

'True, but he might hold it against me in the negotiation.'

'You lawyers. All you think about is money.'

I was telling Lucy how rotten my plants looked when the outer door opened and three children stepped into my office. I cupped the receiver and called, 'Out here.'

The oldest was a girl with long dark hair and pale skin and little oval glasses. I made her for fifteen, but she might have been older. A younger boy trailed in behind her, pulling a much smaller girl. The boy was wearing oversized baggy shorts and Air Nike sneakers. He looked sullen. The younger girl was wearing an *X-Files* T-shirt. I said, 'I'm being invaded.'

Lucy said, 'Tracy just looked in. I have to go.'

The older girl came to the French doors. 'Are you Mr. Cole?'

I held up a finger, and the girl nodded. 'Luce, don't worry about how long it takes. If you run late, it's okay.'

'You're such a doll.'

'I know.'

'Meetcha outside the building at six.'

Lucy made kissy sounds and I made kissy sounds back. The girl pretended not to hear, but the boy muttered something to the younger girl. She giggled. I have never thought of myself as the kissy-sound type of person, but since I've known Lucy I've been doing and saying all manner of silly things. That's love for you.

When I turned off the phone, the older girl was frowning at my plants. 'When they're yellow it means they get too much sun.'

Everyone's an expert.

'Maybe you should consider cactus. They're hard to kill.'

'Thanks for the advice.'

The girl followed me back into my office. The younger girl was sitting on the couch, but the boy was inspecting the photographs and the little figurines of Jiminy Cricket that I keep on my desk. He squinted at everything with disdain, and he carried himself with a kind of round-shouldered skulk. I wanted to tell him to stand up straight. I said, 'What's up, guys? How can I help you?' Maybe they were selling magazine subscriptions.

The older girl said, 'Are you Elvis Cole, the private investigator?'

'Yes, I am.' The boy snuck a glance at the Dan Wesson, then eyed the Pinocchio clock that hangs on the wall above the file cabinet. The clock has eyes that move from side to side as it tocks and is a helluva thing to watch.

She said, 'Your ad in the Yellow Pages said you find missing people.'

'That's right. I'm having a special this week. I'll find two missing people for the price of one.' Maybe she was writing a class report: *A Day in the Life of the World's Greatest Detective.*

She stared at me. Blank.

'I'm kidding. That's what we in the trade call private-eye humor.'

'Oh.'

The boy coughed once, but he wasn't really coughing. He was saying 'Asshole' and masking it with the cough. The younger girl giggled again.

I looked at him hard. 'How's that?'

The boy went sullen and floated back to my desk. He looked like he wanted to steal something. I said, 'Come away from there.'

'I didn't do anything.'

'I want you on this side of the desk.'

The older girl said, 'Charles.' Warning him. I guess he was like this a lot.

'Jeez.' He skulked back to the file cabinet, and snuck another glance at the Dan Wesson. 'What kind of gun is that?'

'It's a Dan Wesson thirty-eight-caliber revolver.'

'How many guys you kill?'

'I'm thinking about adding another notch right now.'

The older girl said, 'Charles, *please.*' She looked back at me. 'Mr. Cole, my name is Teresa Haines. This is my brother, Charles, and our sister, Winona. Our father has been missing for eleven days, and we'd like you to find him.'

I stared at her. I thought it might be a joke, but she didn't look as if she was joking. I looked at the boy, and then at the younger girl, but they didn't appear to be joking either. The boy was watching me from the corner of his eye, and there was a kind of expectancy under the attitude. Winona was all big saucer eyes and unabashed hope. No, they weren't kidding. I went behind my desk, then thought better of it and came around to sit in one of the leather director's chairs opposite the couch. Mr. Informal. Mr. Unthreatening. 'How old are you, Ms. Haines?'

'I'm fifteen, but I'll be sixteen in two months. Charles is twelve, and Winona is nine. Our father travels often, so we're used to being on our own, but he's never been gone this long before, and we're concerned.'

Charles made the coughing sound again, and this time he said, 'Prick.' Only this time he wasn't talking about me.

I nodded. 'What does your father do?'

'He's in the printing business.'

'Unh-hunh. And where's your mother?'

'She died five and a half years ago in an automobile accident.'

Charles said, 'A friggin' drunk driver.' He was scowling at the picture of Lucy Chenier on my file cabinet, and he didn't bother to look over at me when he said it. He drifted from Lucy back to the desk, and now he was sniffing around the Mickey Mouse phone.

I said, 'So your father's been gone for eleven days, he hasn't called, and you don't know when he's coming back.'

'That's right.'

'Do you know where he went?'

Charles smirked. 'If we knew that, he wouldn't be missing, would he?'

I looked at him, but this time I didn't say anything. 'Tell me, Ms. Haines. How did you happen to choose me?'

'You worked on the Teddy Martin murder.' Theodore Martin was a rich man who had murdered his wife. I was hired by his defense attorneys to work on his behalf, but it hadn't gone quite the way Teddy had hoped. I'd been on local television and in the *Times* because of it. 'I looked up the newspapers in the library and read about you, and then I found your ad in the Yellow Pages.'

'Resourceful.' My friend Patty Bell was a licensed social worker with the county. I was thinking that I could call her.

Teri Haines took a plain legal envelope from her back pocket and showed it to me. 'I wrote down his birth date and a description and some things like that.' She put it on the coffee table between us. 'Will you find him for us?'

I looked at the envelope, but did not touch it. It was two-fifteen on a weekday afternoon, but these kids weren't in school. Maybe I would call a lieutenant I know with the LAPD Juvenile Division. Maybe he would know what to do.

Teresa Haines leaned toward me and suddenly looked thirty years old. 'I know what you're thinking. You're thinking that we're just kids, but we have the money to pay you.' She pulled a cheap red wallet from her front pocket, then fanned a deck of twenties and fifties and hundreds that was thick enough to stop a 9mm Parabellum. There had to be two thousand dollars. Maybe three. 'You see? All you have to do is name your price.'

Charles said, 'Jeezis Christ, Teri, don't tell'm that! He'll clean us out!' Charles had moved from the Mickey phone and now he was fingering the Jiminys again. Maybe I could handcuff him to the couch.

Teri was looking at me. 'Well?'

'Where'd you get the money?'

Her right eye flickered, but she did not look away. 'Daddy leaves it for us. It's what we live on.'

Teresa Haines's hair hung loosely below her shoulders and appeared clean and well kept. Her face was heart-shaped, and a couple of pimples had sprouted on her chin, but she didn't seem self-conscious about them. She appeared well nourished and in good health, as did her brother and sister. Maybe she was making all of this up. Maybe the whole thing was their idea of a joke. I said, 'Have you called the police?'

'Oh no.' She said it quickly.

'If my father was missing, I would.'

She shook her head.

'It's what they do, and they won't charge you. I usually get around two grand.'

Charles yelled, 'Ripoff!' A small framed picture fell when he said it, and knocked over three Jiminy figurines. He scuttled toward the door. 'I didn't do anything. Jeezis.'

Teresa straightened herself. 'We don't want to involve the police, Mr. Cole.' You could tell she was struggling to be calm. You could see that it was an effort.

'If your father has been gone for eleven days and you haven't heard from him, you should call the police. They'll help you. You don't have to be afraid of them.'

She shook her head. 'The police will call Children's Services, and they'll take us away.'

I tried to look reassuring. 'They'll just make sure that you guys are safe, that's all. I may have to call them myself.' I spread my hands and smiled, Mr. Nothing-to-Be-Afraid-of-Here, only Teri Haines didn't buy it. Her eyes cooled, growing flinty and hard and shallow with fear.

Teresa Haines slowly stood. Winona stood with her. 'Your ad said confidential.' Like an accusation.

Charles said, 'He's not gonna do frig.' Like they'd had

this discussion before they came, and now Charles had been proven right.

'Look, you guys are children. You shouldn't be by yourselves.' Saying it made me sound like an adult, but sounding that way made me feel small.

Teresa Haines put the money back in the wallet and the wallet back in her pocket. She put the envelope in her pocket, too. 'I'm sorry we bothered you.'

I said, 'C'mon, Teresa. It's the right way to play it.'

Charles coughed, 'Eat me.'

There was a flurry of fast steps, and then Teresa and Charles and Winona were gone. They didn't bother to close the door.

I looked at my desk. One of the little Jiminys was gone, too.

I listened to Cindy's radio, drifting in from the balcony. The Red Hot Chili Peppers were singing 'Music Is My Aeroplane.' I pressed my lips together and let my breath sigh from the corners of my mouth.

'Well, moron, are you just going to let them walk out of here?' Maybe I said it, or maybe it was Pinocchio.

I pulled on a jacket to cover the Dan Wesson, ran down four flights to the lobby, then out to the street in time to see them pull away from the curb in a metallic green Saturn. The legal driving age in the state of California is sixteen, but Teresa was driving. It didn't surprise me.

I ran back through the lobby and down to the parking level and drove hard up out of the building, trying to spot their car. A guy in a six-wheel truck that said LEON'S FISH almost broadsided me as I swung out onto Santa Monica Boulevard, and sat on his horn.

I was so focused on trying to spot the Saturn that I didn't yet see the man who was following me, but I would before long.

CHAPTER 2

Teresa Haines's Saturn turned south past the West Hollywood Sheriff's Station, then east onto Melrose. I didn't career through oncoming traffic to cut her off, and I didn't shoot out her tires. Teri Haines was driving just fine, and I wasn't sure what to do if I stopped them. Hold them at gunpoint for the police?

Fairfax High School was just letting out, and the sidewalks were dotted with boys toting book bags and skateboards, and girls flashing navel rings. Most of the kids were about Teri's age, some younger, some older, only these kids were in school and she wasn't. Charles leaned out of the passenger-side window and flipped off a knot of kids standing at the bus stop. Three of the kids gave back the finger, and somebody threw what appeared to be a Coke can which hit the Saturn's rear wheel.

Teri cruised along Melrose past hypermodern clothing outlets and comic-book shops and tour groups from Asia until she turned south onto a narrow residential street. Modest stucco houses lined the street, and the curbs were jammed with parked cars. Some of the cars probably went with the houses, but most belonged to people who'd come to shop on Melrose. I stopped at the corner and watched. The Saturn crept halfway down the next block, then turned into the drive of a yellow bungalow with an orange tile roof and a single royal palm in the yard. The three Haines children climbed out of the car and disappeared into the bungalow. Retreating to familiar territory after an unsuccessful meeting with the detective.

I cruised past their house, found a parking space on the next block, and walked back. Screams weren't coming from within, no music was blaring, and no smoke was rising from either windows or roof. Charles had probably passed out.

I stood on the sidewalk in front of the house next door and thought about things. When I was following them I had known exactly what I would do: I would locate their residence, then call one of my friends at Children's Services or the LAPD, and that would be that. Only the house and the yard, like the car and the children, appeared well maintained, and now I wasn't so sure. Maybe these kids were fine, and all calling the cops would get me was a house full of frightened children. Still, all I could see was the outside of the house. Inside, there might be rats. Inside, there might be squalor and vermin. Only one way to find out. When in doubt, snoop.

I slipped past the Saturn and walked up the drive and climbed atop their gas meter to peek into the kitchen. I couldn't see the kids, but the kitchen was neat and orderly and clean. No rats, no flies, no towers of unwashed dishes. I moved to the next set of windows, chinned myself on the sill, and peered through a little dining room to the living room. It occurred to me that Charles might see me peeking in the window and bean me with a brick, but these are the chances you take when you're a world-class private eye. Life is risk. The TV was on, and Charles and Winona were watching *Aeon Flux*. No one was pushing, no one was shoving. Like the kitchen, the living room was neat and orderly and in good repair. Eleven days without an adult, and everything looked fine.

I dropped back to the drive, then went to my car. I

watched the house and tried to look unthreatening so that nervous neighbors wouldn't call the cops. A black guy in a gray LeBaron cruised past. I smiled and nodded, but he looked away. Maybe I wasn't unthreatening enough.

Two hours and ten minutes later I started the car and left to pick up Lucy Chenier. I wasn't sure that I was doing the right thing by leaving them alone, but I wasn't sure it would be best to have them scooped up by a herd of social workers and put into a foster home either. Of course, they might be safer in such a home, but they didn't look particularly endangered where they were. Maybe I should stop advertising in the Yellow Pages.

The KROK studio and corporate offices are on Olympic Boulevard, just west of Doheny Drive along the southern edge of Beverly Hills. It's a large, modern building of steel and glass in an area of chain grocery stores and expensive high-rise apartments and upscale health clubs. Twentieth Century-Fox isn't far away, and neither is Century City.

Olympic was jammed with rush-hour traffic, and the valet parking attendants at the health club across the street from KROK were running double time to keep up with the incoming flux of agents and lawyers and studio execs anxious to pump iron and shoot hoops after a hard day telling the truth. Four guys in Versace suits were standing together outside the health club, staring toward KROK, only they weren't staring at the building; they were staring at Lucy Chenier. Lucille Chenier is five inches over five feet, with light auburn hair and green eyes and the rich, healthy tan of someone who spends a lot of time outdoors. She had attended Louisiana State University on a tennis scholarship, and she still played regularly and was serious about it. You could see it in the way she carried herself, and in the way her muscles

21

worked beneath her skin. I pulled to the curb and felt myself smile as she climbed into my car. 'Did you take the job?'

'Not yet, but they made a very interesting offer.' Her green eyes were amazing. Absolutely without bottom.

'How interesting?'

She smiled wider.

'That's pretty interesting.'

She leaned across the shifter and kissed me, and I kissed her back. 'Did you make a reservation at Border Grill?'

'I did.'

'Fantastic!' She settled back in the seat. 'We can eat, then I'll pack, and then we'll have the rest of the evening to sip champagne and do whatever.'

I smiled at her, and felt an enormous warmth grow between us. 'Whatever.'

Lucy told me the particulars of her interview as we drove toward Santa Monica, and then I told her about Teresa Haines. I told her about Charles and Winona, and how I had followed them back to their home, and as I told it, a vertical line grew between Lucy's eyebrows in a kind of frown. She said, 'They've been alone for eleven days?'

'Yep.'

'With no adult supervision?'

'That's right.' The line grew deeper.

'And you looked through the windows?'

'Everything seemed fine.'

Lucy was squirming so hard that I thought she was going to pop out of the seat. She shook her head and held up her hands and said, 'Seeming fine isn't enough. We'd better turn around.'

I said, 'Hunh?'

'*Turn around.* We're going into that house and make sure.'

I turned. Maternal hormones are awesome to behold.

Twenty minutes later, we left Melrose and once more cruised their house. Everything appeared in order and unchanged, and the Saturn was still in the drive. At least they weren't out joyriding. 'They're fine.' The professional detective makes his pronouncement.

'Stop.'

We parked in the drive behind the Saturn, went to the front door, and rang the bell. Charles threw open the door without checking, and when he saw us his eyes bulged and he tried to slam the door. 'Run! They've come to take us away!'

I pushed open the door and stepped inside, Lucy behind me. He was a game kid, grunting and huffing against the door as he slid across the floor. I said, 'Relax, Charles. No one is going to take you away.'

Teresa Haines said, 'Stop it, Charles.' She said it once, sharply, and he stopped.

Teresa and Winona were in the living room. The TV was off, so they probably hadn't been watching it. Winona was standing behind Teresa, and Teresa looked calm and in absolute control of her environment. She wasn't looking at me; she was looking at Lucy. I said, 'I wanted to make sure you guys were okay.'

Charles said, 'I tol' ya we shouldn't'a said anything! They're gonna put us in a home!'

Teresa crossed the living room, and extended her hand to Lucy. 'My name is Teresa Haines. Who are you?'

Lucy took her hand. 'Lucille Chenier. I'm a friend of Mr. Cole's.'

The house smelled faintly of tomato sauce and garlic. Teri said, 'Are you with Children's Services?'

Lucy smiled, friendly and relaxed. 'Not at all. I don't

live in Los Angeles. I'm just visiting.' Lucy released Teresa's hand, but kept the smile as she walked to the kitchen. 'Mr. Cole tells me that you've been without your father for over a week?'

'I'm sure he'll be back soon.'

'I'm sure he will. Do you mind if I look around?' Her smile was warm and reassuring.

Charles said, 'What about a search warrant? You gotta have a search warrant if ya wanna look around!' He was scowling at us from the door, his hand still on the knob as if he might suddenly throw open the door and run for it if we made the wrong move.

Teri said, 'If it will make you feel better.' Ignoring Charles.

Lucy disappeared into the rear. Teresa looked back at me and cocked her head. I shrugged. 'She's a mother.'

'Did you have second thoughts about helping us?'

'I wanted to make sure that you're okay.'

'So you followed us.'

'Sure.' Grilled by a kid. 'I wanted to see your living conditions. Also, Charles stole a figurine from my office.'

Charles yelled, *'I didn't do anything!'* He made a big deal out of waving his arms and pulling at his hair. *'Why does everyone blame me?'* Drama.

Teri said, 'Charles.' Her eyes narrowed and it sounded like a warning.

I held out my hand. 'Give it over, kid.'

Charles dug the Jiminy out of his pocket and threw it on the floor. 'Frig!'

Teri glared lasers at him. 'Charles.'

Charles scooped up the Jiminy, then skulked over with it, ready to run in case I tried to hit him.

He put it in my hand, then scuttled away. I looked at the Jiminy, then tossed it back to him. 'Keep it.'

Charles looked surprised.

Teresa said, 'You don't have to do that.'

'I know.'

She said, 'I'm sorry about this.'

I shook my head. It happens.

Teresa Haines took a breath, then said, 'So you've seen that we're fine.'

'Looks like you've got things under control.'

'So you won't have to call the police.'

I looked into the calm eyes, only they weren't so calm anymore. A tiny flame of fear was burning behind the oval glasses. 'You were aware of that possibility when you came to see me, yet you came anyway. You must be very concerned for your father.'

The flame grew brighter and her face worked, and then the flame was gone and the eyes were calm again. She had fought to control herself, and she had won. Some kid. She said, 'Of course I'm concerned. He's my father.'

Lucy came back and headed into the kitchen. 'Your room is very neat, Teresa. Do you share it with Winona?'

'Yes, ma'am.'

The smile. 'Charles's room is a mess.'

Teresa said, 'I know. You can't get him to make his bed.'

Lucy laughed. 'I know what that's like. I have an eight-year-old son who's the same way.'

Charles made the coughing sound, and this time you could make out the word 'Bitch.'

I said, 'Hey.'

Charles skulked into the dining room as far from me as he could get, put the Jiminy on the table, and pretended to play with it.

I could hear Lucy open the refrigerator and the stove and the pantry. A serious inspection was taking place, and it was coming from somewhere very female. Something was happening between Lucy and Teresa and, in a way I didn't quite understand, I was no longer a part of it. 'What do you and your brother and sister eat, Teresa?'

'I cook for us.'

Winona said, 'I cook, too.'

Lucy came back and smiled at Winona. 'I'll bet you're a good cook, honey.'

'We make spaghetti.'

'My favorite. Did you have spaghetti for breakfast?'

Winona laughed. 'We had Cheerios.'

Lucy smiled at Winona again, then glanced at me and nodded. I said, 'Is there food?'

'Yes.'

Teresa said, 'I shop and cook for us even when Daddy's home. It's no big thing.' She seemed affronted that anyone would think otherwise.

I said, 'We just wondered, that's all. It looks like you're in good shape.'

Teresa looked hopeful. 'Then you aren't going to turn us in to Children's Services?'

I frowned at her. 'You're underage. You can't live here alone.'

Lucy hooked her arm through mine, and squeezed. Tight. She smiled warmly at Teresa. 'He won't call them just yet, dear, but we'll have to consider that as we go.'

Now I frowned at Lucy. 'What's this 'we' business?'

Lucy squeezed tighter. 'But don't you worry about that for now, Teri. Right now, he's going to find your father.'

I said, 'I am?'

Lucy turned the warm smile my way. 'Of course you are. If you know what's good for you.'

I said, 'Mm.'

Lucy turned back to Teresa. 'Have you eaten dinner yet?'

26

'I was about to cook.'

Lucy beamed. 'We were just on our way to a very nice restaurant. Why don't you join us?' She gave my arm a little shake. 'Wouldn't that be fun?'

I said, 'Mm.'

Winona said, 'I want spaghetti.'

I phoned Border Grill and asked if they could make the reservation for a party of five. They could.

The five of us went to dinner – me, Lucy, Teresa, Winona, and Charles. We had to take the Saturn. Winona sat between Lucy and me; Charles threw a sauteed shrimp at the waitress, tried to steal a pepper mill, and ate two desserts. The bill came to a hundred eighty-two fifty.

Mm.

CHAPTER 3

I took Lucy to LAX early the next morning and waited with her at the gate. When it was time to board we held each other, and then she disappeared into the jetway. I went to the observation window, stared at her plane, and tried not to look depressed.

An older gentleman with a walking stick appeared at the glass next to me and shook his head, glum. 'Another visit, another parting.' He shook his head some more. 'Me, I never say good-bye.'

'Good-byes are tough, all right.'

'They're permanent. You say good-bye, you're inviting disaster.'

I looked at him. 'What do you mean, permanent?'

'The big birds come in, the big birds go out, and you never know what's going to happen.' He sighed. 'I hope nobody put a bomb.'

I looked at him harder. 'Do I know you?'

He made a shrug.

'I think I've seen you here before.' He was stooped and balding with baggy, old-man pants.

He shrugged again. 'God knows, it's possible. I spend my whole life in this place, picking people up, sending people off. All without a good-bye.'

'I'm pretty certain.'

He patted my arm and smiled. It was a kindly smile, and wise. 'That's where you're wrong, young man. The only thing certain is death.' He patted my arm again and leaned close. 'I hope you didn't say good-bye. For her sake.'

Great.

I left him at the window, walked out to the car, and took Sepulveda Boulevard north through the city, the footloose and fancy-free detective reentering the workaday world. I was missing Lucy already and feeling grumpy because of it, but I was also excited and hopeful. She felt that the job with KROK was going to work out, and, if it did, she and her son, Ben, would move here and then I could see her all the time. Thinking about that made me smile, and the grumpiness faded. The sun had climbed nicely, the air had warmed, and a slight orange haze was building in the east past Baldwin Hills. Perfect convertible weather even with the coming smog.

I followed Sepulveda north to Washington Boulevard, then turned east past the old MGM Studios to La Cienega when I spotted a gray Chrysler LeBaron edging across the white line three cars behind me. He stayed on the line a few seconds without changing lanes, the way you do when you want to see something ahead of you, and then he disappeared. I thought that maybe it was the same LeBaron I had seen outside Teri Haines's home, but then I said, 'Nah.' I was probably watching too many episodes of *Cops*.

Fifteen minutes later I parked behind Teri Haines's Saturn and went to the door. I kind of expected to find the house in smoking ruins, but I guess Charles had passed out from overeating. *Lighten up, Cole. He's only a kid.* Sure. They probably said that when Attila was a kid, too.

Teresa answered the door in jeans and pink Keds and an oversized white T-shirt. I said, 'Where are Charles and Winona?'

'I took them to school.' I guess she could read my surprise. 'Charles is in sixth grade and Winona is in third. You don't think I'd let them grow up stupid, do you?'

'I guess not.' Put in my place by a fifteen-year-old.

The house was as neat and clean as it had been yesterday, only now it was quiet. A washing machine chunked somewhere beyond the kitchen and street sounds sifted in through the windows. Teresa let me in, and stood well to the side as she showed me into the living room. Watchful. 'Would you like coffee? I always make coffee before I take them to school.' A blue mug sat steaming on the coffee table atop an issue of *Seventeen*.

'What about you?'

'I have a cup.'

'I meant about school.'

She sat at the edge of the couch and laced her fingers over a knee. She was so close to the edge that I thought she might slip off. 'We move around a lot, and I got tired of always being the new kid, so I took the GED exam last year when we moved to Arizona.' GED. General Equivalency diploma. 'I don't go to school.'

'Ah.'

She pursed her lips. 'I'm sorry, but is talking about me going to help you find my father?'

'Maybe. You just told me that you used to live in Arizona, which is something I didn't know. Maybe he went there.'

She flushed a hard red behind the glasses. I guess she didn't like being shown up either.

'If I'm going to find your dad, I'm going to need what we in the trade call a lead. That means I'll ask you a lot of questions, you'll tell me what you know, and maybe we'll get somewhere. You see?'

She nodded, but she wasn't happy about it.

I took out my pen and prepared to make notes. 'Tell me about him.'

Her father's name was Clark Rudy Haines. He was

thirty-nine years old, five feet ten inches tall, one hundred fifty-two pounds. He had light brown hair, though he had lost most of it years ago, and brown eyes. He wore glasses. She told me about the glasses, then she had some of the coffee, and then she stared at me.

I said, 'Okay.'

'Okay, what?'

'I need more than that.'

She looked uncomfortable, as if she couldn't imagine more than that. As if she was suddenly thinking that having me here was a bad idea, and she was wishing that she'd never come to my office.

I tapped my pen on the pad. 'You said he was a printer. Tell me about that.'

'Okay.' She said that her father was a commercial offset operator, and that they had left Tucson for Los Angeles because he had been offered a job with Enright Quality Printing in Culver City. She told me that he had been laid off, and that he had been concerned about finding another job. Then she shut up and watched me some more.

'So you think he left in search of another job?'

'Oh yes.'

'He's done this before?'

'Not for this long.' She explained that printing was a nomadic life because companies got big contract orders and hired printers like her father to fill those orders, but that when the jobs were done, the printers were let go. She said that when her father was let go, he would have to look around for another job and that was why they moved around so much.

'Does he have a girlfriend?'

She looked surprised. 'We move around too much for that.'

'How about friends?'

She frowned, thinking hard. 'I don't think he has any friends here either. He might've in Tucson.'

I thought about her GED. I thought about her not liking being the new kid in school. 'How about you?'

'What?'

'Do you have friends?'

She sipped more coffee and didn't answer. Guess they moved around too much for that, too.

'Does your father have a criminal record?'

'No.'

'Does he gamble? Maybe hit the card clubs down in Belflower or put money on sporting events?'

'No.'

'He drink, or have a history of mental problems?'

'Absolutely not.' The fifteen-year-old face hardened and she gripped the cup with both hands. 'Why are you asking questions like that?'

'Because a man doesn't just walk away from his children.'

'You make it sound like he abandoned us.'

I stared at her, and the washing machine changed cycles.

'He isn't anything like that. He isn't a drunk, or have brain problems. He's a good father. He's kind and sweet, and he's been gone before, but he's always come back.' She shook her head. 'There are too many printers and too few jobs. When you hear of something you have to follow up fast or you'll lose out.' She looked affronted, like how could I suggest anything else? 'I'm worried that he went somewhere and had an accident. What if he has amnesia?' Amnesia.

I circled Enright Printing on the little pad. 'Okay. I'll talk to the folks at Enright and see if they know something. Also, it might help if I had a picture.'

She frowned. 'I don't think we have a picture.'

'Everybody has pictures.'

She bit at her lower lip. 'I don't think so.'

'Well, maybe you have a snapshot.' I knew a friend with a fifteen-year-old daughter. She had about a zillion pictures of her cat and her friends and siblings and vacations and school and things. Boxes of the stuff.

Teresa shook her head. 'I guess we're just not camera people.'

I put away the pad and stood. 'Okay, let's go look in your dad's bedroom.'

She looked horrified. 'I don't think he'd like us snooping in his room.'

I spread my hands. 'When you hire a private eye, you hire a snooper. Snooping is how you find people who walk away without telling you where they've gone. Snooping is what I do.'

She didn't like this either, but we went along a little hall and into a bedroom at the back of the house. It was a small room, sparsely furnished with a double bed and a dresser and a nightstand. There were no photographs on the nightstand or the dresser, but large ink drawings of all three children were thumbtacked to the walls. The drawings were done on coarse construction paper with colored felt-tip pens, and appeared to have been torn from a notebook. They were signed *CH*. 'Wow. Did your father do these?'

'Yes.'

'He's some artist.' The drawings were almost photographic in their realism.

'Unh-hunh.'

When I opened the dresser's top drawer Teresa stiffened, but said nothing. I looked through the dresser and the nightstand. Maybe a half-dozen undershirts and underwear and socks were in the dresser, and not much else. There was a closet, but there wasn't much in it, just a single sport coat and a couple of pairs of thin slacks and a raincoat. 'Does it look like he packed for a long trip?'

She peeked into the closet like something might jump out at her, then shook her head. 'Well, I know he had two coats, and two pairs of pants are missing.'

'Okay. So he packed some things.'

'I guess so.'

I stood in the center of the room and tried to come up with an idea. 'Do you have any pictures of your mother?' If there was a picture of the mother, maybe Clark would be in it, too.

She shook her head. 'I don't think so.' Jesus. I had never seen a house without pictures before.

'Okay. Forget pictures. Where does he keep the credit card receipts and bank statements and things like that?'

'We don't use credit cards.'

I stared at her.

'We pay for everything with cash. When you're on a budget, cash is the best way to manage your money.' She was very certain of herself when she said it.

'Okay. No pictures, no credit cards.' No clues.

'We have a checking account and a savings account, though. Would you like to see them?'

'That, and your phone bills.'

The eyes narrowed again. 'Why would you need to see that?'

'The phone bills will show any toll calls made from or charged to your phone. You see?' My head was starting to throb. I guess she wanted me to find him without clues. Maybe I was supposed to use telepathy.

But she finally said, 'Well, okay.' Grudgingly.

'You know where to find that stuff?'

'Of course I know where to find it.' Offended.

I thought that she might find the stuff in her father's room, or maybe lead me out to the kitchen, but she didn't. She brought me to her room. Two twin beds were set against adjoining walls, a small army of stuffed animals on one, pictures of David Duchovny, Dean Cain, and Gillian Anderson above the other. Again, there were no photographs of Teri or her family. I said, 'Who likes Duchovny?'

Teri turned red and disappeared into her closet. Guess I'd gotten my answer.

She reappeared with a shoe box held together by a large rubber band. She put the box on the empty bed, then sorted out thin packets of paper held together with large paper clips. She knew exactly what was what and where it belonged. 'Are the phone bills in there?'

'Un-huh.' A large wad of cash was mixed in with the packets, even larger than the roll she'd brought to my office. She saw me looking at the cash, frowned, then put it in her pocket. Better safe than sorry.

Far away something chimed, and Teri stood. 'That's the washing machine. I have to put our clothes in the dryer.'

'Okay.'

The checking and savings accounts were from the First Western Bank of Tucson, Arizona. The savings account was a simple passbook account with a balance of $1,104.16, and showed no unusual deposits or withdrawals. The checking account held a balance of $861.47, with the last deposit having been made just before they'd left Tucson for Los Angeles. The entry record was neat and orderly and made in a teenage girl's rounded hand. I put the banking papers aside and paged through the phone bills. Since they had been in Los Angeles for only four and a half months, there were only four bills, and most of the toll calls were in the LA area, with more than half to Culver City. Most of those were in the first month. Probably Clark looking for a job, but maybe not.

Two of the calls were to Tucson, and five to Seattle, three of the Seattle calls made in the last month, and two of them lengthy. When Teri came back, I said, 'Who's in Seattle?'

She stared at me as if she didn't understand what I'd said.

'You've got five calls to Seattle here, three in the last month, two of them for a pretty long time.'

'My mom's up there.'

'That's where she's buried?'

Nod.

'So your dad might have friends there.'

'I doubt it.' She adjusted her glasses. 'We didn't like it there. I'm pretty sure he wouldn't go back.'

'We'll see.'

'I'm positive he wouldn't.'

'Fine.' Like I shouldn't even waste my time.

I tamped the phone bill pages together, folded them, then put them in my pocket. She didn't like it when I did that either. I gave back the rest of her bills. 'Okay, I'm going to try to find your father, but we have to have an understanding.'

She stared at me, watchful and suspicious.

'I will not notify the authorities that three minors are living here alone so long as the three of you appear safe and in good care. Maybe your father will come home today, but maybe not. Maybe I'll find him fast, but maybe not. You're doing okay right now, and that's good, but if at any time I feel it's in your best interest to notify the police, I will do so. Are we clear on that?'

She looked stubborn. 'Will you tell me first?'

'I won't tell you first if I think you'll run.'

She liked that even less.

'I'm willing to let things stay as they are for now, but I won't lie to you. That's the way it has to be.'

She looked at me for a time, and then she looked at her papers. 'Are you finished with these things?'

I nodded. She took the checkbook, secured it to the bank statements and canceled checks with the same paper clips, and returned it to the shoe box. She did the same with the utility bills and the little pack of cash receipts all written in her hand. Fifteen.

'How long have you been paying the bills?'

She knew exactly what I was saying. 'My father is a good man. He loves us very much. He can't help it that she died on him. He can't help it that these things are hard for him.'

'Sure.'

'Someone has to take care of Charles and Winona. Someone has to clean the house.'

I nodded.

'Someone has to hold this family together.'

I thought there might be tears but her eyes were clear and sharp and hard behind the glasses. Determined. She put the remainder of her papers back into the box, put the top on the box, and again sealed it with the big rubber band. The matter-of-fact eyes came back to me and she dug out the wad of bills. 'We never settled the amount of your fee.'

'Forget it.'

The eyes hardened. 'How much?'

We sat like that, and then I sighed. 'A hundred dollars should do it.'

The hard eyes narrowed. 'In your office you said two thousand.'

'It's not as big a job as I thought. A hundred now, a hundred when I find him.'

She peeled off two of the hundreds and gave me both. 'Take it all now. I'd like a receipt.'

I gave her the receipt, and then I left to find her father.

CHAPTER 4

I phoned information for Enright's address, then left Teresa Haines alone with her coffee and laundry, and headed south along La Cienega toward Culver City. I wanted to tell her not to drive, and to be careful if she walked to the mall, but I didn't. She had been living like this for quite a while, and I knew she would ignore me because I would be saying it more for me than for her. That's the way adults often talk to children. You know they're not going to listen, but you want to tell them anyway just so you know that you have.

Enright Quality Printing was located in a two-story industrial building just off Washington Boulevard three blocks from Sony Pictures. On the way down, I was thinking it would be a small copier place like a Kinko's, but it wasn't. Enright was a big commercial outfit with employees and overhead and presses that run twenty-four hours a day, the kind that does large-scale jobs on contract for businesses and government. The building occupied most of the block, and what wasn't building was a neat, manicured parking lot for their corporate customers and a loading dock for the six-wheelers that delivered their product. The loading dock was busy.

I put the car in the parking lot, then went through the front entrance into a little waiting room. An industrial rack was built into one wall, filled with pamphlets and magazines and thick heavy manuals of the kind Enright produced. There were chairs for waiting and a counter with a young woman behind it. I showed her a card and said, 'Is there someone in charge I might see?'

She looked at the card as if it were written in another language. 'Sorry. We don't do cards.'

I took back the card. 'I don't want cards. I'd like to speak with someone in authority.'

She squinted at me. 'You mean Mr. Livermore?'

'Is he in charge?'

'Unh-hunh.'

'Then that's who I'd like to see.'

'Do you have an appointment?'

'Nope.'

'He might be busy.'

'Let's give it a try.'

If we're patient we're often rewarded.

She said something into her phone and a few minutes later a short, thin man who was maybe a hundred years old came out of the offices and scowled at me. 'You want something printed?'

'Nope. I want to ask you about a former employee.'

I gave him the card and he scowled harder. 'This is shit work. Ya oughta get your money back.' He handed the card back and I put it away. Just the way you want to start an interview, getting crapped on by an expert. 'You the cops?'

'Private. Like it says on the card.'

He made a brushing gesture. 'I didn't get that far. I see shit printing, I gotta look away.' This guy wouldn't let up. He said, 'Listen, you wanna talk, I'll talk, but you gotta walk with me. I got some ass to kick.'

'No problem.'

I followed him along the hall and onto the floor of the printing plant, walking fast to keep up with him. I guess he was anxious to start kicking ass.

The plant itself was large and air-conditioned and

brightly lit with fluorescent lights. It smelled of warm paper. Machines that looked like cold-war era computers bumped and clunked and whirred as men and women monitored the progress of paper and cardboard and bindings. The machines were loud, and most of the workers wore hearing protection but not all of them, and most of them smoked. A woman with a cigarette dangling from the corner of her mouth was wearing a T-shirt that said EAT SHIT AND HAVE A CRAPPY DAY. 'I'm looking for an employee you let go three weeks ago, Clark Haines.'

Livermore made the brushing gesture again. 'Got rid of'm.'

'I know. I'm wondering if you have any idea where he might be.'

'Try the morgue. All fuckin' junkies end up in the morgue.'

I said, 'Junkie?' I think my mouth was open.

Livermore stopped so suddenly that I almost walked into him. He glared at two guys who were standing together by a large offset press, then made a big deal out of tapping his watch. 'What is this, vacationland? I ain't payin' you guys to flap gums! We got orders to fill!'

The two men turned back to their machines, Livermore set off again, and I chased after. So much ass to kick, so little time to kick it. I said, 'Are you telling me that Clark Haines is a drug addict?'

'Guy was a mess since day one, always runnin' to the john, always shakin' with the sweats an' callin' in sick. I knew somethin' wasn't right, so I started keepin' my eyes open, y'see?' He pulled the skin beneath his right eye and glared at me. Bloodshot. 'Caught'm in one'a the vans, Haines and another guy.' He jabbed the air with a stiff finger. 'Bammo, they're outta here. I got zero tolerance for that crap.'

I didn't know what to say. It didn't seem to fit, but then it often doesn't. 'Have you heard from Clark since that day?'

'Nah. Why would I?'

'Job reference, maybe? He told his kids he was looking for work.'

'Hey, the guy's a top printer, but what am I gonna say, hire a junkie, they give good value?'

Livermore beelined to a short Hispanic man feeding booklet pages into a binder. He grabbed a thick sheaf of the pages, flipped through them, then shook his head in disgust. 'This looks like shit. Redo the whole fuckin' order.'

I looked over his shoulder. The pages and the printing looked perfect. 'Looks okay to me.'

He waved at the pages. 'Jesus Christ, don'tcha see that mottle? The blacks're uneven. Ya see how it's lighter there?'

'No.'

He threw the pages into a large plastic trash drum, then scowled at the Hispanic man. 'Reprint the whole goddamn run. Whadaya think we're makin' here, tortillas?'

I guess printing isn't a politically correct occupation.

The Hispanic man shrugged like it was no skin off his nose, and began shutting down the binder.

Livermore was again stalking the aisles. I said, 'Who was the man with Haines?'

'One of the drivers. Another fuckin' junkie, but him I could figure. Him, he had asshole written all over'm.'

'What was his name?'

'Tre Michaels. I think Michaels was the dealer.'

'Did you call the police?'

'Nah. Hey, I thought about it, okay, but they put up such a fuss, whinin' and cryin' and all. Michaels is on parole, see? I coulda violated him easy, but I figured, what the hell, I just wanted him outta here.'

'Think I could have his address?'

Livermore made a little waving gesture and walked faster. 'Go back up front, and ask Colleen. Tell'r I said it was okay to give you what you want.'

Colleen was only too happy to oblige.

Tre Michaels lived on the second floor of an apartment building just south of the Santa Monica Freeway in the Palms area, less than ten blocks from Culver City. It was just before eleven when I got there, but Michaels wasn't home. I found the manager's apartment on the ground level, told her that I needed to speak with Mr. Michaels about a loan he had applied for, and asked if she had any idea when he might be back. She didn't, but she was only too happy to tell me that Michaels worked at the new Bestco Electronics that had just opened, and that maybe I could find him there. She smiled when she said it and I smiled back. We are nothing if not the finest in West Coast detection.

Five minutes later I turned off Overland into the Bestco's lot, parked, and went inside. Bestco is one of those enormous discount electronics places, and as soon as I stepped through the doors three salesmen in sport coats and smiles surrounded me, anxious to meet or better any advertised price in town. I said, 'I'm looking for Tre Michaels.'

Two of them didn't know the name, but the third told me that Michaels worked in 'big screens.' I walked back to 'big screens.'

Tre Michaels was drinking black coffee from a Styrofoam cup as a gentleman of Middle Eastern descent argued with him about price surrounded by thirty large-format televisions displaying exactly the same image of

Arnold Schwarzenegger throwing a guy through a window. I recognized Michaels because he wore a little plastic name tag that said TRE. The Middle Eastern guy was saying that he could get a better price elsewhere, but if Bestco matched that price, then gave him five percent for cash and threw in free delivery and a free two-year full-service warranty, he might be willing to deal. Michaels said that if the man could produce a published price he might be able to give him an extra two percent, but he didn't seem in a hurry to do it. He seemed more interested in Arnold.

Michaels was an overweight guy in his early thirties with a wide butt and a hairline that hadn't seen his eyebrows in years. He had pale skin and washed-away eyes and dry lips that he continuously licked. The lips made me think he was feeling short and thinking about his next fix, but that's only because Livermore had said he was a junkie. Tre Michaels didn't look like a junkie, but then I've never met a junkie in real life who looked like Johnny Rotten.

Michaels glanced over when he saw me, and I pointed at a fifty-two-inch Mitsubishi. 'When you've got a moment, I'd like to buy this unit from you.'

He nodded.

'Full price.'

Michaels came over without a second glance at the Middle Eastern man and said, 'Will that be cash or charge, sir?'

The Middle Eastern guy started making a big deal out of it, but another salesman drifted over and pretty soon they were gone. I said, 'Do you have an office?'

Michaels smiled like the thought was silly. 'We'll just write you up over here by the register.'

I lowered my voice and went close to him. 'You don't

43

need to write me up. I want to ask you about Clark Haines.'

Tre Michaels froze as if he was suddenly part of a great still photograph. He glanced at the blond salesclerk. He twisted to look around at the other salespeople and customers, and then he wet his lips some more. He made what he hoped was an innocent smile. 'I'm sorry. I don't know anyone by that name.'

'C'mon, Tre. I'm not here to make trouble for you. I just want some information about Clark Haines.'

More licking. Around us, images of Arnold crashed up through a floor, spraying a hail of lead at faceless bad guys as the world exploded around him. I said, 'That Arnold is something, isn't he? Walks through a world of hurt and all of it slides right off.' I turned the smile back to Tre Michaels. 'Too bad it doesn't slide off the rest of us like that, isn't it?'

Tre nodded, kind of stupid, like he wasn't sure if he should talk to me or not, like he was scared to talk, but scared what I might do if he didn't.

'I'm not the police, Tre. I'm looking for Clark, and I know that you know him. I know that you and Clark know each other from Enright. I know that you're on parole for narcotics, and that you sold Clark drugs at least one time.' I spread my hands. 'Talk to me about Clark and you'll never see me again.'

'Sure.' He kept looking around. He kept licking his lips and looking at Arnold, but Arnold wasn't coming to help.

'Clark's missing and I'm trying to find him.'

'I don't know where he is.'

'Don't lie to me, Tre. I'm betting if I push down your socks or check your arms, I'll find needle tracks. I'll bet if I check your apartment, I'll find dope. If I think you're lying to me, I can call a couple of cops I know. Violation is only a phone call away.'

'I'm not lying. I swear to Christ I don't know where he is.'

'He buy from you often?'

Head shaking. 'A couple of times. Maybe three, four.'

'What did he buy?'

'Dime bags of heroin.' Jesus Christ.

'When's the last time you saw him?'

He shook his head and made a kind of shrug, as if it was tough to remember. 'A couple of weeks ago he calls me. He says he's going away for a few days and he wants to buy enough to get'm through.'

'He say where he was going?'

Michaels shook his head again. An older guy I took to be the floor manager was watching us now. Michaels saw him and didn't like it.

I said, 'Think hard, Tre. Did Clark mention a name or a place? A girlfriend, maybe?'

More shaking. 'Look, that was, what, two weeks ago? I haven't heard from him since, okay? I swear to Christ I haven't.'

The floor manager sidled closer, trying to listen. Michaels leaned toward me. 'These guys beef me out of the job, it's going to go like a bitch with my parole officer. *Please.*'

I left Tre Michaels in the sea of flickering Arnolds and slowly drove north to my office. The day was warm and clear, but the air felt dirty and the weight of the sun seemed heavy as if the light was a burden. I thought about Teresa and Charles and Winona, and how the daddy I was trying to find wasn't the same daddy that Teri was searching for, and I thought how sad it was that we often never really know the people around us, even the people we love.

CHAPTER 5

It was after two that afternoon when I took the winding drive up Laurel Canyon to the A-frame I keep just off Woodrow Wilson Drive in the mountains above Hollywood. It's a long drive up Laurel, but I've found that as you climb through the trees and cut rock to the top of the mountain and leave the city behind, you're often able to leave the clutter and stress of modern life with it. Often, but not always. Less often still when you're thinking about three kids with a missing father who turns out to be a drug addict.

I parked in the carport, turned off the alarm, and let myself in through the kitchen. The home was cool and still and smelled of Lucy's presence, but I probably just imagined it. Wishful thinking. I said, 'Anybody home?'

No answer.

I share the house with a large black cat who has shredded ears and a fine flat head that he carries cocked to the side from when he was shot with a twenty-two. I think it soured him. He is not the world's friendliest cat, and he'd hissed twice when Lucy arrived, then scrambled through his cat door and disappeared. He had watched us drive away that morning, so I thought he'd be inside waiting for me by now, but there you go. He sulks.

I took an Evian from the fridge, had some, then put Clark Haines's phone bills on my kitchen counter and looked at them. Tre Michaels had said that Clark was going on a trip, and the phone bills showed calls both to

Tucson and Seattle, but the dope changed things. People died from drug overdoses, and people were often murdered when they were trying to buy drugs, so there was a very real possibility that the only trip Clark Haines had taken was to the morgue. I spent the next thirty-two minutes on the phone with hospital emergency rooms and the Los Angeles County Medical Examiner's Office asking if anyone named Clark Haines or fitting his description had been admitted, living or dead, but no one had. Whew. Dodged that bullet.

I went through the bills, noting the two calls to Tucson and the five to Seattle. Over four months, there were also eighty-six local-area toll calls. The Tucson calls were to two different numbers. The five calls to Seattle were to two numbers, also, one number once, the other four times. I called the Tucson numbers first, getting a woman who answered, 'Desert Moving and Storage,' and asked her if Clark Haines was there, or if she knew how I could reach him. She told me that she knew no one by that name. Clark had probably used them to move to LA from Tucson, and she didn't remember the name. A woman named Rosemary Teal answered the next call. I asked her if Clark was there, and she told me that he'd moved, though she wasn't sure where. I asked her how she knew that he'd moved, and she told me that she was his neighbor. I asked if she'd heard from him since they moved, and she said only once. She said he'd called to ask her to please check and be sure he'd turned off the gas. When she insisted that I identify myself, I hung up. *Turn off the gas.* The junkie as concerned neighbor. I called the Seattle numbers next. When I called the first number, a young woman's voice answered, 'New World Printing.' I again asked for Clark Haines, and she told me that no one by that name worked there. I dialed the second number, and on the third ring a hoarse male voice said, 'Hello?'

'Hi, is Clark there?' Bright, and kind of cheery.

The voice said, 'Who is this?' Suspicious.

'Tre Michaels. Clark said he was coming up and gave me your number.'

'I think you got the wrong number.' Clark Haines had spoken to someone at this number for over an hour on two separate occasions.

'I'm sure I copied the number right. We're talking Clark Haines, okay? Clark said he'd be at this number or that you'd know how to reach him.'

'I don't know anyone by that name.' He hung up, and he didn't sound anywhere close to credible.

I called my friend at the phone company, gave her the area code and number, and asked for an ID. Forty seconds later she said, 'That service is billed to a Mr. Wilson Brownell. You want his address?'

'Sure.'

I copied the address, then hung up and thought about the two hundred dollars I had taken from Teresa Haines. Wilson Brownell clearly knew Clark and, under normal circumstances, would be the next step in the investigation. A ticket to Seattle and a hotel would normally be a billable expense, but having a fifteen-year-old kid for a client wasn't normal. Teresa and Charles and Winona were minor children living alone because their father, unemployed and now established as a drug user with a spotty employment record, had, for all intents and purposes, abandoned them. There was every real possibility that Clark Haines might never return, or even be found alive, and the smart thing to do would be to call the police and let them handle it. If I went to Seattle, I couldn't reasonably expect to recover the cost.

Only I had promised Teresa Haines that I would try to

find her father, and it bothered me to leave the lead to Wilson Brownell untested and unresolved. I thought about the two hundred dollars again, and then I picked up the phone and dialed another number.

First ring, and a man's voice said, 'Pike.' Joe Pike owns the agency with me.

'I'm looking for a guy named Clark Haines, and I believe he's gone to Seattle. He has three kids and I need you to keep an eye on them while I'm up there.'

Pike didn't respond.

'Joe?'

We might as well have been disconnected.

'They're doing okay, but I don't like the idea of them not having an adult around if they need help.'

Pike said, 'Three children.'

'I just want to make sure they don't burn down the house.'

More silence.

I was still waiting for him to say something when the cat came in through his cat door and growled so loud that Joe Pike said, 'Is that your cat?'

The cat trotted into the living room and growled again. Angry. He went from the living room into the kitchen and then back out to the front entry. He would trot hard, then stop and sniff, then growl some more. I said, 'I'll call you back in a few minutes.'

I hung up and watched the cat. 'You okay, buddy?'

His eyes narrowed but he didn't come near.

I sat on the kitchen floor, held out my hand, and after a while he finally came over. His fur was warm and coarse, and he needed a bath. I stroked his back, then felt his ribs and hips and legs. I was thinking that someone had shot him again or that a coyote had gotten him, but nothing seemed broken or tender or cut. I said, 'What's wrong?'

He jumped away from me and disappeared through his door and that's when I saw the blood.

Three drops of red were on the kitchen floor by the door jamb, two overlapping small drops, with a third larger drop nearby. I had stepped over them when I had let myself in. I said, 'Sonofagun.'

I touched the large drop and it was tacky.

I thought that maybe he'd brought in a ground squirrel or a field mouse, but there was no dirt or debris or fur. Sometimes he'll bring a kill up to my loft, so I went upstairs to check. Nothing. I went back down and looked through the living room and the dining room and the pantry, but there were no remains there either, and my scalp began tingling. I checked the doors and the windows, then went upstairs again and once more worked my way through the house. The handguns I keep locked in my nightstand were still there, as was the ammunition. The shotgun and rifle were still secure in the closet. My watches, jewelry, cash, and credit cards were all in their places, and their places looked unchanged, yet maybe not. I was pretty sure that the clothes hanging in my closet had been pushed to the right, but now they were spread evenly across the bar, and someone or something had smudged the dust on the two top shelves of my bookcase. Yet maybe not. Nothing was missing, but I felt an acute sense of difference in the shape and way of things, and a growing suspicion that someone had been in my house, and that they hadn't been here to steal. I went down the slope to check the alarm box on the side of my house. Fresh scratches gleamed in the metal around the screw heads. It looked like someone had beat the alarm, then let himself in through the kitchen. The cat had probably nailed him or her going out because he'd already completed his search. I said, 'Man, this really sucks.'

The cat was stalking around at the top of the slope, still growling, still pissed. He is an obsessive animal and does not let go of anger easily.

I said, 'Come here, you.'

He stalked over, surly and growling and making little noises.

I picked him up and held him close. 'I'm glad you weren't hurt.'

He squirmed until I put him down. Pity any dog that tried to grab him now.

I went back inside, washed my hands twice, then called Joe. 'Someone went through my house.'

'Have anything to do with the father?'

I thought about it. 'I don't know why it would, but I'm not sure.'

'Maybe I should watch you instead of these kids.'

'Maybe.' I told him their address. 'Meet me there and I'll introduce you. I'll take a flight out early in the morning.'

'Whatever.'

Pike hung up, and I stood in the center of the kitchen and listened to the silence. Someone had been in my home, and it made me feel creepy and violated and angry. I pulled out the Dan Wesson, sat it on the kitchen counter, and crossed my arms. 'Let's see'm come back now.'

Acting tough will sometimes help, but not always, and the gun did not lessen the feeling that I was vulnerable and at risk. They seldom do.

I shut off the lights, locked the house, and reset the alarm. It hadn't helped, but you do what you can.

I drove down to see Teri Haines.

CHAPTER 6

It was just after six that evening when I rang their bell and Charles threw open the door. He threw it wide, just as he had before, without regard to who might be on the other side. I said, 'Always ask who it is.'

Charles showed me a twelve-inch serrated carving knife. 'You don't have to ask when you're ready.'

Sometimes you just have to shake your head.

Today Charles was wearing the oversized shoes, the monstrously baggy shorts, and a black Wolverine T-shirt that hung almost to his knees. Teresa appeared over his shoulder, and said, 'Did you find him?' Hopeful.

'Nope. But I've got a couple of ideas. How about I come in and we talk about them?'

Winona was sitting at the dining table, and plates were there for Charles and Teresa. I'd interrupted dinner. Spaghetti, again. Maybe it was all they knew how to make. 'Smells great.' Mr. Cheery.

Teresa said, 'We were just finished, but there's more if you'd like some.'

'That's okay, but thanks.'

'Just let us clear the table.'

'Sure.' I wandered into the living room and sat on the couch. I had to move a library book to sit. Brennert's *Her Pilgrim Soul*.

Winona slid from her seat, placed her silverware onto her plate, then carried the plate and her glass into the kitchen. Teresa gathered her things, too, and so did

Charles. No one had to badger him. Everyone knew what to do and everyone did their job as if it were part of a larger accepted pattern. They gathered their things and brought them into the kitchen, and then Teresa and Charles returned, Teresa picking up the place mats and Charles wiping off the table with a damp cloth. Like they had done it a thousand times and would do it a thousand more, and had accepted it as a natural part of their lives. A ritual. I watched them and wondered at the secrets families keep. Teresa wanted me to find her father, but the man I was finding didn't appear to be the man she knew. And the man that I would eventually find would be different still. It is often that way in my line of work.

When the table was clean, Teresa came over, sat in the big chair, and gave me a smile. 'Would you like a cup of coffee?'

'No, thanks.'

'Well, if you change your mind.' Prim and proper. In absolute control of her environment, and of this meeting with the employee. 'Now, what have you found?'

Water was running in the kitchen. Winona's night to do the dishes. 'Has your father mentioned a man named Tre Michaels to you?'

She shook her head. 'No. No, I don't think so.'

'How about Wilson Brownell?'

She stared thoughtfully as if maybe this rang a bell, but then she shook her head. 'Unh-unh.' Charles skulked in from the dining room and leaned against the wall.

'Tre Michaels worked with your father. He saw your dad a couple of weeks ago, and your father said that he was thinking of taking a trip, but he didn't say where. At about that same time, your dad made five long-distance calls to Seattle and spoke with Wilson Brownell, twice at considerable length.' When I mentioned Seattle Teri and Charles glanced at each other, and Charles crossed his arms. 'I phoned Mr. Brownell, but Brownell denied knowing your father. I think he's lying, and I think maybe your dad went to Seattle to see him. I'm going to fly up tomorrow to ask Mr. Brownell in person.' I didn't mention the drugs, or why Clark had been fired from Enright.

Teresa looked nervous. 'Why do you have to go to Seattle?'

'I told you why.'

She frowned harder. I thought she wanted to object some more, but you could tell that whatever her objections might be, her desire to find her father was stronger. 'Okay. I guess I should pay you some more money.'

I raised a palm. 'Forget the money. I'll take up that part of it up with your father when I find him.'

Charles was frowning, too. He seemed less happy about my going to Seattle than Teresa. She said, 'How long will you be gone?'

'Two days, maybe three. Less if I get what I'm after right away.'

They were watching me now, all big eyes.

'I've asked my partner to come over. His name is Joe Pike, and he'll be around if you need anything.'

Charles looked sulky. 'What are we gonna need? You think we're babies?'

'No, but I'll sleep better if I know there's someone to help you if you need it.'

The doorbell rang. Charles grabbed his knife and raced for the door. I said, 'Ask who it is.'

Charles threw open the door and there was Joe Pike, filling the frame, motionless. Pike is six-one, with long ropy muscles, short dark hair, and a face that gives you nothing unless you know him well. His arms are laced with veins, and bright red arrows had been tattooed onto the outside of his deltoids a long time ago. They point forward. He was wearing a gray sweatshirt with the sleeves cut off and blue Levis and bottomless black pilot's glasses. The glasses tilted toward Charles.

Charles dropped the knife and screamed, *'Run!'* He tried to slam the door, but Pike caught the door without effort, and gently pushed it open.

I said, 'Lighten up, Charles. This is Joe Pike. Joe works with me.'

Charles was leaning into the door with everything he had, making little sounds like 'Grr, grr, grr.'

Teresa snapped, *'Charles!'*

Charles jumped away from the door and ran past Winona into the kitchen, breathing hard. Winona was standing in the kitchen door, hands soapy and dripping, sniffling like she was about to cry.

Teresa said, 'It's okay, honey. He's one of the good guys.' She looked back at me and shook her head. 'We can take care of ourselves. We don't need a baby-sitter.' Charles peeked out from behind the door.

Joe Pike looked at the knife on the floor, then at the children, and then at me. 'Baby-sitter?'

I spread my hands. 'He won't live with you. He'll just be around, and you'll have his phone number. If there's anything you need, you can call him.' I looked at Joe. 'Right?'

Joe's head swiveled so that the flat black lenses angled my way. I thought he might be amused, but you never know.

Teresa's mouth set in a stubborn line. 'It's all right. We're fine.'

I said, 'Look, I'm not leaving you guys here alone. Joe will be outside, and he might drop in a time or two, and that's the way it has to be.'

Teresa wasn't liking it, but I wasn't giving her a lot of

choice. 'Well, I guess there isn't much I can do about it, is there?' Stiff.

I shook my head. 'No.'

Charles finished eyeing Joe and skulked out from behind Winona. 'Lemme see your gun.'

Pike picked up the serrated knife, flipped it into the air, then caught it by the blade. He looked at Charles, and Charles ducked behind Winona. Pike walked over and held out the knife. Handle first. 'Put this away before someone gets hurt.'

Charles took the knife and disappeared into the kitchen.

Pike turned to Teresa. 'It's a pleasure to meet you, Ms. Haines. My name is Joe.' He held out his hand and she took it. I think she blushed.

Winona smiled. 'My name's Winona.'

Pike glanced over at me and said, 'Go ahead and leave. We'll be fine.'

That Joe. To know him is to love him.

I left them like that in the deepening purple of twilight, and went home.

I approached my house with a suspicion I do not often feel and let myself in. The three drops of blood were still by the cat's door, and the quiet house still held an air of alienness that I resented. The cat slipped in through his cat door, sniffed the three drops, then snicked across the floor and sat by his bowl. Guess he had moved past it.

I gave him a can of Star Kist tuna, then opened the sliding glass doors that lead to my deck. The twilight air was cool and scented with wild sage. I put Jimmy Buffett on the CD player, then poured a glass of Cuervo Gold, had some, then went out to the side of my house and selected a fat green lime from the tree I planted two years ago. It went well with the Cuervo. My home had been invaded, and I could either let my feelings for the place be changed by that event or not, but either way would be my choice. The event is what you make of it.

I spent the next two hours cleaning both bathrooms and the kitchen and the floors. I threw out my toothbrush and opened a new one, and I washed the sheets and pillowcases and towels. I pulled the plates and the silver from the cupboards and drawers and loaded them into the dishwasher, and vacuumed the couch and the chairs and the carpets. I scrubbed the floors hard, and spent the remains of the day cleaning and drinking until, very early the next morning, I had once more made peace with my home.

I packed, then fell into a fitful sleep as Jimmy Buffett sang about Caribbean sunsets, over-the-hill pirates, and a world where fifteen-year-old girls didn't have to carry the emotional weight of their families.

Later that morning I went to Seattle.

CHAPTER 7

Seattle is one of my favorite cities, and I often think that if I did not live in LA, I might live there. Where the sky over Los Angeles is more often dimensionless and ill-defined, Seattle is capped by a continually redefined skyscape of clouds that makes the sky there a visibly living thing, breathing as it moves, cooling the city and its people with a protective cloak, and washing the air and the land with frequent rains that come and go in a way that freshens the place and its people. You can get the best coffee in America in Seattle, and browse in some of the best bookstores, and fish for silver and blackmouth salmon, and, until recently, the real estate prices were so low compared to those in Southern California that herds of Californians moved there. A friend of mine from Orange County sold her house and used the equity to buy a beautiful home on the water at Bainbridge Island. Cash. She used the balance of her equity to invest in mutual funds, and now she spends the bulk of each day painting in watercolors and digging for butter clams. So many Californians did this that property values in the Seattle area went through the roof and many native Seattleites could no longer afford to live in their own town. Whenever I visit I say I'm from Oregon.

I picked up a Ford Mustang and a street map from the Sea-Tac rental people, then followed Highway 509 north toward Elliot Bay and a seafood house I know that lies in the shadow of the Space Needle. I had a crab cake sandwich and fried new potatoes and mango iced tea for lunch, then asked a parking meter cop for directions to Wilson Brownell's address. With any luck, Brownell and Clark might be sitting around Brownell's place right now. With any luck, I might be on the next flight back to LA and not even have to spend the night. It happens.

Brownell lived across the Duwamish Waterway in an older, working-class part of West Seattle called White Center. It is a community of narrow streets and old apartments and wood-framed homes surrounding a steel mill. Young guys with lean, angry faces hung around near the mill, looking like they wished they could get work there. The ground floor of Brownell's building fronted the street with a secondhand clothing store, a place that refinished maritime metalwork, and a video rental place called Extreme Video. The video place was papered with posters of Jackie Chan and young Asian women tied to chairs with thousands of ropes. Extreme.

I missed Brownell's building twice because I couldn't find the building numbers, then found it but couldn't find a place to park. I finally left the car by a hydrant six blocks away. Flexibility in the art of detection.

Three young guys in T-shirts were hanging outside the video place when I got back, drinking Snapple. One of them was wearing a Seattle Mariners cap, and all of them were sporting black Gorilla boots and rolled-cuff jeans. A stairwell protected by an unlocked wire door had been carved from the corner of the building just past the metalwork place. There was a directory on the wall, and a row of mailboxes with little masking-tape tags for names and apartment numbers, only Brownell wasn't one of the names on the directory and the names on the masking tape had faded to oblivion. I said, 'Any of you guys know Wilson Brownell?'

The one with the cap said, 'Sure. He comes in all the time.'

'You know which apartment he's in?'

'I'm pretty sure it's apartment B. On the second floor.' You see how friendly it is in Seattle?

I took the stairs two at a time, then went along the hall looking for B. I found it, but the apartment across the hall was open and an older woman with frizzy hair was perched inside on an overstuffed chair, squinting out at me. She was clutching a TV remote the size of a cop's baton and watching C-Span. I gave her a smile. 'Hi.'

She squinted harder.

I couldn't hear anything inside Brownell's apartment. No radio, no TV, no voices making furtive plans, just the C-Span and street noises. It was an older building without air-conditioning, so there would be open windows. I knocked, and then I rang his bell.

The woman said, 'He's at work, ya dope.' Just like that, ya dope. 'Middle'a the day, any worthwhile man finds himself at work.' Eyeing me like that's where I should be.

She was maybe seventy, but she might've been eighty, with leathery ochre skin and salt and pepper hair that went straight up and back like the Bride of Frankenstein. She was wearing a thin cotton housecoat and floppy slippers and she was pointing the remote at me. Maybe trying to make me disappear.

'Sorry if I disturbed you.' I gave her my relaxed smile, the one that says I'm just a regular guy going about a regular guy's business, then made a big deal out of checking my watch. 'I could've sworn he said to come by at two.' It was six minutes before two. 'Do you know what time he's due back?' The World's Greatest Detective swings into full detection mode to fake out the Housebound Old Lady.

The squint softened, and she waved the remote. Inside, congressional voices disappeared. 'Not till five-thirty, quarter to six, something like that.'

'Wow, that's a lot later than I planned.' I shook my head and tried for a concerned disappointment. 'An old buddy of ours is in town and we're supposed to get together. I wonder if he's been around.' For all I knew Clark was inside asleep on the couch. You cast a line, you hope for a bite.

She made herself huffy. 'I wouldn't know. I don't spy on people.'

'Of course.'

'People come and people go. You're old and livin' alone, no one gives you the time a day.' She went back to C-Span, and now I could smell cat litter and turnips.

'Well, he's a little shorter than me, thinner, glasses, a hairline back to here.'

She turned up the sound and waved the remote. 'People come, people go.'

I nodded, Mr. Understanding, Mr. Of-Course-I-Wouldn't-Expect-You-to-Remember. Then I slapped my head and made like I'd just realized that I was the world's biggest moron. 'Jeez, he must've wanted me to meet him at work! I'll bet we're supposed to meet there, then go out! Of course!' The World's Greatest Detective employs the Relatable Human Failing technique in an effort to cultivate rapport.

The woman frowned at her television, then muted the sound again. 'What a bullshit story.'

'Excuse me?'

Her face cracked into a thin, angry smile that said she was as sharp as a straight razor, and if a guy like me didn't watch out she would hand back his head. 'If there's something you wanna know, just ask. You don't

61

have to make up a bullshit story about old friends getting together. What a crock!'

I smiled again, but now the smile was saying, okay, you nailed me. 'Sorry about that.' Shown up by the Bride of Frankenstein.

She made a little shrug, like it wasn't a big thing. 'You hadda try, you just went too far with it. A guy making out as nice as you wouldn't be caught dead being friends with an asswipe like Will Brownell.' I guess they didn't get along. 'What's the real story?'

'Brownell's friend owes me six hundred dollars.'

She cackled and shook her head. 'I mighta known. Sooner or later it always gets down to money, doesn't it?'

'Uh-huh.' Everyone relates to greed. 'How about the guy I described? Has he been around?'

She made the shrug again, but it seemed sincere. 'That's not much of a description, young man. Could be anyone.'

'Fair enough. Can you tell me where Brownell works?'

'He works at some printing place.'

'New World Printing?'

'Maybe.' The other Seattle number that Clark had phoned.

I said, 'You won't tell Brownell that I was around, will you?'

She turned back to the television. 'What'd the sonofabitch ever do for me?' Nope, I don't guess they got along.

I went back down the stairs to the street and checked out the building. Two of the kids were gone, but the kid in the Mariners cap was sitting in the doorway to the video store on a wooden stool, inspecting a car magazine. The C-Span Lady's apartment was above the metalwork place at the front of the building, which meant Brownell's apartment was in the rear. I walked down to the end of the block, rounded the corner, then came up the service alley. A rickety fire escape ran up the back of the building to the roof like a metal spiderweb. I counted windows and visualized the location of the C-Span Lady's apartment so that I would know which windows belonged to Brownell. There were a lot of windows. Potted plants nested around some of the windows and drying clothes hung from the rails outside others, and a kid's tricycle rested on the fire escape outside still another. Figure that one. Brownell's windows were closed.

I used a Dumpster to reach the fire escape ladder, chinned myself to the rail, and let myself into Wilson Brownell's dining area. One should always lock one's windows, even in friendly cities like Seattle.

Clark Haines was not asleep on the couch. The apartment was quiet and warm from having been closed, and smelled of coffee and Jiffy Pop. The dining area opened into a living room ahead of me and a kichenette to my right. Beyond the kitchenette was a door that probably led to a bedroom and a bath. A vinyl couch and a mismatched chair filled one corner of the living room opposite a Sony Trinitron and a VCR. A coffee table was angled between the couch and the chair, scattered with magazines and a yellow rotary phone. A small pine table and three chairs sat in the dining area, along with an Ikea shelving unit showing a couple of plants, a bright orange goldfish in an oversized pickle jar, and some photographs of an African-American woman with a pretty smile. The woman looked young, but the photographs looked old, and I thought that the woman might now be, also. Precise, photo-realistic drawings of the woman had been framed and hung on the walls. They were signed *Wilson*, but in style and technique they looked exactly like the drawings that Clark Haines had done of his children.

You hope for the obvious: a sleeping bag and pillows

on the couch, a suitcase, a note stuck to the fridge saying 'meet Clark at 5,' anything that might indicate an out-of-town guest, or the location of same. Nada. A case of beer cooled in the fridge and the cabinets were filled with enough booze for a booksellers' convention, but that didn't mean Brownell had company. Maybe he was just a lush. The magazines turned out to be trade catalogs for commercial printing equipment and industry magazines with dog-eared pages and supply brochures. The marked pages all noted paper and ink suppliers in Europe and Asia. Four of the catalogs still had their mailing labels, and all of the labels were addressed to Wilson Brownell. A hot topic in most of the magazines seemed to be *Digital Micro-scanning Architecture for Zero Generation Loss*. Whatever that meant. I guess if you're a printer, you like to read about printing.

I took a quick peek in the bath, then went to the bedroom. Clark Haines wasn't there either. A neatly made double bed sat against the wall, along with a chest and a dresser and a drafting table. I glanced into the closet. One bed, one toothbrush, one set of toiletries, one used towel, no luggage or alternative bedding. More photographs of the same woman sat upon the chest and the dresser, only some of these showed a smiling African-American man. Wilson Brownell. An in-progress drawing was tacked down onto the drafting table, pen and ink, done with very fine lines, showing an almost photographic reproduction of the Seattle skyline. Wilson Brownell might be a lush, but he was also a gifted artist and I wondered if it was he who had trained Clark. Maybe Clark had come up here for art lessons.

I went through the nightstand and the chest, and was working through the dresser when I noticed a small Kodak snapshot wedged along the bottom edge of the dresser's mirror, half hidden behind yet more photographs of the woman. It was a color shot of two couples standing on a fishing pier, one of the couples Brownell and the woman, the other a much younger Caucasian couple. The Caucasian woman had dark wavy hair, pale skin, and glasses. She looked exactly like an older, adult version of Teresa Haines. She was smiling at the camera, and holding hands with a thin guy whose hairline was already starting to recede. I took down the picture and turned it over. On the back, someone had written: *Me and Edna, Clark and Rachel Hewitt,* **1986**. I looked at the picture again. The Caucasian woman had to be Teri's mother, and the man had to be Clark, only the name wasn't Haines, it was *Hewitt*.

I put the picture in my pocket, made sure everything else was like I had found it, then let myself out the window, walked around to the street, and once more climbed the stairs. The C-Span Lady's door was still open, and she was still shaking her remote at her television. Guess if I watched Congress all day I'd want to shake something, too.

I said, 'One more thing.'

Her eyes narrowed, and she muted the sound.

I held out the picture, and this time I didn't bother to smile. 'Is this one of the people who come and go?'

She looked at the picture, then she looked back at me. 'He owe you money, too?'

'Everybody owes me money. I have a generous nature.'

She held out her hand and brushed her thumb across her fingers. 'How about extendin' some'a that generosity my way?'

I gave her a crisp new twenty.

'He showed up a week ago, Thursday. Stayed a couple of days, then left. You shoulda heard all the carryin' on.'

'What do you mean?'

65

She made a sour face and waved the remote. 'Moanin' and cryin', moanin' and cryin'. I don't know what all was goin' on in there.' She made a little shudder, like she didn't want to know. 'I ain't seen him since.'

'Appreciate the help.'

She turned back to the C-Span and made the twenty disappear. 'Don't mention it.'

Sooner or later it always gets down to money.

CHAPTER 8

New World Printing was east of the Duwamish Waterway between Georgetown and Boeing Field in a tract of older industrial buildings that were built when red bricks and ironwork were cheap. The front of the building contained a fancy glass entrance and a receptionist who would pick up her phone and tell Mr. Brownell that a Mr. Cole wanted to see him. Considering Mr. Brownell's uncooperative response when I phoned, it was likely that Brownell would (at worst) refuse to see me, or (at best) be warned of my approach and therefore prepared to stonewall. This was not good. I have found that if you can surprise people in their workplace, they are often concerned with avoiding an embarrassing scene, and you can jam them into cooperating. This is advanced detective work at its finest.

I parked at the curb and walked around to the loading dock on the side of the building where two men were wrestling a dolly stacked with about ten thousand pounds of boxed paper into a six-wheel truck. 'You guys know where I can find Wilson Brownell?'

One of the men was younger, with a thick mustache and a hoop earring and a red bandana tied over his head like a skullcap. 'Yeah.' He pointed inside. 'Down the aisle, past the desk, and through the swinging door. You'll see him.'

'Thanks.'

I followed an endless aisle past shipping flats stacked

with boxes of brochures and magazines and pamphlets. I picked up two boxes and carried them with what I hoped was a purposeful expression, just another worker bee lugging paper through the hive.

A balding guy with a potbelly and tiny, mean eyes was sitting at the desk, talking to a younger guy with a prominent Adam's apple. The balding guy was thin in the arms and chest and neck, but his belly poked out beneath his belt-line as if someone had slipped a bowling ball in his pants. He squinted at me the way people do when they're trying to remember who you are, but then I was past him and through the swinging door and into a cavernous room filled with whirring, ka-chunking, humming machines and the men and women who operated them. A woman pushed a dolly past me and I smiled. 'Wilson Brownell?'

She pointed and I saw him across the room, standing at a large machine with two other people, one a kid in a KURT LIVES T-shirt, and the other a middle-aged guy in a suit. A large plate had been removed from the side of the machine so that they could see inside.

Wilson Brownell was in his early sixties, and taller than he looked in the pictures at his home. He was dressed in khaki slacks and a simple plaid shirt, with short hair more gray than not and black horn-rimmed glasses. Professorial. He was using a pen to point at something inside the machine. The guy in the suit was standing with his arms crossed, not liking what he heard. Brownell finally stopped pointing, and the suit walked away, still with crossed arms. Brownell said something to the younger guy, and the younger guy got down on the floor and began working his way into the machine. I walked over and said, 'Mr. Brownell?'

'Yes?' Brownell looked at me with damp, hazel eyes.

68

You could smell the booze on him, faint and far away. It was probably always with him.

I positioned myself with my back to the kid so that only Wilson Brownell would hear. 'My name is Elvis Cole. I've phoned you twice trying to find a man named Clark Haines.'

Brownell shook his head. 'I don't know anyone by that name.'

'How about Clark Hewitt?'

Brownell glanced at the kid, then wet his lips. 'You're not supposed to be here.' He looked past me. 'Did they let you in?'

'Come on, Mr. Brownell. I know that Clark phoned you six times from Los Angeles because I've seen his phone record. I know that he's been at your apartment.' He wasn't just stonewalling; he was scared. 'I'm not here to make trouble for you or for Clark. He walked out on his kids eleven days ago, and they need him. If he isn't coming home, someone has to deal with that.' Elvis Cole, detective for the nineties, the detective who can feel your pain.

'I don't know anything. I don't know what you're talking about.' He shook his head, and the booze smell came stronger.

'Jesus Christ, those kids are alone. All I want to do is find out if Clark's coming home.' You'd think I wanted to kill the guy.

He held up both hands, palms toward me, shaking his head some more.

'This isn't an earth-shaker, Wilson. Either I'm going to find Clark, or I'm going to turn his kids over to Children's Services, and they're going to take custody away from him. You see what I'm saying here?' I wanted to smack him. I wanted to grab him by the ears and shake him. 'Clark is going to lose his kids unless he talks

69

to me, and you're going to be part of it.' Maybe I could guilt him into cooperating.

Wilson Brownell looked past me, and his eyes widened. The bald guy with the bowling-ball paunch was standing in the swinging doors, frowning at us. Brownell's face hardened and he stepped close to me. 'Do everybody a favor and get your ass out of here. I'd help you if I could, but I can't, and that's that.'

He turned away but I turned with him. 'What do you mean, that's that? Didn't you hear what I said about his kids?'

'I said I can't help you.' Wilson Brownell's voice came out loud enough so that the kid on the floor peeked out at us.

Two men had joined the bald guy in the swinging doors. They were older, with thin gray hair and wind-burned skin and the kind of heavy, going-to-fat builds that said they were probably pretty good hitters twenty years ago. The bald guy pointed our way and one of the new men said something, and then the bald guy started toward us. Brownell grabbed my shoulder like a man grabbing a life preserver. 'Listen to me, goddamnit.' His voice was a harsh whisper, lower now and urgent. 'Don't you mention Clark. Don't even say his goddamn name, you wanna walk outta here alive.' Wilson Brownell suddenly broke into a big laugh and clapped me on the shoulder as if I'd told him the world's funniest joke. He said, 'You tell Lisa I can get my own date, thank you very much! I need any help, I'll give'r a call!' He said it so loud that half of British Columbia could hear.

I stared at him.

The bald guy reached us, the two new guys still in the swinging door, watching through interested eyes. The bald guy said, 'I don't know who this guy is. He just walked in here.'

70

Brownell kept his hand on my shoulder, letting the laugh fade to a grin. 'Sorry about that, Donnie. I knew this guy was coming by, and I shoulda told you. He's a friend of mine.'

I glanced from Brownell to Donnie, then back to Brownell, wondering just what in hell I had walked into.

Brownell shook his head like, man, this was just the silliest thing. 'This guy's wife has been tryin' to set me up with this friend of hers for three months now. I keep sayin', what on earth am I going to do with a new woman when I'm still in love with my Edna?'

Donnie squinted the ferret eyes at me like he was deciding something. 'What, are you a mute or something? Don't you have anything to say?'

Brownell was looking at me so hard that his eyes felt like lasers. I shook my head. 'Nope.'

Donnie made his decision, then glanced back at the two guys in the swinging door, and shook his head once. The two guys vanished. 'You know better'n this.'

Brownell said, 'I'm sorry, Donnie. Jesus Christ.'

The tiny eyes flicked back to me, and then a smile even smaller than the eyes played at the edges of his mouth. 'C'mon, I'll show you the way out.'

I followed the bald guy out, got into my car, and drove to a Seattle's Best Coffee, where I bought a double-tall mochachino and sat there feeling confused, a more or less natural state. I had flown to Seattle expecting some difficulty in dealing with Wilson Brownell, but nothing like this. Wilson Brownell seemed stark raving terrified to mention Clark's name. In fact, Brownell seemed not only terrified of me but also of his fellow employees. Maybe there was something to it, or maybe Brownell was just a goofball suffering from some sort of paranoid psychosis. Goofballs are common. I could sit here and guess, but all I would have are guesses. I needed to ask

Wilson Brownell, and there were only two options: I could shoot my way back into New World and pistol-whip the information out of him, or I could wait and ask him when Wilson left work. The C-Span Lady had said that Brownell got home between five-thirty and a quarter to six, which meant that he probably left work between five and five-fifteen. It was now forty-three minutes after two, giving me two hours and twenty minutes to fill, and I decided to visit Rachel Hewitt's grave. If Clark had visited her grave, he might've left flowers. If he left flowers, there might be a florist's tag, and if there was a florist's tag, I might be able to get a line on Clark. A lot of ifs and maybes, but ifs and maybes define my life.

The Seattle's Best people let me use their Yellow Pages. Twelve cemeteries were listed in the greater Seattle, Mercer Island, and Bellevue area. I copied their numbers on a napkin, traded three dollar bills for quarters, and started dialing. The first four cemeteries I phoned did not have a Rachel Hewitt listed, but a woman who answered the phone at the fifth said, 'Why, yes, we do have a Rachel Hewitt as a client.' Client.

I said, 'Did you know Rachel Hewitt?'

'Oh, goodness, no.'

'You knew she was there without having to look it up.' She had said it that quickly.

'Oh, well, I had to look it up just last week for another gentleman. On a Monday, I believe. Yes, that's right, a Monday.'

'Over the phone, or in person?'

'Oh, he was here.'

I described Clark. 'Did he look like that?'

'Oh, no. Nothing like that. This gentleman was tall and blond, with short hair.'

I got directions, hung up, and eighteen minutes later I

pulled through the gate onto the grounds of the Resthaven Views Cemetery and parked at the office. The woman I'd spoken with was older and sweet, and named Mrs. Lawrence. She showed me a large plot map of the grounds, and directed me to Rachel Hewitt's grave site. I said, 'The man last Monday, do you know who he was?'

'Oh, a friend or relative, I imagine. Like you.' Like me.

Rachel Hewitt had been laid to rest on the side of a grassy knoll near the western edge of the cemetery with a clear and pleasant view of Lake Washington. I left my car in the shade of a sycamore tree and walked north counting headstones. Rachel Hewitt's was the fifth headstone in, but the headstone was bare. Guess Clark hadn't been out, or if he had, he'd skipped the flowers.

I said, 'Well, damn.'

No flowers meant no lead.

Three cars were parked below me, and I could see people trudging among the graves, some sitting on the grass, some standing, one older gentleman in a lawn chair he'd brought, visiting old friends or loved ones. Above me, twin mausoleums stood on the crest of the hill with what would be sweeping views of the lake. Trees stood sentry around the mausoleums, lending shade, and a couple of cars were parked among the trees, one a faded tan pickup, the other a black Lexus. Someone was sitting in the Lexus, but they were so far away I couldn't see them clearly. Something flashed, and I thought they must be looking through field glasses. Admiring the view, no doubt. Enjoying another fine day with the dead.

I brushed at the headstone and took out the photograph that I'd taken from Brownell's apartment and again thought how very much Teri looked like her mother. I put the picture away and stared at Lake Washington and tried not to feel sour. No mean feat when you've spent your own money to fly a thousand miles to stand clueless beside a woman's grave. I was still confident that I could find Clark, but the odds that I could do it within a reasonable amount of time were diminishing, and I would need to do something about the kids. Of course, even if I found Clark, I was thinking that I still might have to call Children's Services. Clark wasn't shaping up as the World's Finest Dad. Rachel might not like it, but there you go. Maybe she should've done a better job of selecting their father.

I left the cemetery and drove south along the lake. It was a lovely afternoon, and the lake was flat. People Rollerbladed along the water and sunbathed on short strips of beach, and none of them were bummed because they had just visited a woman's grave.

I turned west at Seward Park and stopped at a red light next to a woman in a green Toyota. I smiled at her, and she smiled back. Friendly. Then I glanced in the mirror and saw a black Lexus two cars behind. It looked like the Lexus from the mausoleum, but I couldn't get a clear enough look at it to be sure. I said, 'Come on, Cole, you've got to be kidding. First LA and now Seattle?'

The woman in the green Toyota was staring at me. I looked away, embarrassed. 'Get a grip, Cole. Now you're talking to yourself.'

I snuck another glance, and now she locked her door.

The light changed and the Lexus stayed behind me, but two blocks later I slowed, and the Lexus sped by. A guy with a blond buzz cut was driving and a dark man who looked about as big as a Kodiak bear was in the passenger seat. Neither of them looked at me. I said, 'You see? It was nothing.'

The woman in the green Toyota passed me, too. Fast.

I parked a block and a half from the New World main gate at eighteen minutes before five. At five, employees started filtering out both on foot and in cars; at six minutes after, Wilson Brownell nosed out of the lot in a small yellow Plymouth hatchback. I let him get one block ahead, then I pulled out after him. He went west across the Duwamish directly to his apartment and parked at the curb in sight of the C-Span Lady's window. I pulled into the mouth of an alley a block away and waited for him to go into his building, but he didn't. He locked his car, then walked north to the next corner and disappeared. I left the car blocking the alley, trotted after him, and made it to the corner in time to see him go into a place called Lou's Bar. There was a case of beer and damn near a dozen bottles of booze in his apartment, but I guess he wanted to stop off for a couple before he went home for the serious drinking. Or maybe he just didn't want to be alone.

Wilson Brownell watched the bartender pour Popov vodka over ice as I entered. I waited for the bartender to finish and move away, then I took the stool next to Brownell. Two women were hunched together over a little table in the shadows, and three of us were at the bar, but the third guy was facedown on the wood. Brownell saw me and said, 'Jesus Christ.'

I looked serene. 'No, but we're often confused.'

'I got nothing to say to you.' Brownell tried to get up, but I hooked one of his feet behind the stool and pushed down hard on his shoulder, digging my thumb into the pressure point at the front of his neck. I didn't like being tough, but I was willing to if that's what it took to find Clark Hewitt and get his butt home to his kids. No one in the bar seemed to give a damn. He said, 'Ow. My goddamned neck.'

'Relax and I'll let go. If you try to get up, I'll knock you on your ass.'

He stopped trying to get up and I released the pressure.

As soon as I let go, he took a belt of the Popov. 'Goddamn. That hurt.'

I took out my wallet and opened it to the license. 'A fifteen-year-old girl who told me that her name was Teresa Haines gave me two hundred dollars to find her father.'

Brownell took another belt of the vodka.

'I have come up here at my own expense because Teresa, whose name I now discover is really Hewitt, and her two younger siblings have a missing father who has apparently abandoned them.'

Another belt.

'I have discovered that Clark Haines, whose name is also Hewitt, is a drug addict. I have discovered that Mr. Hewitt has come to Seattle, has spent time with his old friend, Mr. Brownell, but that Mr. Brownell doesn't give enough of a damn about these minor children to cooperate in helping me find their father.' I put away the wallet, then took out the picture of Brownell and Clark and their wives and put that on the bar.

The picture was creased from having been in my pocket. Brownell's jaw tightened. 'You went into my home.'

'Yes.'

His jaw flexed some more, then he picked up the picture and put it in his own pocket. He had more of the vodka, and I saw that his hand was shaking. 'You don't know a goddamn thing about anything.' His voice was soft and far away.

'I know Clark was with you.'

He shook his head, and the soft voice came again. 'You're in somethin' now you don't know anything about. If you're smart, you'll just go home.'

'So tell me and I'll go.'

He shook his head and tried to lift the Popov, but his

hand was shaking too badly. I didn't think it was shaking from the booze. 'I can't help you and I got nothing to tell you.' He blinked hard, almost as if he were blinking back tears. 'I love Clark, you see? But there ain't nothing I can do. I don't know where he went and you shouldn't be asking about him. I'm sorry about his children, but there ain't nothing I can do about that. Not one goddamned thing.' Brownell's hand shook so badly that the Popov splashed out the glass.

'Jesus Christ, Brownell. What in hell's got you so scared?'

The bar door opened and the blond guy from the Lexus came in. He was maybe six-two, with hard shoulders and sharp features and ice blue eyes that looked at you without blinking. He stepped out of the door to make room for his friend, and the friend needed all the room he could get: He was a huge man, maybe six-five, with great sloping shoulders, an enormous protruding gut, and the kind of waddle serious powerlifters get. His thighs were as thick as a couple of twenty gallon garbage cans. The buzz cut was wearing a blue sport coat over a yellow T-shirt and jeans, but his friend was decked out in a truly bad islander shirt, baggy shorts, and high-top Keds. The big guy had a great dopey grin on his face, and he was slurping on a yellow sucker. The buzz cut said, 'Willie.'

Wilson Brownell said, 'Oh, shit.' He knocked over his stool as he lurched from the bar, then hurried through a door in the rear. Gone. The bartender didn't look. The women didn't look. The guy sleeping on the bar stayed down.

The buzz cut and his friend came over. 'You are coming with us.' The buzz cut spoke the words with a careful, starched pronunciation that made me think of Arnold Schwarzenegger, only the accent was Russian.

'Sez who?' I can slay 'em with these comebacks.

The weightlifter reached under his shirt and came out with a Sig automatic. 'You'll come or we will shoot you.' He said it in a normal speaking voice, as if he didn't give a damn who heard. Another Russian.

I said, 'Have you guys been following me from Los Angeles?'

The weightlifter shoved me, and it felt like getting blindsided by a backhoe. 'Shut up. Walk.'

I shut up. I walked.

Maybe Wilson Brownell was right. Maybe I was in something deeper than I realized, and now it was too late to get out.

Isn't hindsight wonderful?

CHAPTER 9

The buzz cut held the door as the lifter walked me out, then followed behind us. The big guy let the gun dangle along his leg but made no effort to hide it. A woman with two kids came out of a bakery across the street, saw the gun, then grabbed her kids and stumbled back into the bakery. I said, 'Don't you guys know it's illegal to walk around with that thing?'

The big guy said, 'This is America. In America, you can do what you want.'

'I'd put it away if I were you. The cops will be here in seconds.' Maybe I could scare him into letting me go.

He made a little gesture with the gun, as if it were the gun shrugging, not him. 'Let them come.' Guess not.

'Who are you guys?'

The buzz cut shook his head. 'Nobody.'

'Where are we going?'

'To the car.' Everybody's a comedian.

The black Lexus was parked by a fire hydrant at the end of the block. This morning I was boarding a jet to fly to Seattle to find the missing father of three children in what should have been a no-big-deal job, and now I was being taken for a ride by two unknown Russian maniacs. I was willing to walk with these guys, but I did not want to get into the car. There are two crime scenes at every kidnapping. The first crime scene is where they snatch you, the second is where the cops find your body.

The lifter didn't seem to be paying a lot of attention,

but the buzz cut was looking at everything. He scanned the storefronts and alleys and roof lines, his ice blue eyes moving in an unhurried, practiced sweep. I wondered what he was looking for, and I wondered where he had picked up the habit. I said, 'Afghanistan.'

The ice blue eyes never stopped their search.

The big guy said, 'Da. Alexei was Spetnaz. You know Spetnaz?'

The ice blue eyes flicked at the big guy, and Alexei mumbled something soft in Russian. The big guy's eyebrows bunched like dancing caterpillars. Nervous. I guess he was scared of Alexei, too.

I said, 'I know Spetnaz.' Spetnaz was the former Soviet army's version of our Special Forces, but they were really more like Hitler's SS. Motivated zealots with a penchant for murder. 'That's a kind of Austrian noodle, isn't it?'

The ice blue eyes flicked my way, and Alexei smiled. The smile was wide and thin and empty. 'Da, that's right. A little noodle.'

I wondered how many Afghan kids had seen that smile before they died.

The big guy was walking behind me, but Alexei was maybe three paces back and to the side so that he wasn't between me and the gun. If I could put Alexei between me and the lifter, I could use him as a shield from the gun and perhaps effect an escape. Superman could probably do it, and so could the Flash. Why not me?

I slowed my pace, and almost at once Alexei slid sideways, brought up a Glock semiautomatic, and locked-out in a perfect two-hand combat stance. Guess they both had guns. He said, 'The car is safer, my friend.'

I showed him my palms and we went on to the car. So much for effecting an escape.

They put me in the front seat. Alexei got behind the wheel and the big guy got into the back. When he got in, the car tilted. Steroids. We started away and the big guy leaned forward and pushed a CD into the player. James Brown screamed that he felt good, and the big guy bobbed his head in time with the music. He said, 'You like James Brown, the king of soul?'

I looked at him.

Alexei said, 'Turn it down, Dmitri.'

Dmitri turned it down, but not very much. He made little hand moves with the music as if he were dancing, looking first out one side of the Lexus, then out the other, as if he wanted to take everything in and miss nothing. 'I enjoy the king of soul, and the Hootie and the Blowfish, and the Ronald McDonald's. Do you enjoy the Big Mac?'

I looked at Alexei, but Alexei wasn't paying attention. 'I prefer Burger King.'

Dmitri seemed troubled. 'But there is no special sauce.' He spoke Russian to Alexei.

Alexei shook his head, irritated. 'No. No special sauce.'

I said, 'Are you guys for real?'

The lifter said, 'What is that, 'for real'?'

Alexei pointed the Glock at me. 'This is real. Would you like to see?'

'No.'

'Then keep your mouth shut.'

Grump.

A light patter of rain began to fall, and Alexei put on the windshield wipers. We took the Alaskan Way Viaduct up past Elliot Bay into Ballard, then turned toward the water and bumped along an older part of the wharf to a warehouse at the edge of a pier. The warehouse, like the pier, was old and unkempt, with great rusted doors that slid along tracks and peeling paint and an air of poverty. Dmitri climbed out, pushed open the door, and we drove inside to park between a brand-new $100,000 Porsche Carrera and an $80,000 Mercedes SL convertible. Guess the air of poverty only went so far.

The warehouse was a great dim cavern that smelled of fish and rain and marine oil. Dust motes floated in pale light that speared down through skylights and gaps in the corrugated metal walls, and water dripped from the roof. Men who looked like longshoremen were driving forklifts laden with crates in and out of the far end of the warehouse, and did their best to ignore us. Alexei blew the horn twice, then cut the engine and told me to get out. A row of little offices was built along the side of the warehouse, and, with the horn, a pudgy guy with a cigarette dangling from his lips stepped out of the last office and motioned us over. We were expected.

The three of us went through the door into a shabby office in which it was even harder to see. The only light in the place came from a single cheap lamp sitting atop a file cabinet in the corner. Three men were around an oak desk that had probably been secondhand in the thirties, two of the men in their mid-fifties, the third maybe younger. The younger guy was the one who'd waved us in. I had hoped that maybe Clark would be there, but he wasn't. Probably just as well.

An empty folding chair was in the center of the room. The pudgy guy gestured at it and said something in Russian. Alexei said, 'For you.'

'I'll stand, thanks.'

Alexei glanced past me to Dmitri and then an M-80 went off in my ear. I rocked sideways and went down to one knee, then felt myself put into the chair. Alexei leaned toward me. 'No more jokes, now.' His voice was far away. 'That was a slap, do you see? If Dmitri closes his hand, it will kill you.'

'Sure.' His face tilted crazily first to one side, then the other, and I thought I was going to throw up.

A fourth man entered, this guy a little shorter than the others, but wider, and hard to see when your eyes are blurring. He was in his fifties, with crinkly gray hair and a florid face and a dark blue shirt open at the neck to show a lot of grizzled chest hair. He was also holding a McDonald's soft drink cup. Large. I guess that's where Dmitri got it from.

When the new guy entered the other men stood, and murmured greetings of respect. The new man spoke more Russian, and Alexei handed over my wallet. The new man put his cup down and sat on the edge of the desk to look through my wallet. Deciding my fate, no doubt.

I rolled my head one way, then the other. The disorientation was beginning to pass, but the soft tissue around my ear felt tight and hot.

The new guy finished going through my wallet, then tossed it to the floor. His eyes were tired and lifeless and uncaring. Just what you want to see when you're being held in a chair by a four-hundred-pound Russian with steel fingers. The new man said, 'I am Andrei Markov.'

'All right.' He spoke pretty good English.

'Where is Clark Hewitt?' It hung like a chime tone in an empty room. All of this was about Clark.

'I don't know.'

Markov nodded and the steel fingers tightened into my shoulders like pliers. Alexei backhanded me with the Glock and a starburst of pain erupted from my other ear. Some days suck. Some days you shouldn't even get out of bed. I said, 'Who is Clark Hewitt and why is he so important?'

Markov said, 'Tell me where he is, or I will kill you.'

'I don't know.' My ears were ringing. I shook my head to stop the ringing but the shaking made it worse.

Another nod, and this time Alexei hammered back the Glock and pressed it hard into my neck. Dmitri stepped back to get clear of the splatter.

I said, 'I've never seen Clark Hewitt, and I don't know where he is. I don't know anything about him.'

Markov said something to Alexei and Alexei answered in Russian. Markov said, 'Do not lie. You were asking about him. You were at his wife's grave.'

'His name came up in something I'm working on so I came up here to find out about him.'

'What thing?'

'I'm trying to find a drug importer from San Francisco. Before he disappeared he said he was going to buy some dope in Seattle off a connection named Clark Hewitt. I came up here to find out.' Good lying is an art.

Markov stared at me some more, thinking about what I had said, trying to decide whether or not he believed me and how far to take this if he didn't. The Glock hovered like a living thing three inches from my left ear. I thought that I might be able to block it away and drive up into Dmitri, and if I was lucky I might be able to live another ten seconds.

Far away a dog barked. Deep and throaty and coming closer.

I said, 'I don't know Hewitt. I don't know you guys. What in hell is going on here?'

The phone rang, and the man to Markov's right answered it and listened without speaking. He put down the phone and said something and Markov's steady eyes wavered.

Something was happening out in the warehouse. The dog sounded closer now, and men were moving and there were voices. Markov murmured more Russian. The

Glock disappeared and Alexei stepped away and the barking came to the door. A guy in a suit stepped inside, holding out a federal badge, and announced, 'Federal Marshal.' He was a tall guy and the suit fit well. He glanced at me, then came over and jabbed a finger into Dmitri's chest. 'Step back, fatso.'

Dmitri squinted at Markov, and Markov nodded. Dmitri stepped back.

The guy in the suit looked at me. 'You okay?'

'Do I look okay?'

'We'll get you some ice.' He turned back to Markov. 'My name is Special Agent Reed Jasper, United States Federal Marshal. The men behind me are with United States Customs. They have some paperwork they'd like to discuss with you.' A powerfully built guy wearing an assault suit and a Browning 9mm was outside the door with the dog, and the dog was straining to get into the room. It was a big, muscular mix, maybe shepherd and Akita, and it looked like it wanted to bite. Behind him, other men were moving through the warehouse.

Andrei Markov spread his hands. 'I am always happy to cooperate with the authorities, Special Agent.'

I said, 'My name is Cole. I'm a private investigator from Los Angeles. These men brought me here against my will and assaulted me. I'd like to press charges.'

Jasper put away his badge, then picked up my wallet and lifted me off the chair as the guy with the dog came in. Jasper never again looked at the Russians, but kept all his attention on me, as if I was the reason he had come and the Russians were now someone else's problem. He said, 'You'll live.'

'I said that I want to press charges.'

'Sure.' He led me out of the room.

Maybe a dozen federal agents were moving through the warehouse. There were a couple more dog handlers in assault suits, but most were wearing blue rain shells that said POLICE – *U.S. Customs*. Jasper led me past them without another word and out into the rain. Maybe Jasper could tell me what was going on. Maybe Jasper could tell me why Clark Hewitt was so important, and why I had been grabbed, and why Andrei Markov had come maybe three seconds from blowing my brains out. I said, 'Man, am I glad to see you guys.'

Jasper said, 'You won't be.'

'What does that mean?'

A guy in a blue shell was waiting beside a nondescript government G-ride. 'Is this the dude?'

Jasper tossed him my wallet. 'Yeah.'

The new guy slipped my wallet into his pocket without looking at it, then went around and climbed in behind the wheel. His blue shell said MARSHAL. I said, 'Would you guys tell me what's going on?' I seemed to be saying it a lot, and no one seemed willing to answer.

Jasper pushed me against his ride, pulled my hands behind my back, and cuffed me. 'You're under arrest, asshole. If you know any good lawyers, you'd better get ready to call 'em.'

Wilson Brownell had been right. I had stepped into something deep, and now I was drowning.

CHAPTER 10

The rain came harder, raging at the G-ride as we made our way southeast across Seattle to the Federal Court Building. Jasper mumbled at the driver a couple of times and the driver mumbled back, but neither of them mumbled to me. The driver's name was Lemming.

First irate Russian thugs, now irate federal cops. Maybe Rod Serling was next.

The rain vanished as we slid beneath the building into the parking garage. We didn't bother with a parking spot; Lemming stopped the car at the elevator where a bald African-American agent was waiting with the elevator locked open. He was wearing a plastic security ID that said SCULLY, WILLIAM P. 'That him?'

'Yeah.'

He stepped into the elevator and unlocked the doors. 'Get his ass upstairs.'

I said, 'If you're Scully, where's Mulder?'

No one answered. Guess they didn't watch the X-Files.

They hustled me up to the sixth floor, then along a general issue federal hall as if I were a presidential candidate with an active death threat against him. We went through a door that said UNITED STATES MARSHALS, and into a department room with maybe half a dozen desks and four more agents gathered at one of the desks, talking. Scully took a bag of blue ice from a little fridge by the coffee machine, uncuffed me, then told me to put the blue ice on my eye. 'Put'm in the cold room.'

I said, 'I think I need medical attention. How about calling nine-one-one?'

'Keep the ice on it.'

They brought me to a small room with a table, four chairs, and no windows. Lemming put me in the far chair and said, 'Sit.'

'How about a lawyer?'

'Sit.'

I sat. Jasper sat at the table across from me, but Scully and Lemming stayed on their feet. Scully whispered something to Lemming, and Lemming left. Jasper said, 'First, I want you to know that we're holding you for questioning. We do not plan to file charges against you at this time, but we reserve the option to do so at a later time.'

'Questioning about what?'

'The murder of a federal officer.'

'Come again?'

Scully said, 'Why are you looking for Clark Hewitt?'

I looked at him. First Markov, now these guys. I looked from Scully to Jasper, then back to Scully. They were staring at me the way a circling hawk eyes a field mouse just before she folds her wings and slips down through the air to feed. I said, 'I'm sorry, I didn't catch that name.'

Scully said, 'Knock off the bullshit. We ask, you answer.'

I grinned at him. 'Is that the way it works, Scully?'

'Yeah. That's the way it works.' My eye was burning and flushed with blood. I put the blue ice on it.

Jasper said, 'Who are you working for?'

'I just went through this with Markov. I didn't like it then either.'

'Tough.'

Scully said, 'How do you know Markov?'

'I don't. Two goons scooped me off the street and brought me to see him.'

Scully glanced at Jasper, and Jasper said, 'Alexei Dobcek and Dmitri Sautin.'

Scully looked back at me. 'Why?'

'So they could ask the same questions you people are asking.'

'What'd you tell them?'

'The same thing I'm telling you.'

'It might go easier if you were more cooperative.'

'You might get more cooperation if you told me what was going on.' I'd had enough, and my voice was getting loud. My back was tight and my cheek and ear were throbbing, and the blue ice had lost its cold. I didn't know why any of this was happening, and the not knowing made me feel like a chump. I had flown up on my own nickel to find a runaway dad, only nothing appeared to be quite what I had thought it was, and that made me feel like a chump, too.

I put the ice packet on the table and stood. 'If you're going to charge me, then do it. If you're going to keep me, I want a lawyer.'

'Sit down.'

I looked at Scully. 'No, Scully, I don't think so.'

Jasper stood and leaned across the table at me. 'Get in the goddamned chair.' Yelling.

'You're going to have to put me in the chair, and it's not going to be as easy as you're thinking.' I didn't shout. I was proud of myself for not shouting.

Jasper started to move around the table, but Scully caught him. 'Reed.'

Jasper stood there, breathing hard. I was breathing hard, too, but I was tired of getting shoved around and kept in the dark. Something was going on and everybody seemed in on it but me. I was seeing bits and pieces of it, and I wasn't liking what I was seeing, but I knew there was still more to the picture. Maybe it was time to start sulking. Maybe I could phone Charles for a couple of pointers and sulk these guys into submission. Or maybe Jasper would try to put me in the chair and I could get in two or three good shots before half a dozen federal marshals boiled through the door and rode me down. Might be worth it.

Scully, William P., had stared at me for what seemed like an hour when the door opened and Lemming whispered something in his ear. Scully listened without saying anything, then nodded and the tension seemed somehow lessened. 'Hang on for a minute.'

He patted Jasper's shoulder and the two of them stepped out with Lemming, but now I was feeling better about things. I was probably thirty seconds away from being thrown into jail, but you always feel better when you tough off to a guy.

Three minutes later Scully and Jasper came back without Lemming. Jasper had a nine-by-twelve manila folder and Scully had two Styrofoam cups of coffee and a baggie filled with fresh ice. Scully tossed me the ice, then put one of the cups by me on the table. He sipped from the other. 'We came on too strong and that was a mistake.' He gestured at the envelope. 'The office down in LA faxed up some information on you. You seem like a square guy, Cole, so let's take a step back and start again.'

'I'm listening.' I put the ice where the Glock had bitten me.

Scully said, 'Andrei Markov is looking for Clark Hewitt to kill him. We're looking for Clark to protect him. That's the difference between us and Markov.'

I looked at him without responding. The tough detective refusing to cut them any slack. Or maybe I was just the sulky detective. 'Don't tell me: Clark Hewitt used to be involved with Markov, but he turned state's evidence, and now he's in witness protection.'

Jasper smiled, but there wasn't a lot of humor in it. 'What else do you know?'

'I don't know any of it, Jasper, but I'm a hell of a guesser. Markov wants Hewitt, and so do you. You aren't the cops or the Treasury or the FBI. You guys are U.S. Marshals, and the marshals oversee the federal witness protection program.' I moved the ice to my ear and leaned back. 'And since you guys don't seem to know Clark's location, that means you've lost him.'

Reed Jasper frowned. 'We didn't lose him, goddamnit. He left. You don't have to stay in the program once you're in. You can leave any damn time you want.'

Scully said, 'Did Markov have any idea as to Clark's location or current identity?'

'Nope. That's what he wanted from me.'

'How'd he pick you up?'

'They had someone on Rachel Hewitt's grave.'

Scully whistled. 'Jesus Christ, three years and they're still on that place.' He shook his head. 'When that Russian swears an oath, he means it.'

I said, 'Who's Markov?'

Jasper said, 'Markov is a big macher in the Ukrainian mob. He came over here a few years ago with his brother, Vasily. Vasily was the boss. They set up shop and began expanding the business, and one of these new ventures was printing counterfeit dollars to ship back home and sell on the Ukrainian black market.'

I nodded. Clark the printer. Clark the artist. 'Clark was a counterfeiter.'

Scully said, 'Yeah.'

'So what happened between Clark and Markov?'

'Vasily thought Clark was skimming his print and

laying it off on a couple of locals. Clark got word that Vasily was planning to bump him off, and came to us for help.'

'He turned state's evidence to buy into the program.'

'Didn't have a lot of choice. The Markovs never made a threat they didn't carry out.'

'Was Clark skimming?'

Jasper shrugged. 'Who knows? Because of Clark, Vasily's doing twelve to twenty on Mercer Island, and Andrei swore he'd spend the rest of his life hunting down Clark and his family, and that's what he's doing. It's been three years, and he's still got people on it. Now you show up, and he sees you as a lead back to Clark.' Great.

I said, 'If Clark went into the program, how come you guys lost track of him?'

Jasper stared at me for a time, then wet his lips and looked away.

Scully made a little mouth move as if his lips had gone dry, too. 'The night we brought Clark in things went bad. Middle of the night, raining, we were going to put him and his kids into a safe house, then begin the relocation. We told him not to worry. We told him it was safe.'

I was watching him. 'Only it wasn't safe.'

Jasper's eyes narrowed and he looked back at me. 'Somehow Markov's people found out. We had everything in the truck, we were five minutes from driving away, and they surprised us.' He stopped and stared past me some more and I wondered if he wasn't reliving that night. 'My partner was a guy named Dan Peterson. He was killed.'

Scully said, 'Go get some water, Reed.'

Jasper shook his head.

I said, 'You couldn't get Markov for the shooting.'

Jasper sucked a breath, then focused on me. 'Peterson ordered me to get Clark and those kids out of the kill zone, and that's what I did. He stayed. I didn't see it, and I still don't know for sure what happened. SPD moved on our call. They found Danny inside. He'd been shot in the backyard, then dragged himself in.' He shook his head again. 'We never had a name or a face, but we know it was Markov.' He shook his head some more. 'Everything went wrong that night. It shouldn't have happened.'

Scully said, 'We finished the relocation, but Clark never trusted us after that. He changed his name as soon as they got to the relocation city and the whole family disappeared.' He shrugged yet again. 'That's his choice, of course. You don't have to stay in the program.'

Jasper made a little wave, then suddenly sat straighter, folding his feelings and putting them away. Every cop I've ever known could do that when he or she had to. 'And now you show up, asking about Clark Hewitt.'

Scully nodded. 'A guy from Los Angeles.'

I stared at Reed Jasper, and then at William P. Scully, and then I thought about Teri and Charles and Winona, waiting for Clark to come home. I wondered how much of this they knew, and I thought they must know some of it. Probably why they weren't thrilled about my coming to Seattle. I thought how terribly afraid they must be of losing him to risk bringing me into their affairs. I thought about what it must've been like for them three years ago, and what it must be like to live a life defined by secrets and lies. Secrets never stay secret, do they? Not even when you want them to. Not even when lives are at stake.

I looked Scully squarely in the eyes and spread my hands. 'I don't know where Clark is, or his kids, or anything about him.'

Jasper stared at me, and you could see he didn't believe me. Neither did Scully. 'Look, Cole, it's not our job to protect him anymore, but we feel what you might call a sense of obligation, you see?'

I smiled my best relaxed grin, and said, 'Man, this has to be one of the world's biggest screw-ups.' I told him the exact same story I'd told Andrei Markov. 'I came here looking for a drug connection named Clark Hewitt. I was just following a name, and the name's the same, but my guy doesn't have anything to do with Russians or counterfeiting or any of this other stuff.' I let the grin widen, like I was enjoying the enormous coincidence of it all. 'All of this is news to me.'

Scully nodded, but you could tell he didn't believe me. 'Who are you working for?'

'You know I'm not going to tell you. The card says confidential.'

'This is important, Cole. Clark is in grave danger. So are those kids.'

I shrugged. They had been in grave danger three years ago, too.

Scully said, 'I think you know something. I'm thinking maybe Clark left some footsteps in LA, and if I'm thinking it, Markov will be thinking it, too.'

I shrugged again. 'I'd help you if I could.'

Special Agent Reed Jasper nodded and stood. You could tell he didn't believe me, but there wasn't anything he could do about it. 'Sure.'

'Can I go?'

Scully opened the door. 'Get the hell out of here.'

It was twenty-two minutes after eleven that night when I walked out of the federal courthouse into a hard steady rain. The rain, like the air, was warm, but now felt oppressive rather than cleansing. Maybe that was me.

The world had changed. It often does, I've found, yet

the changes are still surprising and, more often than not, frightening. You have to adjust.

I had come to Seattle to find a man named Clark Haines, and in a way I had, though that no longer seemed to matter. What mattered was those kids, alone in a house with a Russian mobster wanting them dead.

CHAPTER 11

My left cheek was tight and discolored the next morning where Alexei Dobcek hit me. I had been up most of the night, trying to keep ice on my cheek, but the ice had been too little, too late, and I felt grumpy and discouraged, though not very much of it had to do with the ice. I packed my things, brought the rental car back to Sea-Tac, and boarded the plane. Grumpy.

A sandy-haired flight attendant in her early thirties clucked sympathetically and said, 'Rough week?'

I grumped.

She put her fists on her hips. 'Pouting won't help.'

These flight attendants are something.

I settled in beside an overweight man with very short hair and glasses so thick that his eyes looked the size of BBs. He smiled, but I didn't smile back. Tough.

I crossed my arms, frowned real hard, and thought about Teri and Winona and Charles as we lifted up through the northwest cloud layer into a brilliant clear sunshine that stretched from southern Washington to the tip of the Baha Peninsula and the Sea of Cortez. Maybe it would help if I stuck out my lower lip. I had flown to Seattle to find an ordinary missing father, and instead had found that Clark Haines was really Clark Hewitt, and that Clark Hewitt, along with being a drug addict, was a criminal, a former participant in the federal witness protection program, and was actively being sought by both the Russian mob and various federal law enforcement agencies. These are not good things to discover, and were even less good when one considered that, if the mobsters were after Clark, they would also be after his children. For all I knew, Clark Hewitt was dead and would never return, or, if he wasn't dead, perhaps had no interest in returning. I thought that maybe I could get his kids into foster care without revealing their true identities, but this somehow seemed to leave them more vulnerable and exposed. The obvious solution was to take them to the police, identify them by their original names, and allow Jasper and Scully to see to their well-being. Charles and Winona and Teri would still end up in foster care, only an awful lot of people would know who and where they were, and the more people who knew, the greater the possibility that word would get back to the Markovs. This was yet another problem, and all these problems were making me grumpier still. Maybe I should try to get into a problem-free occupation of some kind. Hunting lions, maybe. Or raising the *Titanic*.

The flight attendant stood over me. 'Are we feeling any better yet?'

I stared at her, and then I sighed. 'Is it that obvious?'

'Mm-hm. Could I bring you a nice cup of tea?'

'A cup of tea would be fine.'

She brought the tea, a couple of Tylenol, and a reassuring smile. Two hours and fifty minutes later we let down through a cloudless cathedral of sky and faint orange haze into the wonderland that is Southern California. I still wasn't sure what I wanted to do, but I felt better about not knowing. The attendant smiled a good-bye at the door. 'You look much better.'

'I've achieved a measure of peace with my uncertainty.'

'Sometimes that's the best we can do.' I guess you

develop a certain wisdom when you spend your life at thirty-five thousand feet.

I kissed her hand, then picked up my car from long-term parking, and made the drive up through the city to Teresa Hewitt's house.

It was after three when I arrived, and that meant Charles and Winona would be home. I would've preferred to speak with Teri alone, but there you go. *Tell me, Winona, can you spell 'foster care'?*

I parked at the opposite curb, crossed to their front door, and rang the bell. I couldn't see Joe Pike or his Jeep, but I waved to him anyway. He would be someplace near, and he would be watching. Unobtrusive.

The Saturn was in the drive, and I figured that Charles would throw open the door and we'd go through the same opera again, but this time it wasn't Charles. This time it was a half-bald guy two inches shorter than me with faded hair and skinny arms and glasses. I said, 'You're a hard guy to find, Mr. Hewitt.'

Clark Hewitt made a soft smile that seemed confused. 'I'm sorry, but my name is Haines. I don't use the other name anymore.' He said it as if there were no value to its secrecy, or, if there had been, he'd forgotten. He was heavier now than in the picture with Rachel and the Brownells, and somehow less distinct. He was wearing a loose cotton shirt and ValuMart chinos and brush-burned Hush Puppies that were screaming for a retread. Winona ran up, grabbed him around the legs with an *oomph!*, and looked at me. 'Hi, Elvis. Our daddy's home!'

'Hi, Winona. So I see.' *Can you spell 'reunion'?*

She dangled one of those ugly little trolls that kids have. It had purple hair and a horrible leer. 'You see what my daddy brought me?'

I nodded.

'It's a key chain.'

Clark Hewitt beamed at her and patted her head. 'Because she always has the key to my heart.'

Winona giggled, and I wanted to shoot him. Clark looked back at me, and said, 'You must be the detective! Please come in.' The detective.

The house smelled of fresh coffee and baked cookies, and, as we entered, Teresa came out of the kitchen carrying a plate heaped with the cookies. Charles peeked out of the hall that led back to the bedrooms, scowling and hunched, with his hands jammed into his pockets. He didn't look happy, and he didn't come out. Lurking. Teri said, 'I left a message on your machine. Daddy came home this morning.'

'I just got back. I haven't checked my messages.'

Clark Hewitt made himself comfortable in his easy chair. I didn't sit. 'Were you on a trip?'

'Seattle. I guess we just missed each other.'

'Ah. Seattle is a wonderful city, but I haven't been there in years.' He gestured at the cookies. 'Teri baked these cookies, Mr. Cole. Won't you have some?'

Teri said, 'Chocolate chip raisin.'

She held the plate close to Clark, who bent to smell. 'Ah! My favorite!'

Clark beamed at Teri and Teri beamed at Clark. Winona beamed at everyone. Charles stayed back in the hall and glowered, but that was Charles. Maybe this wasn't the Hewitt house. Maybe my plane hadn't really landed in Los Angeles, but had somehow jumped dimensions and brought me to an alternate Los Angeles and these people were the Bradys.

I stayed on my feet, and I didn't take the cookies. 'Clark, you and I need to talk.'

He selected a fat, round cookie and settled back in the chair. 'Mmm.'

'Clark.'

Winona perched on the couch and Teresa put the plate on the coffee table near her father. 'Come out here, Charles, and have a cookie with Daddy.'

Charles made a single cough. 'Eff'm.'

Teresa's face flashed into a hard white mask, and her voice came out as rough as a rat-tail file. '*Charles.*'

Charles coughed again, stomped down the hall, and slammed his door. Daddy might be home, but I guess everything wasn't hunky-dory with the Bradys.

Clark chewed and swallowed and smacked his lips as if he hadn't heard. Maybe he lived in one world and they lived in another and the two worlds overlapped only on occasion. 'I'm sorry the kids bothered you with all of this, Mr. Cole, but it's my fault they were worried. A business opportunity came up and I had to leave on such short notice that I couldn't get home to explain.'

'Such short notice that you left three underage children to fend for themselves.' No one had mentioned my face. No one had asked about the swelling or the bruise.

He eyed the plate for another cookie. 'Well, I tried phoning, but I always called at the wrong time.'

Teresa said, 'He phoned during the day when I was out.'

'You told me you don't go out.'

She frowned. 'Well, to the market and to pick up the kids. You know.'

Clark snagged a second cookie. 'I guess I should've tried more often, but there was so much to do.'

Winona said, 'We're going to be rich. We're going to buy a house and a Sega and a really big TV.'

Clark chuckled. 'Well, let's not buy that house just yet, but life is certainly looking up. Yes, it is.' He gave Winona a hug and smiled at Teri, but Teri wasn't looking at him. She was looking at me. He said, 'Our luck is about to change, and, boy, we deserve it. I'll be printing documents for a group of international investors with a long-term contract. A contract spells job security. None of this seasonal employment. No more of this moving every few months.' He tickled Winona and she giggled. 'We'll be able to buy our own home and settle down and not move around so much. Won't that be good, Teri?'

Teri nodded without looking at him. 'Yes sir. Yes, it will be good to stay put.'

Winona twirled the little troll. 'Can I have my own room? I want my own room!'

Clark laughed. 'Well, we'll see.'

I stared at Teri, and Teri stared back. Her lips were a thin tight line and her eyes fluttered and she mouthed the words 'Well, we'll see' as if they'd had this conversation a thousand times, and she knew deep in her soul that it was just talk, that the money would never come, and they would move and move and move. Then she seemed to get the fluttering under control and said, 'Would you like a cup of coffee?'

I said, 'Clark, could I see you outside, please?'

Clark said, 'It's hard being a single parent, but these little guys are just such a help. Their mother would be so proud.' Maybe he hadn't heard me. Maybe he was so filled with wonderful plans and the intricacies of big deals that the words had just flown right past him. Or maybe he was high.

I leaned toward him. 'Markov.'

Clark's eyes focused for the first time, and he stood. 'Well, kids, I'm sure Mr. Cole is very busy, so I'll see him out to his car. Everybody say good-bye.'

Teri and Winona said good-bye, and Clark followed me out to my car. The heat had risen and the sun was bright and hot and the grass on the front lawn looked wilted and spotty. A stocky Hispanic woman walked past on her way up to Melrose. She carried a shopping bag in one hand and used the other to shield her eyes from the sun. She did not look at us. 'Clark, I know who you were and what you did. I was in Seattle. I spoke with Wilson Brownell and a U.S. Federal Marshal named Reed Jasper. I also met Andrei Markov. I did not tell Jasper where you were, or what name you were living under, though I think you should contact him.'

Clark Hewitt was shaking his head before I finished. 'I couldn't do that. I don't want anything to do with those people.'

'The Markovs suspect that there's some kind of connection between us, and they know I'm from Los Angeles. That means they might show up here, nosing around, and even if they don't they're still out there, waiting. Jasper wants to help.'

Clark raised a hand as if I were telling him about a great place to buy discount tires but he was about to tell me of an even better place, his discount-tire secret. 'Thank you, but everything is going to be fine. We're going to leave soon.'

'You should leave *now*, Clark. If you don't have the money, call Jasper. He'll help. So will I.'

Clark shook his head.

'Are you high?'

He blinked at me, then shook his head. 'Oh no. I don't do that.'

I took a breath and let it out. I wanted to shout at him to knock off the bullshit, but Winona and Teri were standing in the front door, watching us. I said, 'I know why you lost the job at Enright Printing. I spoke with Tre Michaels.'

He didn't answer. He was pale, with dark lines under his eyes, and he looked tired. His eyes seemed sad, and I thought he might cry. 'Are you going to tell?'

'Of course not.' Like we were six years old.

Clark Hewitt's eyes filled and he blinked fast. 'Please don't tell.'

My head hurt and my scalp felt tight and the tightness was moving down to my neck. 'Do your children know about any of this?'

He shrugged.

'Do they know what you were, and why you move around so much?'

Another shrug.

'They must know something, Clark. It was only three years ago. You changed their names.'

He looked at the ground. Talk about denial.

Charles appeared in the window, stuck out his tongue, and gave us the finger with both hands. He seemed to be looking more at his father, but maybe it was the angle. 'Clark, I can help you get into a substance abuse program. There are people at the county and at a couple of private places I know who can help. You've got these kids to think about.'

Clark glanced at Teri and Winona. He smiled at them like we were discussing the weather. 'We'll be fine. Everything is going to be okay real soon. I won't leave them again.'

I took out a card and wrote a name and number on it. 'I want you call this number and speak with a woman named Carol Hillegas. If you don't enroll in a program I'm going to call Children's Services. Do you see where I'm going with this?'

Clark took the card, but didn't look at it. 'I understand. I won't leave them again.'

'Clark.'

'Everything's going to be fine. I'll call and I promise I won't leave them again.' He reached into his pocket and came out with an enormous fold of cash. 'I want to apologize for the trouble, and I want to thank you again for taking care of my children. I think you deserve a bonus.'

I stared at him.

He fumbled with the bills, riffling through a roll of hundreds that was even larger than Teri's. 'It's the least I can do.'

Teri noticed Charles in the window and said something. Charles gave us the finger still harder, and started crying. Teri disappeared from the door, reappeared in the window, and grabbed Charles by the arm. He shoved her and ran, and she chased him. She was crying, too. Winona was still in the door, smiling and oblivious and waving. Her face was filled with light.

I said, 'Just call the goddamned number.'

Clark Hewitt was still fumbling with his bonus money when I crossed the street, climbed into my car, and drove away.

CHAPTER 12

Fourteen minutes after leaving the Hewitts, I carved my way through the trees along Woodrow Wilson Drive, then turned onto my little road and saw Joe Pike. Pike's Jeep was parked at the front of my house, and Pike was leaning against the rear hatch, as motionless as a tree or the house or the earth. I put my Corvette in the carport, and met him at the kitchen door. Pike said, 'Nice eye.' No hello, no hey, are you all right? 'Clark do that?' You can always count on your friends for humor.

'How long you been here?'

'I left my position when you and Haines came out of the house.' You see? He'd seen everything.

I let us in, put my overnight bag on the kitchen counter, took two Falstaffs out the fridge, gave one to Pike, then drank a long pull of mine.

I turned on the kitchen tap and cupped the water to my face. I drank most of what was left of the beer, then took a deep breath and let it out. I had pulled the drapes when I left, and the house was dim and still from the close air. Dim and still was good. When it was dark it was easier to pretend that there weren't three kids on the run from the Russian mob with a junkie for a father. Maybe that was why Pike never took off his dark glasses. Maybe it was easier when you couldn't see so much.

Pike said, 'What's wrong?'

'His name isn't Haines. It's Hewitt, and he isn't just your ordinary junkie. He's on the run from the Russian mob, he used to be in the federal witness protection program, and he doesn't have a clue that he or those children are in danger.'

Pike nodded. 'So where's the surprise?' You never know if he means it.

I opened the house, then poked around to see if anyone had been in while I was away. As I poked, I told Pike about Wilson Brownell and Reed Jasper and what Jasper had said about Clark. I described what had happened with the Markov brothers, and how I got the eye. When I told him about the Markovs, Pike's head swiveled about a quarter micron. 'He really Spetnaz?'

'That's what he said.'

'People say anything.' You could tell Pike was interested.

'It's the new world order, Joe. Equal opportunity crime.'

Pike went to the glass doors and looked out. He slid back the glass and the silky mountain air rolled in. 'This isn't good.'

'No,' I said. 'It's not.'

'It won't matter what you told the Russians. They'll figure you've got a line on Clark, and they'll show up.'

'That's what I told Clark. I told him to leave town, or go back to the marshals. They're still willing to help.'

'Will he?'

'I don't know. I told him to call Carol Hillegas. He won't be worth a damn to those kids until he's clean, but who knows what he'll do?' We went out to the deck and stood at the rail and looked down at the canyon. 'Talking to Clark is like talking to your television. He doesn't see that his actions have consequences.'

Pike crossed his arms.

'Also, he told me that our services were no longer needed.'

The corner of Pike's mouth twitched. He'll never smile, but sometimes you'll get the twitch. 'Fired.'

'Well, yeah.'

Another twitch. 'How much money we make?'

'Two hundred, less the cost of airfare and hotel. I'd say we're down about three hundred.'

Pike finished his beer.

'But we picked up some frequent flyer miles.'

Pike said, 'You thinking it was the feds or the Russians who went through your house?'

I thought about it, then shook my head. 'It's possible, but I don't think so. If these Russians had a line on Clark, they wouldn't't've bothered with me up in Seattle, and the feds would've just knocked on the door. Besides that, I think I've been followed by a guy in a gray LeBaron, and I'm pretty sure the following started before those kids came to my office.' I told him about the black guy in the LeBaron.

'So maybe there's still someone stalking you.'

'Could be.' Always a pleasant thought. 'You want to stay for dinner?'

'No.'

Pike watched a car move along the canyon floor beneath us for a time, then left without another word. No so long, no see you later. Just left.

I finished the Falstaff, crimped the can, and tossed it in my can bag. Recycling. I unpacked, did laundry, and wandered through the house. I felt empty and unfinished, as if there were more to be done only I didn't yet know what to do. Maybe I was bored.

Clark was home, his kids weren't alone anymore, and he was going to do whatever he was going to do. They would leave or they would stay, he would call Carol Hillegas or he wouldn't, he would ask Jasper for help or not, and there wasn't a whole helluva lot I could do about it short of putting a gun to his head. Life in a free society.

I opened another Falstaff, then called Lucy Chenier at her office. 'It's the world's greatest human being, calling for Ms. Chenier.'

Lucy's assistant, Darlene, laughed. 'I see we've upgraded from the world's greatest detective.'

'They're one and the same, are they not?'

'Only when we're talking about you, Mr. Cole.' To know Darlene is to love her. 'I'm sorry, but Ms. Chenier isn't in.' It was just before six in Baton Rouge. Lucy normally stayed in her office until six, unless her son, Ben, had a soccer game.

'Is she at home?'

'You could call her there and find out, I suppose.'

I kidded with Darlene for a few more minutes, then hung up and phoned Lucy's home. She answered on the first ring with 'Hi, David!'

'David?'

'Oh. It's you.'

'Maybe we should hang up and start this conversation again.'

Lucy laughed and said, 'David is David Shapiro, who just happens to be the most experienced news talent attorney in New Orleans, and who also happens to be representing me.'

'KROK made a firm offer?'

She said, 'Negotiations are officially under way.'

The grin started deep and came out big. 'Lucille, that is totally wonderful.'

'It's only their opening offer, and we have to counter, but we're close, Elvis. We are really, really close, and this is going to happen.' You could hear the energy and excitement in her voice. 'David thinks we'll conclude by the end of next week. After that, it's just a matter of waiting for Ben's school year to end, and then we can move out.' The end of Ben's school year was less than six weeks away.

'KROK doesn't have a problem with waiting?'

'Not at all. They've even offered to put me in touch with a real estate agent to help us find a place to live.'

We talked, and as we did the tension slowly seeped away with our sharing, and my home became my home again, warm and enveloping and no longer a place that had been invaded by another. The cat's door clacked, and the cat walked over, bumped against me, and purred. Maybe he could feel the change, too.

Lucy asked about the Hewitt children, and listened as I told her about my trip to Seattle, and the uncomfortable facts that I had learned about their father. She said, 'You took it upon yourself to fly to Seattle to look for him?'

'There's a sucker born every minute, Lucille.'

She sighed, and I could almost see her smile. I could see her in the big overstuffed chair in her living room. I could see Ben on the floor surrounded by Incredible Hulk comic books while he watched 'Babylon 5'. I could smell the bay leaf and sassafras of the oyster gumbo simmering for their dinner in the warm safe house near LSU. Exactly the kind of house that Teri and Charles and Winona did not have. Or maybe I'd just drunk too much Falstaff and all of it was wishful thinking. She said, 'You're not a sucker, you nut. You're the man I love.'

'Thanks, Luce.'

We talked for another hour, sharing our excitment and the evolution of our love, and then we hung up, Lucy promising to call with periodic updates on her status with KROK, and me promising to send her the real estate section from the Los Angeles Times, and both of us making those sugary kissing sounds. Sometimes I'm so schmaltzy I embarrass myself.

I brought the remains of my beer out onto the deck and listened to the breeze ruffling the leaves and to the shush of the cars down in the canyon and to the silence in my home. The cat came out and sat with me. I said, 'Lucy will be here soon. You'd best get used to it.'

He rubbed his head against my leg and purred.

It hadn't been such a bad day, after all.

CHAPTER 13

I woke the next morning telling myself that I should take a free day and relax. After all, I was officially unemployed, and when you get beat up by Russian weightlifters in Seattle you deserve time off. Teri and Charles and Winona were no longer my responsibility, and Clark had been warned, so there you go. Portrait of the detective with time on his hands. Unemployment had its advantages.

I fed the cat, then worked my way through forty minutes of tae kwon do *katas* in the hot morning sun and considered my options: I could run along the Pacific Coast Highway with Joe Pike or drive up to the Antelope Valley to pick fresh peaches or lay on the deck all day eating venison sandwiches and reading the new Dean Koontz. These all seemed like ideal ways to spend a day, but by nine that morning I had shaved, showered, and made my way down the mountains to the Beverly Hills Public Library to learn what I could about the Markov brothers, and what Clark did to get them so pissed off.

Being unemployed is easier said than done.

The Beverly Hills Library is one of the more wonderful libraries in the city. It is clean and neat and Spanish in its architecture, smack in the heart of BH between the Beverly Hills Police Department and the BH City Hall. A slim woman with very short hair showed me how to use their on-line search service and helped me connect with the *Seattle Times*. I downloaded every article they had about the Markov brothers and Vasily Markov's prosecution and subsequent sentencing, and when I printed the download it came to eighty-six pages. What's a day at the beach when you can spend your time reading about the Russian mob?

It was a crowded morning with no free tables, so I sat at a table opposite a couple of young women who looked about right for UCLA. I smiled at them when I sat, and they smiled back. One of them was tall and blond, with blue glitter nail polish and short, ropy hair. The other was short and dark and might've been Persian. Her nail polish was black. The blonde whispered something to her friend when I sat, and they giggled. I said, 'No giggling.'

The blonde frowned at me. 'No one was talking to you.'

'My mistake.'

The first headline read: MOB BOSS INDICTED ON 39 COUNTS. The basic story was as Reed Jasper described: Vasily Markov headed an organization of Russian émigrés who had long been suspected of involvement in counterfeiting, black marketeering, smuggling, extortion, and murder, but that it wasn't until 'an insider in Markov's counterfeiting ring' turned state's evidence that the grand jury could get an indictment. That insider was Clark Hewitt.

The blonde and her friend giggled again, but when I glanced over they pretended to be studying.

The articles described Hewitt as a professional printer who had been 'coerced' by Markov into printing counterfeit U.S. dollars for export to the former Soviet Union. No mention was made of Clark's family, and no mention was made that Markov suspected that Clark had been skimming and had targeted him for death. Other than minor details, there was nothing new or revealing in the first seventy-four of the eighty-six pages, and I was beginning to feel that I would've been better off reading the Koontz.

More whispering, more giggling.

I glanced over. Fast. 'Caught you.'

The blonde blinked at me with innocent eyes. 'Now that you've caught us, what're you going to do with us?'

I turned red and continued skimming. Flirting can be an ugly business. Especially when your girlfriend is soon to move in.

The blonde leaned toward me and looked at the downloads. 'Why are you reading about criminals?'

'Term paper.'

'You're not writing a term paper.'

'You're right. I'm with the library police, and I'm about to bust you for unlawful flirting.'

Her friend said, 'You started it.'

Three pages later I came to an article that wasn't about Markov, though the headline read MARKOV ONLY THE LATEST. It was a sidebar article about counterfeiting in the Pacific Northwest, and its star subject wasn't Clark Hewitt. I sat up straight and I read the name twice, the second time aloud. 'Wilson Brownell.'

The blond girl said, 'Excuse me?'

I raised a hand and kept reading.

The article labeled Wilson Brownell as 'Seattle's Master Printer' and described Brownell as a key figure in a funny-money ring operating in the late sixties and early seventies. The article said that Brownell had put together a printing operation in his garage and had developed a coffee-based aging process that enabled him to turn out fake currency that, except for the quality of the paper, was almost indistinguishable from the real thing. They estimated that he had placed almost ten million fake dollars into circulation before, in an attempt to acquire actual government currency paper, Brownell met with an undercover Treasury agent whom he believed to be a European paper supplier. The article finished by saying that Brownell had served eight years of a twenty-year federal sentence, was paroled, and was reputed to be living in the Seattle area, though he could not be reached for comment.

I pushed back from the table, crossed my arms, and stared at the articles. The blond girl was concerned. 'Is everything all right?'

I shook my head, went back on-line, and tried to pull up more stories about Brownell, but none were available. Too far back.

I thanked the librarian for her help, said good-bye to the tag team from UCLA, then drove to my office and phoned the North Hollywood Division of LAPD. A woman's voice answered on the third ring. 'North Hollywood detectives.'

'Lou Poitras, please.'

'Who's calling?'

'The world's greatest detective.'

She laughed. 'Sorry, bud. You're talking to the world's greatest.' These cops are something.

'Tell him J. Edgar Hoover.'

She laughed again and told me to hold on.

I hung for maybe forty seconds, then Lou Poitras came on the line. 'It's gotta be you. No one else would have the balls.'

'Hi, Louis. I need to find out about a guy in Seattle named Wilson Brownell. Got time to make the call for me?'

'No.' He hung up. I never met a cop who didn't think he was a riot.

I called back and the same woman answered.

I said, 'This time tell him I've got pictures of the goat.'

She said, 'You sure you wouldn't rather talk to me? I'll bet I could help you.'

'I'd rather talk to you, but Poitras owes me money and this is how he works it off.'

'Hold on.'

Poitras came on maybe ten seconds later and sounded tired. 'Christ, I guess it's go along or have my lines tied up the rest of the day. Beverly's in love with you.'

I could hear Beverly shriek in the background. 'Jesus, Sarge, don't tell him *that*!'

Poitras said, 'What's the guy's name again?'

I spelled it for him. Lou Poitras is a detective sergeant at North Hollywood Division, married, three kids, the youngest of whom is my godchild. He's been pumping iron six mornings every week for as long as I've known him, and he is roughly the size of a Lincoln Continental. I'm pretty sure he could lift one.

Poitras said, 'You know, the taxpayers probably don't like funding your research.'

'At least they're getting something for their money.'

Poitras didn't say anything.

'Sorry, Lou. Just kidding.' Sometimes these cops are sensitive. 'Brownell did time on a federal beef, but now he's out. I need to know if he's keeping clean or if the feds think he's into something.'

'You think he is?'

'If I knew I wouldn't have to put the arm on my friends for free information, would I?'

Poitras said, 'Free?'

A kidder, that Lou.

He said, 'I'll call you later.' Then he hung up.

I pushed back in my chair, put my feet up, and thought about Wilson Brownell and Clark Hewitt, and why Clark would risk returning to Seattle where both the Russian mob and the federal marshals were looking for him. It was obvious that Brownell and Clark were more than just friends. Brownell had probably taught Clark everything he knew about printing money, which is probably how Clark had gotten involved with the Markovs. If Clark was willing to risk going back to Seattle to see Brownell, it had to be because Brownell knew or possessed something that Clark needed, and that suggested Clark's new business plan probably involved counterfeiting. Clark might be goofy, but he probably wouldn't risk getting tagged by the Russians just to pal around with an old bud. Maybe Brownell was even going into business with him.

I pulled out the two one-hundred-dollar bills that Teresa had given me and examined them. They were older bills, well worn and used, and they looked fine to me. I rubbed at the ink and held them to the light and examined the paper. They still looked fine, but I wasn't an expert.

I put them away and leaned back again when two men came through the outer door. The first guy was tall and black, with a shiny bald head and a plain navy suit and a grim demeanor. The second guy might've been a fashion model posing as a cutting-edge corporate executive. He was in his late thirties and in good shape, with immaculate dark hair and a conservative Brooks Brothers suit. I smiled when I saw the black guy because he was the same guy I'd seen in the gray LeBaron outside Teri Hewitt's house. I smiled wider when I saw a thick bandage on the back of his left hand, and I kept smiling as I reached under my jacket, took out the Dan Wesson, and pointed it at them.

The white guy said, 'You won't need that.' He had a light southern accent, and he didn't seem concerned about the gun.

I said, 'That's up to you. We might be here a while waiting for the police.'

The black guy closed the door and leaned against it. I guess he wanted to make sure I couldn't escape.

The white guy inspected my office. He looked at the figurines, and the Pinocchio clock, and then the picture of Lucy Chenier. Especially the picture of Lucy. I said, 'None of it's for sale. You want to tell me why you were in my house, or should I just start shooting?'

The white guy turned away from the picture. Now he was inspecting me.

I said, 'Pal, it's been a rough couple of days and I'm feeling a mite testy.'

He smiled, like me being testy was just what he wanted. He said, 'This is my associate, Mr. Epps. My name is Richard Chenier. I'm Lucy's ex-husband.'

My eyes clicked from Epps to Richard Chenier and I stared. So much for Russian mobsters. So much for federal agents.

Richard Chenier said, 'The gun?'

I remembered the gun and put it away.

'We were going to meet sooner or later, so I decided to introduce myself.' He didn't offer his hand, and neither did I.

'There might've been a friendlier way to say hello.'

Richard nodded. 'Perhaps.' I guess this wasn't going to be a friendly visit.

'Tell me something, Richard. Do you have your man Epps here follow every guy Lucy dates?'

'No. Only the ones who tempt her into moving two thousand miles. And take my son with her.'

I said, 'Richard.'

He smiled, then sat in one of the director's chairs across from my desk. 'My son likes you, so I wanted to find out what kind of guy you are. You can understand that, can't you?'

'I can understand your wanting to know about me. Hiring a guy to B and E my home is stepping over the line.'

'Oh, I didn't hire Mr. Epps for *you*. He works for my company. We're in international oil.'

'Mm.' Maybe I was supposed to be impressed.

'He's very good at what he does, and he tells me that you seem to be a solid man. Stable. Good reputation. All of that.'

'I'm glad you approve.'

'And small. A person we might describe as a minor player in an insignificant game, well beneath what I would want for my wife and my son.'

I stared at him some more, and then I looked at Pinocchio. I sighed, then stood. 'Okay, Richard. We've met. It's been fun. I'm sorry it's going to be like this, but now it's time to leave.'

He didn't move. Neither did Epps. 'Small, but reasonable, so I decided that I should explain things to you so that you understand.'

'I can ask nice, Richard, but, believe me, I don't have to ask, or be nice.' Epps shifted his weight forward slightly, away from the door. 'Epps, you won't believe it even while it's happening.' That probably scared him.

Richard raised both hands and smiled. 'I'm not here to threaten you. Look, I love this woman, and I love my son. What you don't understand is that she still loves me. We just have to work out a few problems, and then she'll come to see that.'

'Good-bye, Richard.' So much for civil discourse. So much for modern men discussing a modern problem in an enlightened manner. I was thinking that it might be fun to beat him to death.

He still didn't move. 'I just want you to consider what's best for Lucy. I know she's been offered this job, but it'll be much better for her to stay in Baton Rouge, and much better for Ben. I'm hoping that you're the kind of guy who wants what's best for them. If you cared, you'd tell her to stay home.'

He really believed it. I glanced at Epps, but Epps didn't seem to care one way or the other. I shook my head. 'You think I should tell Lucy to stay home?'

Richard smiled like a pleased teacher whose slow pupil was finally catching on. 'That's right.'

Maybe that's why their marriage failed. 'Richard, here's something that you don't seem to understand. This decision isn't mine or yours. It's Lucy's.'

Richard frowned, as if I'd failed him in my attempt to understand.

'I love her, and I want her here, but I can't make her come and I can't make her stay, and neither can you. It's her life, and her decision. You see?'

Richard Chenier frowned harder. 'There's always a way to get what you want. That's how I make my living.'

I stared at him. I tried to picture them as a couple, and couldn't.

Richard Chenier glanced at Epps, then stood. Epps opened the door. Richard said, 'You don't think I intend to just let them leave, do you?'

'I don't think you have any choice.'

'You'd be surprised.' He smiled at me, and I didn't like it. I didn't like him.

Richard Chenier walked out of my office without looking back. Epps stared at me, then grinned and turned away, too.

'Hey, Epps.'

He looked back, still grinning.

'That's some cat, huh?'

Epps dropped the smile, walked out, and closed the door. Hard.

I stared at the door for a very long time, and then I shook my head.

'Pleased to meet you, Richard.'

CHAPTER 14

I watched Richard and Epps drive away, then went back to my desk and stared at the Mickey phone and thought about calling Lucy, but what would I say? *Your ex-husband dropped by and told me he loved you?* Nope. *Richard hired some guy to break into my house.* It sounded like tattling.

I looked at the Pinocchio clock, and gave it Stan Laurel. 'Isn't this a fine development?'

Pinocchio's eyes went from side to side, but he didn't say anything. He never does.

I tried to think about Markov. I took out the two one-hundred-dollar bills, looked at them again, but I kept seeing Richard on the bills instead of Ben Franklin. 'For chrissakes, Cole, get over it. You're onto something with Clark. Follow up your lead.'

What kind of guy hires someone to break into his ex-wife's boyfriend's house?

Would you stop?!

I knew from Lucy that Richard Chenier was an attorney with the firm of Benton, Meyers & Dane, and I knew he had graduated from law school at LSU, where Lucy had been an undergraduate, but that was all I knew, and I had never given him much thought. Now he had entered my home and my office in a belligerent and threatening manner, which I could handle, but he had also indicated that he had no intention of allowing Lucy to leave Baton Rouge, which I didn't like at all. Whatever that meant.

I decided that if I couldn't stop thinking about Lucy's ex-husband, the smart thing would be to deal with it. I had met Lucy when I worked a case in Louisiana last year, and while I was there I had made friends with a couple of people on the Louisiana State Police and the Baton Rouge PD. Now I called them, told them what I knew about Richard and Epps, and asked if they could give me a fast background check. They told me that they'd get back to me as soon as possible.

While they were working on that, I called Joe Pike. 'Clark went to Seattle to see a man named Wilson Brownell. Brownell is a master counterfeiter. He taught Clark how to print, and I'm thinking that Clark went back to Brownell because he's getting back in the trade.'

'You think he's printing money?'

'I've got two one-hundred-dollar bills that I'm wondering about, and maybe this explains why Clark won't go to Jasper. If he's setting something up, it might be coming together and he wants to see it through.'

Pike didn't say anything for a moment, like maybe he was thinking. 'There's a woman named Marsha Fields at the Treasury office downtown. I could call her tonight, see if you can drop by with the bills tomorrow.'

'Okay.'

Then he said, 'What?' Like he could hear something in my voice.

'The guy who broke into my house is named Epps. He's the same guy in the LeBaron, and he works for Lucy's ex-husband. They just left my office.'

More silence. 'Want me to do anything?'

'I don't think we need to kill him just yet.'

'Maybe later.' Pike hung up. Sometimes the silence says it all.

I stared at the phone some more, then called the LSU Alumni Office. A little bit after that I phoned Benton, Meyers & Dane, pretending to be a prospective client, and six minutes after that the first of my cop friends called back. One hour and twenty-seven minutes after Richard Chenier walked out of my office, I knew that he had been a second-string cornerback for the LSU frosh team until a blown knee ended his collegiate career. He had dallied in campus politics, graduated summa cum laude, was an unsuccessful Rhodes candidate, and had never been arrested. Impressive. I also knew that he was a full partner at BM&D, a firm specializing in corporate law for international oil concerns, but was currently out of the office (yeah, he was in mine!) and not scheduled to return until next week. Lawrence Epps was a former Louisiana state trooper who had left the job and who now worked as an investigator for BM&D. He had been arrested four times, three of those for assault, and had been convicted one time for misdemeanor battery. One of those arrests was for beating his first wife. Sweet.

All in all, I was feeling better about things when I went home. I still wasn't liking Richard very much, but he seemed like a square guy, and if I tried real hard I thought that I might be going a little crazy, too, thinking that I might lose my child. After all, Lucy had married the guy, and that said something. Of course, she had also divorced him, but that didn't dawn on me until later.

When I got home that evening the cat was sitting by his bowl in the kitchen. I talked it over with him while I was making dinner, and said, 'What would you do?'

The cat blinked, then bent over and licked his anus. Cats lead simple lives.

Joe Pike called me at nine the next morning, telling me that Special Agent Marsha Fields of the U.S. Secret Service was expecting me. I made boiled eggs and English muffins for breakfast, then took my time showering and dressing before winding my way across town to the Treasury Department.

The Treasury has its offices on the seventeenth floor of the Roybal Federal Building in downtown Los Angeles, between the LAPD's Parker Center on one side and the Los Angeles Federal Metropolitan Correctional Center on the other. Cops feel safer when they cluster.

I parked in the basement, then took an elevator to the lobby where I went through a metal detector and gave my name to a guy who looked like he ate a Pontiac for breakfast. Then I took another elevator up to seventeen.

When I stepped off the elevator, a tall, athletic-looking woman with short red hair in a navy pants suit was waiting. She said, 'Mr. Cole? I'm Marsha Fields. Joe Pike asked me to examine some currency for you.' She took my hand with a firm grip and smiled nicely.

'That's right.' I smiled nicely, too, and tried to get my hand back. She didn't let go.

'Mm-hm. And how did you get these bills?' She kept the hand and I was thinking that maybe she wouldn't let go, as if the bills were funny or my answer was wrong she'd slap the cuffs on me and whisk me away to Secret Service Land.

'I cashed a check at a market in Hollywood.'

She kept the hand and the smile a little bit longer and then she dropped both. 'Well, come with me and let's see what we have.'

I followed her along a nondescript hall, past men and women who wouldn't make eye contact. All the better to keep secrets. She said, 'Joe says that you and he work together.'

'That's right. Joe owns the agency with me.'

'Joe's a very interesting man.'

'Mm-hm.'

'We met when Joe was on LAPD. We got to be friends.'

I nodded. She seemed interested.

'We were close.'

I looked at her. 'Joe speaks well of you.'

She brightened and didn't look so suspicious anymore. 'I imagine he's married by now.' I guess love was in the air. Or at least lust.

'Not yet. But there's always hope.'

She blushed and we went into a small lab that looked not unlike a doctor's office and smelled of naphtha. A black Formica counter ran along one wall with a shelf of little bottles above it and three light trays. A single steel sink was sunk into the counter, with a binocular microscope on one side of it and a large magnifying glass on a gooseneck stand on the other. Modern crime fighting at its cutting-edge finest.

Someone had taped cutout pictures of the president, the vice president, and the speaker of the house above the counter and used a Marks-a-lot to label them Manny, Moe, and Curley. Someone else had drawn a bozo face on the president and written *Would YOU take a bullet for this clown?* These Secret Service agents are a riot, aren't they?

Marsha Fields said, 'May I see the bills?'

I gave her both hundreds. She put one down and worked with the other. She examined both sides, then folded the bill and rubbed it together, then looked at the face again. She put it on one of the light boxes, then pulled over the magnifying glass and inspected first the front face, then the back. She made a clucking sound. 'These babies are righteous fakes.'

'Funny money.' Clark. You doofus.

'You bet. But not schlock. This is good stuff.'

'How can you tell?'

She held the bill under the big magnifier for me to see

and pointed with a Uniball pen. 'Look at the scrollwork around the edge of the bill. You see the vertical lines behind the portrait of Ben Franklin and the spokes in the Treasury seal? All of these lines should be clean and unbroken.'

I looked where she was indicating and I could see that the lines weren't clean and unbroken. The parallel lines were smudged together in some places and in other places were broken or separated. 'Yeah. I see.'

'Real money is made from engraved plates, so all of these lines are clearly resolved and separate. These bills were made from offset plates. The counterfeiter takes a picture of real money, then makes a plate from the picture, only you lose a little resolution with each step so the lines become smudged. Understand?'

She was looking at me expectantly, so I nodded. 'Sure.' If you can at least look smart, people will assume that you are smart.

'The other giveaway is the paper. Real money is printed on a cotton blend made by the Crane Paper Mill in Dalton, Massachusetts. You see these little red and blue lines?'

She showed me the little red and blue filaments we've all seen in money. There were little red and blue lines in this bill, too. 'Sure. I thought counterfeit money didn't have those lines.'

She nodded, pleased not only with me, but with the funny money. 'It doesn't and neither does this.'

'I'm looking at it.'

'Nope, you only think you're seeing it.' She put a drop of something from one of the little bottles on the bill and nothing happened. She frowned, selected another bottle, and put a different drop on another red fiber. This time the fiber dissolved and she smiled. 'The red and blue marks in real money are rayon fibers that are mixed in the cotton and linen mash when Crane makes the paper.' She tore the edge of the bill and looked at the fibers. 'This is a pretty good linen fiber, probably from a European mill, but the red and blue marks were printed on top of the paper in two separate processes.' She was smiling broadly now. She was beaming. 'This isn't schlock work. Someone went to a lot of trouble and they did a good job.' I guess she could appreciate the counterfeiter's art.

'Are these new bills?' I was thinking that if Clark was printing again, this is what he was printing.

'Oh no. I'd say these were eight, ten years old, at least.' She snapped off the light tray, but didn't offer the money back to me. 'Looks like you're out two hundred bucks.'

'That's the way it goes.'

She crossed her arms and nodded. 'You want to tell me where you really picked up this money?'

'I did.'

She smiled again, and stood. 'Sure.'

'You keep the money?'

'That's the way it works. You can file a claim for reimbursement through this office or any bank.'

'Thanks.'

'Tell Joe to call me sometime.'

I went out through security, down to my car, and started back toward my office. So Clark and his kids were living on counterfeit money. That's why they paid for everything in cash. If they tried to deposit their money into a savings or checking account, they'd risk being discovered. The few hundred bucks they had in checking was probably the only real money they had, but Teri probably didn't know that, just as she didn't know that her father was a counterfeiter.

Of course, knowing that they were living on counterfeit money didn't mean Clark was currently printing it or intending to. This stuff was probably the money he'd skimmed from Markov.

I nosed up onto Temple, then left toward the Hollywood Freeway. The downtown traffic combined with Caltrans construction projects was slowing the streets. I had gone three slow blocks and had just squeaked past a red light when about four thousand horns started blowing behind me. I looked in my rearview and saw the reason for all the noise: A nice new metallic tan Camaro had jumped into the oncoming lane to muscle its way through the intersection against the traffic. A blond guy with a buzz cut was driving, and a man who looked like the Incredible Hulk was filling the passenger seat.

Alexei Dobcek and Dmitri Sautin.

For the first time since Richard Chenier had walked into my office, it was easy to stop thinking about him. The Russians had arrived.

CHAPTER 15

It was just before lunch in downtown Los Angeles, and maybe eighty thousand people were jamming the sidewalks and streets around us, flooding through the crosswalks against the DON'T WALK lights. In New York that would get you killed, but in LA where pedestrians have the right of way, cars collect in turn lanes like debris in a drain cover. Dobcek wasn't used to that; people in Seattle obey the crosswalk signs.

They didn't close the gap between us; they just tried to keep me in sight. Probably picked me up at my office. Probably hoping that I'd lead them to Clark.

I drove with the traffic flow, letting Dobcek stay with me, and turned north under the freeway to Sunset Boulevard, then into a strip mall. Mr. Nonchalant. Mr. Taking-Care-of-a-Little-Errand. Dobcek and Sautin pulled to the curb in front of a menudo shop a block behind and tried to look inconspicuous. Hard to do when you weigh three hundred pounds.

I called Joe Pike from a pay phone outside a florist. 'Dobcek and Sautin are sitting in a tan Camaro fifty yards away, watching me.'

'Shoot them.' Life is simple for Pike. Like with the cat.

'I was thinking more along the lines of delaying them. They probably picked me up at my office, and they're probably hoping I'll lead them to Clark.'

Pike grunted. 'Or they're hoping for another chance to beat it out of you.'

'Well, there's that, too.' I told him where I was, and what I wanted.

Pike said, 'Try to stay alive until I get there.'

Always the encouraging word.

I pretended to talk for another five minutes, went into the florist to kill more time, then climbed back into my car and continued north along Sunset, making sure that Dobcek and Sautin made every light with me.

When I reached Elysian Park Avenue I turned toward Dodger Stadium, and wound my way up past small residential homes through the mountains to Chavez Ravine. Traffic thinned, and I thought that Dobcek might break off the tail, but he didn't.

Chavez Ravine is a broad flat bowl surrounded by low mountains that wall the stadium from the city. Dodger Stadium sits in the center of the bowl, surrounded by black tarmac parking lots like some kind of alien spacecraft resting alone on its launching pad. All you'd need was a big shiny robot, and you'd think Michael Rennie had come back to Earth.

An hour before game time on a cool spring evening and there'd be fifty thousand people driving past. Noontime on a day when the Dodgers were out of town, and the place was deserted. An ideal place for a conversation or a murder.

The roads there loop and roll around the base of the ravine, and little signs direct you toward the stadium or Elysian Park or any number of interesting places. I followed the signs past palm tree sentinels toward the ticket booth, and increased my speed enough to pull away from the Russians. Dobcek would want to stay with me, but not enough to get crazy and blow his tail. After all, he'd figure that he could always go back to my office and wait until I returned, but he would follow because for all he knew I was heading toward a safe house where I'd stashed Clark and his kids. I pressed it going up the hill to the turnoff to the ticket booth, but I didn't turn there. I turned off the road into the grass and backed my car behind a stand of scrub oak and brush. We hadn't had rain in weeks and the soil was hard as the pavement.

Forty seconds later the Camaro cruised past through the gate. I saw his brake lights come on, and I pulled back onto the road, and stopped in the gate, blocking their exit. Pike's Jeep was across the road in front of them. Pike was leaning across the Jeep's hood, pointing a twelve-gauge Beretta autoloader at them. I got out, walked up to their car, and smiled at them. 'Baseball. The great American pastime.'

Dobcek's hands were on his steering wheel. He nodded. 'Nicely done.'

'Welcome to LA, boys. Now get out of the car, keeping your hands where we can see them.'

Dobcek got out first. When Dmitri Sautin climbed out, the little Camaro rocked.

I said, 'Guns.'

Pike came around the Jeep, the shotgun still at his shoulder. Dobcek fingered the Glock from under his left arm and held it out. I tossed it into my Corvette. I looked at Dmitri Sautin. 'Now you.'

Sautin shook his head. 'No.'

Dobcek said, 'Dmitri.'

Sautin said, 'I think they have to take it, if they can.' He lowered his hands and grinned at Pike. Dmitri Sautin was four inches taller than Pike, and outweighed him by a hundred pounds.

Pike said, 'It's going to hurt.'

Sautin said, 'Ha.'

Sautin was still grinning when Pike hit him on the side of the head with a hard fast roundhouse kick. Sautin took one step to the side and looked surprised, but he didn't go down. Pike kicked him again, and this time Sautin staggered. His eyes filled and his lower lip quivered and he began crying. Pike said, 'Gun.'

Dmitri Sautin held out the Sig. I took it and tossed it in with the Glock.

Dobcek smiled, and it was ugly and predatory. His eyes sparkled in the bright sun and stayed with Joe Pike.

I patted them down, took their wallets, and then I told them to step away from the car. They did. I went through their car and found the rental papers. They had arrived at LAX that morning. I took the keys from the ignition and found two overnight bags in the trunk. I looked through them but found nothing but clothes and toiletries. I put their bags in the Corvette, too. Dmitri Sautin wiped at his nose, and said, 'But we will not have underwear.'

'A criminal's life is an ugly one.' I looked through their wallets, didn't learn anything new, and tossed the wallets in with the guns. I said, 'Markov's really going to be impressed when you tell him about this.'

Sautin said, 'You must be stupid to think we would tell him.'

Dobcek said, 'Shut up, fool.' Dobcek's eyes never left Pike.

I said, 'It's like I told you in Seattle, I don't know Clark Hewitt and I don't know where he is. You guys are wasting your time.'

Dobcek said, 'Da.'

'If you're smart, you'll go back to Seattle. If you try to tag me again, I'll kill you.' Mr. Threat.

Dobcek made the little smile again.

Pike said, 'He won't, but I will.'

Dobcek's smile faded.

I said, 'See the little building at the bottom of the hill?'

They could see it.

'Start walking.'

Sautin started toward the ticket building, but Dobcek didn't. Dobcek looked at Pike. 'This one goes to you, but I think we see each other again, yes?'

The corner of Pike's mouth twitched, saying here we are, saying we can take this anyplace you want, but wherever we go I will win and you will lose.

Dobcek made a small nod and followed Sautin.

We watched them for a time, and then Pike said, 'You lie well. Too bad they didn't believe you.'

'Yeah, but it'll buy us enough time to warn Clark. I told Clark they were going to come and now they have, and he'll have to do something. He won't like it, but there you go.'

Pike went to his Jeep and came back with an eight-inch stainless-steel hunting knife. He went around the Camaro and cut all four tires. Buy us even more time.

I said, 'By the way.'

He looked at me.

'The two C-notes were counterfeit.'

Pike nodded.

'Your friend Marsha Fields kept them.'

Another nod.

'Means we're down about five hundred now.'

Pike went back to his Jeep. 'A criminal's life is an ugly one.'

I got into my car and went to warn Clark Hewitt.

CHAPTER 16

Twenty minutes later I turned off Melrose and saw the green Saturn. I parked behind it, then went to the door and rang the bell three times. I was thinking that maybe everyone was pretending they weren't home when Teri opened the door. She wasn't smiling, and she opened the door only wide enough to look out. 'Oh, hello.'

'Great to see you, too.'

Blank.

'I need to see your father.'

'He isn't home.'

I glanced at the Saturn.

'He walked up to Melrose to go shopping.'

I edged closer to the door. 'That's okay. I'll wait.'

She didn't move or open the door. 'He might be a while.'

'No problem. When you make the big bucks like me, time is your servant.'

Something crashed through the house like a runaway buffalo and Charles appeared behind her, his face falling when he saw me. 'Oh, it's him.' Him.

I said, 'Are you going to open the door or make me wait out here?'

Charles jabbed at Teri's back and whispered loud enough for me to hear. 'Tell'm to eff himself.'

I said, 'Charles, for chrissake.'

Teri stepped back to let me in.

134

Charles screamed, 'Oh, frig!' He thundered back through the house and slammed his door.

I went into the living room, adjusted the blinds, and sat on the couch so that I could see the street. The Russians hadn't arrived, and I didn't expect them to, but you never know. If they found us, maybe I could just give them Charles. 'Where's Winona?'

'In her room.'

The TV wasn't going and Winona hadn't come out to see me. The house did not smell of baking cookies. I watched Teri and Teri watched me, and the close living room somehow felt expectant and tenuous. 'Quiet.'

Teri looked smaller than before, and tired. Her eyes were dark caves. I said, 'What did he go shopping for?'

'Clothes.'

I sat and listened, and her uneasiness was a physical thing that seemed to magnify sounds. I tapped the couch arm, and the tapping echoed like thunder. I sighed, and heard it as a rush of dry wind clawing across the desert. 'He's gone again, isn't he?'

She looked at the floor.

'How long?'

She didn't answer, and I imagined Dobcek and Sautin bombing around town, getting closer and closer, and finally showing up. Maybe it wouldn't be just Dobcek and Sautin. Maybe it would be other guys. Better guys. 'How long has he been gone, Teri?'

'Since yesterday morning.' A voice so small you could barely hear her.

'He didn't take the Saturn.'

'He walked up to Melrose. He said someone was picking him up.'

'He say who?'

She shook her head.

'Did he say when he'd be back, or where he was

going?' I wanted to roll my head and hear the bones crack and feel the relief.

She shook her head again. Of course not.

'And he hasn't called?'

'Uh-uh.'

I took a deep breath and let it out. The Russians had landed and Clark had disappeared. Again. Maybe he would be home by supper, but maybe not. Maybe Dobcek and Sautin weren't the only Russians who'd come down, and maybe those guys had Clark right now, but that probably wasn't the case either. Clark might be sitting with the U.S. Marshals right now, asking to get back into the program, but I wasn't willing to bet on it. Either way I wasn't going to leave these kids alone anymore. I said, 'Do you have any Tylenol?'

When I had the Tylenol, I excused myself, went to the kitchen, drank one glass of tap water, then went back to the living room. Teri had not moved, and the house seemed even more still. I wondered how often it had been like this. Maybe more often than I thought. I said, 'You and I need to talk.'

'He'll be back soon.' She tried to sound hopeful. 'He always comes back.'

'I hope you're right.' I sat very close to her and spoke in a quiet voice. I wanted her to know before Charles and Winona. 'We have to talk about some hard things. I don't know how much you know, or what you've guessed, but I don't see any other way.'

'About Seattle.' A statement. Like she knew what was coming and dreaded it.

'That's right. Seattle.'

She remembered the night her family had left, and she remembered the men who had taken them in a dull beige van in the middle of a rainstorm, and the thunder that had not been thunder. She remembered gray federal buildings and airplanes, and she knew that they had moved to Salt Lake City and change their names because bad men were after her father, though she did not know why. I told her. I didn't want to tell her, and I didn't like myself for it, but she needed to know. 'Your father counterfeited money for a man named Vasily Markov. Markov wanted to have your father killed, so your father turned state's evidence in order to buy his way into the witness protection program. Do you know what that is?'

Her lips had formed a hard little knot. 'I'm not an idiot.'

'Your father learned his trade from a man named Wilson Brownell, up in Seattle. Markov's people have been watching Brownell, and they figured that something was going on. They staked Brownell and your mother's grave, and that's where they saw me.'

The hard lips softened. 'You went to my mother's grave?'

'The men who are after your father have come to Los Angeles. They've already found me, because they suspect that I know your whereabouts, and that means they'll stay here until they find your father, too. Do you understand that?'

'Yes.' Without expression.

'These men are dangerous, and I am not going to walk out of here and leave you alone. That is no longer an option.'

She looked from my left eye to my right, not really seeing me, breathing softly. You could tell she was thinking. I heard something creak in the hall. Charles, probably. Eavesdropping. 'What about my father?'

'I think he's going to print money again, but I don't know that. I'm pretty sure that's why he went to see Brownell.' I couldn't bring myself to tell her about the drugs.

Her eyes narrowed, and her lips moved, but I couldn't make out what she was saying. She blinked, and I thought she might be trying to keep back the tears.

'I know it's hard.' I said it as softly as I could.

She was hunched over, elbows on knees, arms crossed, lips pursed. A hard, tight knot. She said something, but I couldn't hear her.

'I didn't hear you, Teri.'

She said it again. 'He's such a loser.'

I didn't know what to say.

'He screws up everything. He's screwed up all of our lives.' The blinking grew harder, and her eyes filled. 'I try to make it better, but it just gets worse. I try so hard.' Tears leaked down across her cheeks and into the corners of her mouth, and I put a hand on her shoulder and squeezed, and I started blinking, too.

'Teri.' Something creaked in the hall again and a door closed.

Teri said, 'Please don't let them hurt him.'

For all I knew they had him now. For all I knew he was dead. 'The only way I can help him is to find him before they do, you see?'

She wiped her eyes on her wrist, then took a breath. She hadn't broken all the way, and now she was pulling herself back together. I guess she'd had a lot of practice.

'But not with you here. I am either going to call the feds and have them take you in, or you're coming with me. Either way, you can't stay here.'

She wiped her eyes again, and now the tears were gone. As if they'd never been. 'Where will you take us?'

'We'll go to my house for now, but we'll have to move to a safe house. I'm easy to find, and the Russians might show up there.'

'What about my daddy?'

'I'll look for him when you guys are safe.'

'He's going to come back here.'

'Then I'll wait here for him, but first we have to get you guys to a safe place.'

She was small and folded, sitting on the edge of the couch, and then she adjusted her glasses and stood. 'Okay.' Just like that. 'I'd better get Charles and Winona.' The fifteen-year-old mother again. Taking care of her family.

We went along the hall to their rooms. Both doors were closed. I rapped at each door. 'Charles. Winona. You guys come here.'

Winona's door quietly opened, and she stepped into the hall. Charles's voice came muffled from behind his. 'Eff you!' He'd been listening, all right.

Teri said, 'Charles, we're going away for a few days. We have to pack.'

'Eff!'

I smiled at Winona. 'Hi, honey.' Mr. Friendly. Mr. Don't-Be-Scared-of-the-Man-Who's-Going-to-Take-You-Away.

'Hi.' She smiled back, but it was uncertain. It was the first time I had seen Winona as anything but bubbling. I guess if my dad had blown in and out without warning I would've been uncertain, too. The little troll key chain was clipped to her belt loop. Guess if you couldn't have Daddy, you might as well have the troll. Maybe, sometimes, the two were one and the same.

I said, 'Teri, why don't you help Winona with her things. I'll talk to Charles.'

Charles yelled, 'I ain't goin'!'

Teri said, 'C'mon, Winona. You help me pack and I'll help you.'

They went into their room, and I tapped at Charles's door. 'C'mon, bud.'

'Eff!'

I tapped again, then opened the door, and when I did he ran over and pushed against it as hard as he could, shouting, 'Eff you! Stay out of here! Eff!' He was red-faced and crying, and I felt like a turd.

I forced the door, Charles on the other side, crying louder and pushing hard, sobbing from the mucus in his throat, thin chest heaving, shouting 'You get outta here!' until I had the door open, and then he ran at me, butting head first into me, punching and spitting and screaming for me to get out and I pulled him close and held him, and after a while all the yelling and crying subsided into a sobbing hack. It was a barren room, holding only a single frame bed and a chest, with none of the posters and toys and things you'd expect to see in the room of a twelve-year-old boy. Maybe Charles didn't think he'd live here long enough to bother. I said, 'It's okay, kid.'

'I hope he never comes back!'

I held him.

'I wish he was dead!'

I held him tighter.

Teri said, 'Charles?' She was standing in the door.

I said, 'We're okay, Teri.'

Charles and I stood for a very long time, and when the sobbing subsided I tried to let go, but by then Charles was holding on to me, arms locked tight around my ribs, face buried in my chest. I could feel the wet soaking through my shirt. 'It's okay, kid.' I said it five or six times. Maybe I said it more.

I let Charles hang on to me for another couple of minutes, and then I told him to pack enough for two nights. I told him that we were going to my place, and that when they were safe I would find his father. Charles turned away without looking at me, wiped his nose on the back of his hand, and packed. He said, 'Eff'm.'

Maybe I would kill Clark if the Russians didn't.

140

CHAPTER 17

I phoned Joe Pike while they packed. 'Clark's gone,' I said. 'Again.'

Pike didn't say anything for a moment. 'You're going to move the kids.'

'That's right. I'm going to take them to my place, but I don't want to keep them there overnight. Sautin and Dobcek could show up anytime.'

'Okay.'

'Think you could come up with a safe house?' Pike knew people, and he'd come up with safe places to stay before. Once an abandoned mansion in Bel Air, once an Airstream trailer in the high desert near Edwards Air Force Base. You never knew. Maybe he owned these places and just didn't bother to tell me.

'Let me make some calls. I'll meet you at your place later.'

By the time I was off the phone, Teri and Winona and Charles were ready to go. Guess they didn't have much to pack, or maybe it was because they'd had so much practice.

We locked their house, put their bags behind the seats, and the four of us made the drive up Laurel Canyon, the three of them bunched together in the passenger seat. Teri had offered to drive their car, but I said no. I wasn't worried that she'd have an accident; I was more concerned that when we got wherever we were going she would simply drive away. Charles said, 'I'm all squished up.'

Teri said, 'Live with it.'

I took it slow because no one was wearing a seat belt. Elvis Cole, the not-quite-responsible parent, looking over his shoulder for a load of Russian hit men.

Teri and Charles were quiet, but after a while Winona began to chatter about how much she liked riding in the convertible. The top was down and the wind blew through our hair, and Winona said that it made her feel like she was in a parade. Charles neither glowered nor flipped off anyone, and Teri seemed lost in herself. I guess everyone had their own way of dealing with what was going on.

Pretty soon we left the city behind and wound through the trees, and a little bit after that we turned into the carport. Winona said, 'Is this your house?'

'Yes.'

'It looks like a tepee.'

'It's called an A-frame. It's tall and steep and shaped like the letter.'

Charles slunk out of the car and peered at the trees and natural hillsides. 'Are there bears?'

'No bears. Just a few coyotes and rattlesnakes.'

He glanced at the ground, then made a sour face. 'What's that smell?'

Winona giggled. 'Charles cut the cheese.'

Teri said, 'Don't be rude.'

'It's the eucalyptus trees.' I pointed them out to him. 'The sun splits their bark, and their sap smells like mouthwash.'

They followed me inside through the kitchen to the living room. I told them to put their bags on the stairs, and I opened the drapes and the big glass doors to let the breeze in from the deck, then checked my answering machine. Lucy had left a message, asking me to call. Teri said, 'Is that Ms. Chenier?'

'Yep.'

'Aren't you going to call her?'

'As soon as we get squared away. You guys can go out on the deck if you want, but nobody climb on the rail. You can play on the slope, just watch out for the snakes.' Summer camp at the Cole residence. They stood in the door and looked at the deck and the slope, but nobody went outside. The snakes.

'There's soft drinks and milk and water in the fridge. You can help yourself. After we get settled, I'll make dinner.'

Teri said, 'You don't have to cook for us.' She hadn't come to the deck. She was standing in the living room by the stairs with her arms crossed.

'Of course I do. But you can help if you like. Is meatloaf okay?'

The three of them shrugged at each other, and Teri said, 'That would be nice. Thank you.'

Charles eyed the loft. 'What's up there?'

'That's my loft. Come on. I'll show you.'

I showed them the downstairs bathroom, then took them up. Charles and Winona wandered through the loft, but Teri went to the rail and looked down into the house. From the rail you can see the living room and the dining area and through the glass out to the canyon. She looked at the big glass triangle of my back wall, then up at the high pointed ceiling. She looked at my bed, and the built-in dresser, and then down at the living room again. 'Do you live here alone?'

'Yes. Except for my cat.'

She let her touch drift along the rail, and then she looked around the room again. 'It's nice.'

'Thank you.' I thought of my house as ordinary, but I

realized then that it was probably a different world to her. Life for them had been a series of temporary furnished rentals, other people's homes and other people's furniture, just a place to stay until their father decided it was time to leave, no more permanent than a daily newspaper.

I showed them the upstairs bath, and then we went downstairs. When we got down again, Joe Pike was standing silently in the entry. Just standing there.

Charles yelped in surprise and shouted, 'Jeezis, you scared me!'

Pike said, 'Yes.'

Charles scrambled outside and peered in from the deck. Guess Joe scared him more than the snakes.

I said, 'I'll make dinner in a minute, but first we have to talk. Charles, come back inside.'

Charles crept back inside and the three of them stared at me, Charles snapping nervous glances toward Joe.

'I'm going to look for your father tomorrow, so I need clues. Did he say anything to anyone while he was home?'

They looked at each other, and shook their heads. Teri said, 'Not like you mean.'

'Nothing that might indicate where he was going?'

Winona said, 'He said we were going to move away soon. He said we could have a really big TV.' Great.

Teri said, 'He made some phone calls.'

'Anyone listen in?'

They shook their heads some more, but Charles wasn't particularly convincing.

'Charles?'

'I didn't do anything.'

'No. But you might've heard something.'

Charles squirmed, then shrugged. 'He said something about going to see someone.'

'You hear a name?'

'Ray.'

'He said the name 'Ray'?'

Shrug.

Pike said, 'How about "Tre"?'

Charles scrunched his face, but this time he didn't shrug. 'Yeah, maybe that was it.'

Pike shook his head and went out onto the deck.

I showed them my videotapes and told them to pick one. Winona picked *Independence Day*. I got them going with that, put two pounds of ground turkey in the microwave to thaw, and was just getting ready to join Pike on the deck when Lucy Chenier called again. I said, 'I was about to call you. Did you close the deal?'

There was a great silence from the other end of the line. 'I'm not sure there's a job offer to be closed.'

I stood in the kitchen with the phone in my hand. Winona and Charles watched great elliptical spaceships enter the atmosphere, but Teri watched me. I said, 'What do you mean, no job offer?' Pike looked in from the deck, curious as to what was keeping me.

'God, I've really needed to talk to you, Elvis.' Her voice sounded hollow and empty.

I held the phone tighter. 'Lucy?'

'When David got back to them, they reduced the term of the contract. They changed every one of the deal points, and said they were reconsidering the amount of my salary.' I could hear the hurt in her voice. 'I just don't understand it.'

'Maybe it's just a negotiating tactic.'

'David doesn't think so. He's done this a hundred times, and he says it's as if they've changed their minds about hiring me.'

I leaned against the counter and frowned. 'Maybe you should call Tracy Mannos.'

'I did. She hasn't returned my call.'

I frowned harder. I thought about Richard in my office, telling me that he wouldn't just let Lucy leave. I thought about it some more and shook my head.

'Richard came to see me.'

Silence.

'He hired a man named Epps to follow us when you were here.' I told her about Epps having searched my house, and about Richard coming to my office. *You don't think I'm going to let her leave, do you?*

She cleared her throat. 'My ex-husband, Richard. Ben's father.' She cleared her throat again. 'He came to see you?'

'Yesterday.'

'And you didn't call me.' It wasn't a question. More a statement, more just wanting to make sure she had the facts of her life straight. 'You didn't think that was worth calling me about.'

I sighed. 'Mistake, huh?'

Silence again. Pike and Teri were watching me until Pike shook his head and turned away. Sometimes you can't win.

'I thought about calling you, but it seemed small. It seemed like something between Richard and me, and I didn't want to bring you into it.'

'A boy thing.' *How do you spell 'moron'?*

'He's upset because you and Ben are moving away, and he stepped over the line with Epps and this other stuff, but it's a stretch to think he could have anything to do with KROK.'

'You don't know, Elvis. This is exactly the kind of thing he would do.' I could hear her breathing. I had never asked about her former marriage, or what led to her divorce, and I didn't want to go there now. She said, 'I think I should come out there.'

146

'Talk to Tracy first. You don't want to come out until you know what you're up against because if you're wrong, it will look bad for you.'

She didn't say anything for several seconds, and then she said, 'Elvis, I'm really sorry about this.'

'You don't have anything to be sorry for.'

'Richard.'

She hung up without another word. I stood in my kitchen, holding the phone and listening to the dial tone, and then I hung up and joined Pike on the deck. The end of the day was approaching, and the sky to the east was hazy with smoke the color of bone. Somewhere, something was burning. Pike said, 'What?'

I told him.

Pike listened without comment, then said, 'Figured we should kill him.' Always with the helpful comment.

'I just don't see it, but you never know. What could some guy from Louisiana have to do with a television station here in Los Angeles?'

Pike crossed his arms and leaned against the deck rail. His head tilted ever so slightly, like maybe it was beyond him. I could see the TV reflected in his glasses. 'First the Russians, now this. You've got a lot to think about.'

'Yes, but I am large.'

He nodded. 'Keep your head in the game. Think about the wrong thing at the wrong time, it'll mean your ass.'

'Thanks.'

'Maybe mine, or those kids'.' You see the way he is?

I said, 'You get a safe house?'

'Place in Studio City. Three bedrooms, furnished, phones. We can use it as long as we want.' He told me the address.

'Sounds good. I'm thinking maybe I should stay at Clark's house tonight. If the Russians haven't gotten him, Clark might go back there. He might be there now.'

Pike's mouth twitched. 'Sure.'

'Well, miracles happen.'

Pike told me he needed to buy supplies for the safe house and that he would be back later. I went into the kitchen to start dinner. I had half a head of iceberg lettuce and a fresh bag of spring greens and a couple of tomatoes that would do for a salad, and maybe half a dozen new potatoes that I could roast with the turkey loaf. I was gathering things together when Teri came into the kitchen and said, 'Can I help?'

'Sure.'

I told her what I planned, then showed her the cutting boards and knives, and gave her a small Maui onion and two carrots to dice. She said, 'What are you going to do with the carrots?'

'For the turkey loaf.'

She looked at me.

'We'll toss in raisins, too, along with a little soy sauce and maybe some peas. You'll see.'

'Winona doesn't like peas.'

'Okay, ix-nay the peas.'

She started with the onion. I worked with the potatoes. Teri used the knife carefully and well, and cut the onion into uniform pieces while Charles and Winona watched the destruction of the Earth. Twice I glanced up at her, and twice I caught her looking at me. Both times I smiled, and both times she looked away. After the second time, she said, 'How can Lucy be your girlfriend if she lives in Louisiana?'

'We didn't plan it that way, it just kind of happened.' I guess she'd been listening to my conversation.

'Do you date other girls?'

'No. I did for a while, but I kept thinking about Lucy, so I stopped seeing other people.'

'Does she date other men?'

'No.'

'How do you know?'

I frowned at her. 'She's been offered a job out here and she may move out – if she can work out the terms of the job.' If the job is still hers to be had.

Chopping. 'What if she can't move here?'

I chopped harder. 'We'll deal with it.' This kid was worse than Joe Pike.

When Teri was finished with the carrots I had her add them to the turkey, and then we mixed in the raisins and the soy sauce and a couple of eggs. I let Teri shape the loaf while I dug out a roasting pan. We put the meat in the pan and surrounded it with the potatoes. The fresh potatoes didn't look like enough, so I added a can of whole peeled new potatoes, and sprinkled everything with paprika. We put it in the oven at four hundred and set the timer for an hour. Teri said, 'I'm sorry about what happened at our house.'

'What do you mean?'

She looked embarrassed. 'When I cried.'

I remembered her eyes filling. I remembered a few tears. Then I remembered her packing it away and shutting it down like a SWAT team cop with twenty years on the job. I said, 'You don't have to apologize for that.'

She shook her head. 'I can't afford to lose control.'

'You're fifteen. It's okay to cry.'

She looked at the floor. 'I'm all they have. If I fall apart, who will take care of Winona and Charles?'

I stared at her. 'What about you? Who do you have?'

She pursed her lips. When she spoke, her voice was soft. 'I don't have anyone.'

I shook my head. 'No, that's not true. You have me.'

She frowned at me, then cocked her head. 'Oh, sure.' She stalked out of the kitchen and went up the stairs.

I said, 'Huh?'

I stayed in the kitchen, opened a Falstaff, and stared at the oven. The living room was rocked by alien explosions and Winona laughed. It seemed safer in the kitchen.

Charles edged into the dining room, fidgeting like something was bothering him. I said, 'What?'

'Nothing.'

I had more of the Falstaff. I glanced at my watch and wondered when Pike would get back. This baby-sitting was damned tough work.

Charles sidled into the door. 'I didn't mean it.'

'You didn't mean what?'

His hands were in his pockets and his face was red. 'I don't want him to be dead.'

I looked at him and sighed. 'I know, Charles. It's okay.'

Charles edged back into the living room. I stayed in the kitchen.

Joe Pike got back forty minutes later, and not long after that the timer dinged. Joe and Winona ate. The rest of us weren't hungry.

When the dishes were cleared I drove back to their house to wait for Clark Hewitt.

CHAPTER 18

The Saturn was still in its place. The Hewitts' house was dark, one of only two sleeping houses on their street.

I cruised the house once, parked around the corner, then walked back. The night air was cool, and traffic sounds from Melrose blended with the voices and laughter of children playing and adults taking an evening stroll.

I waited until two young women walking a dog were beyond me, then sauntered up the drive and let myself in using Teri's key. The lights were off, and I did not turn them on. I wanted to search the house again, but not at the risk of alerting either Clark or a passing car filled with Russians. I took off my jacket and holster, put the Dan Wesson near at hand, and settled in on the couch. After a while I slept, but I woke often at sounds made by the strange house, rising when I did to make sure that those sounds weren't Clark or Russian thugs. They never were, and little by little the dark brightened to dawn. Clark Hewitt did not return.

Fourteen minutes after six the next morning, it was light enough to work. I did a more detailed search now than I had with Teri, stripping Clark's bed and checking the mattress seams and the box spring liner, taking out every drawer in the dresser and chest to see if anything was taped behind or beneath them. I didn't know what I was looking for, or even think that I would find something, but you never know. When the phone company offices opened at nine I planned on checking the calls that Clark had made while he was home, but until then it was either search or stay on the couch and watch Regis and Kathie Lee. At least this way I could pretend to be a detective.

I went through Clark's closet, checking the pockets in his shirts and pants and coats, and I looked in his shoes. He didn't have many, so it didn't take long. I went through the bathroom, then once more went through the kitchen, and then the kids' rooms and the living room. At sixteen minutes after eight I was finished, and still hadn't found anything.

I went back into the kitchen, located a jar of Taster's Choice instant, and made a cup with hot water from the tap. At least I found the coffee.

I was sipping the coffee and thinking about phoning Tracy Mannos when I noticed a ceiling hatch in the hall. I hadn't noticed it before because the cord that's supposed to be there so you can pull down the door had been clipped, and also because most houses in Southern California are built without attics because of the heat. If you have anything, you might have a crawl space. I went into the hall and looked up at the door. It had been painted over a few hundred times, but the door seemed free and usable, and, with finger smudges around the edges, looked as if it had been used. Maybe I could detect more than instant coffee after all.

I used one of the dining room chairs, pulled down the door, unfolded the ladder, and climbed far enough to stick my head into the crawl space. Twelve minutes after eight in the morning and it was already a hundred degrees up there.

I went back to the kitchen for a flashlight, took off my shirt, and went up into the crawl space. Maybe ten feet back along one of the rafter wells was a dark, lumpy shape. I boosted myself up, then duckwalked along the prewar two-by-eights to a military surplus duffel bag, as clean and dust-free as if it had just been put there. I opened it enough to look inside and saw banded packs of hundred-dollar bills. I said, 'Aha.'

You hang around an empty house by yourself long enough, you'll say damn near anything.

I dropped the duffel out of the crawl space, opened it on the living room floor, and counted out a little more than twenty-three thousand dollars in worn C-notes that were perfect mates to the bills Special Agent Marsha Fields had confiscated. Markov money. Money that the Hewitts had been living on for the past three years, money good enough to get by with as long as you didn't flash it at a bank or in front of a Secret Service agent. Then I said 'Aha' again.

Mixed with the money were half a dozen printer's catalogs, all of which bore a mailing label addressed to one Wilson Brownell in Seattle, Washington. Clark was definitely printing again, and probably with Brownell's help. Maybe they were partners.

It was two minutes after nine when I put the money back into the duffel, and the duffel back into the attic. I kept the catalogs. I had a pretty good idea who Clark had phoned, and after I stowed the duffel I called my friend at the phone company and had her run a line check on the Hewitts' number covering the past three days just to be sure. It didn't take long. She told me that three calls had been made to two numbers, one of which lasted twenty-six minutes and showed a Seattle area code. Brownell. The other two numbers were both in the Los Angeles calling area, and belonged to Tre Michaels. Charles had called it right on that one.

If I hung around the house long enough, Clark would

return. The money was here, and, as far as Clark knew, so were his kids, but considering Clark's track record I might have to wait for days. Since Clark had phoned Tre Michaels, I was sure he was looking to connect, and that meant either he had been or would be visiting Culver City. Junkies may never go home, but they always go back to their connection. Ergo, Tre Michaels might know something. Maybe they were shooting up together right now.

I washed up, locked the house, and drove south to Culver City and the Bestco. I asked a Pakistani sales-clerk named Rahsheed for Tre, but Rahsheed told me that Tre had the day off. Great. I went along Overland to his apartment, figuring it was a long shot, but as I turned onto his street Michaels passed me going in the opposite direction in a dark blue Acura. Lucky is better than good every time.

I swung around in a fast K-turn, thinking my luck might hold and he might bring me to Clark. He didn't. He turned into the Culver City park and parked next to a rusted-out Dodge van where a couple of younger guys with long, sun-bleached hair were jumping skateboards. The younger guys were well muscled and shirtless, with dark tans and baggy shorts and high-top felony flyers, and they stopped the jumping and opened the van's side door when Tre got out of the Acura. Michaels opened the Acura's trunk, and everybody carried brand-new Sony laser-disc players to the van. Still in their boxes and almost certainly ripped off from Bestco. Tre closed his trunk, and everybody climbed into the van. The van didn't start and didn't move, and its windows were curtained over. Your friendly neighborhood dopemobile.

I parked at the far end of the lot, then crept back to the van and listened. Nothing. Out in the park, two women were jogging with babies in three-wheel strollers and a couple of guys had their shirts off to catch the sun and a half-dozen Latin guys were playing soccer and here in the parking lot Tre Michaels was scoring dope. Life in the big city.

I took out the Dan Wesson, waited for the women with the strollers to pass, then threw open the sliding door, and yelled, 'Police!'

Tre Michaels and the two young guys were sitting cross-legged on the bare metal deck, dividing up money and nickel bags of white powder amid the laser-disc players, all three of them frozen in mid-count, staring at the Dan Wesson with bulging wet eyes. The money was a short stack of worn hundreds, and I wondered if Tre had gotten them from Clark. One of the kids said, 'Oh, shit.'

Tre Michaels said, 'It's you.'

I lowered the gun. 'Good job, Officer Michaels. Couldn't've done it without you.'

The two kids looked at Tre.

Tre Michaels opened his mouth, then closed it and looked at the kids. 'I'm not a cop.'

The bigger kid's eyes narrowed. 'You prick.'

Michaels said, 'Hey. This is bullshit.'

I pulled Michaels out of the van. 'I think we can cut these kids a deal, don't you?' I jerked him harder, then slammed the side door and walked him away. The van's engine roared to life and its tires smoked. Michaels said, 'Are you nuts? Do you know what you did to me?'

'They're kids, Tre. You're not scared of a couple of kids, are you?'

His eyes were wide and bright, and his face was sheened with sweat. 'Jesus, you gotta be nuts.'

I walked him to the car. 'Tell me something. You think Bestco would press charges if they knew you were ripping off goods to turn over for dope?'

Michaels chewed at his lip and didn't say anything, staring after the departing van like it was the last bus to salvation and he had missed it. Across the park, the driver gave us the finger and yelled something I couldn't understand. Charles in five years.

I said, 'Clark Haines.' Tre wouldn't know 'Hewitt.'

Michaels stared at the van.

I jerked his arm. 'Wake up, Tre.'

He looked at me. 'That was my whole score. They got my money. They got the goods. Now what am I going to do?'

I jerked him again. Harder. 'Me or Bestco.'

Tre Michaels wet his lips, still staring after the van. 'Jesus, didn't we go through this before? I dunno where Clark is.'

Another jerk. 'He called you, Tre. Twice.'

He finally looked at me and his eyes were confused. I've never known an addict who wasn't. 'Well, yeah. He came by last night and scored a couple bags.'

Another jerk. 'C'mon, Tre. He's up to something and a crummy two bags wouldn't cut it.'

'He bought eight bags, okay? That was all I had.' He scrunched up his face like he was regretting something. 'I gave him a really good price.'

Eight bags was a lot. Maybe enough to travel on. Maybe he was going back to Seattle. 'Did he say why he needed so much?'

'He said he'd be gone for a few days.'

'He say where he was going?' I was thinking Seattle. I was thinking Wilson Brownell, again.

'Long Beach.'

I looked at him. 'He said he was going to Long Beach?'

Michaels made the scrunched face again. 'Well, he didn't say he was going to Long Beach, but he asked me

for a connection down there, so what would you think?'
Long Beach.

'Did you give him a name?'

Michaels frowned. 'Hell, I don't know anyone in Long Beach.' He started to shake. 'You really screwed me with those guys.' He waved his hands. 'Now what am I gonna do, you tell me that? Now what?'

He was crying when I walked away.

I drove to my office. I still wanted to call Tracy Mannos, but first I needed to call Brownell and ask him about Long Beach. I would also call Teri and ask her. Maybe saying the words would ring a bell.

At fourteen minutes after eleven, I left my car in the parking garage, walked up the four flights to my office, and found the place filled with cops.

Reed Jasper was sitting at my desk, while three other guys that I'd never seen before were going through my files. Papers were scattered around on the floor and the place had been turned upside down. Jasper smiled when he saw me, and said, 'Well, well, well. Just the guy we wanted to see.'

I looked from Jasper to the other guys, then back to Jasper. They were heavy men in dark rumpled suits with anonymous faces. Feds. I said, 'What the hell are you doing, Jasper?'

'Trying to get a line on Clark Hewitt, my man.' He took a folded sheet of paper from his inside coat pocket and dropped it on my desk. 'Federal order to search and seize, duly signed and hereby presented.' He leaned back in my chair and crossed his arms.

The other three guys were staring at me, and I felt myself run cold. 'Why?'

'Wilson Brownell was found tortured to death yesterday afternoon. I think Clark Hewitt might've been involved.'

CHAPTER 19

I said, 'If I wanted to remodel, I wouldn't have called the government.'

Jasper said, 'These are Agents Warren and Pigozzi of your Los Angeles Marshals' Office, and this is Special Agent Stansfield of the FBI.' Warren was black. Pigozzi sported bright red hair, and Stansfield's chin was littered with serious zit-craters. 'We're here because we believe you have knowledge of Clark Hewitt, either under that name or another.'

I dropped onto the couch and frowned at him. 'Didn't we go through this in Seattle?'

Warren said, 'I would encourage you to contact an attorney at this time.'

'Why?'

'Because anything you say will be used against you.'

I spread my hands. 'I've got nothing to hide.' Mr. Confident. 'Other than being pissed off that you guys are ransacking my office.'

Warren went back to the files like it didn't really matter to him either way.

Jasper shook his head. 'I don't get you, Cole. I know you're holding out, but I don't get why.'

I didn't say anything. How do you explain a promise to a fifteen-year-old?

He said, 'Your buddies the Markovs have come to town. If they haven't been around to see you, they will.'

'I hope they're neater than you guys.'

The red-haired agent looked up from the file cabinet, then let six or seven files dribble through his fingers to the floor. The floor was covered with yellow work sheets and billing statements and slim stapled reports. I said, 'That's really bush.'

Jasper looked over and frowned. 'Jesus Christ, Leo.'

Leo said, 'Maybe he shouldn't try to be funny.'

I said, 'That's a good line, Leo. You practice in front of the mirror?'

Leo made a ragged smile. 'Let's see if you're that good when it comes time to renew your license.'

'Pardon me while I catch my breath.'

Leo let more files dribble to the floor.

Jasper came around the desk like we were in his office, not mine. 'Look, Cole, all I want is a little cooperation.'

'You got a great way of showing it.'

'Clark Hewitt is up to his ass here, and so are his kids. You've met the Markovs. You know what I'm talking about.'

I tried to look like it didn't matter.

'My partner got blown away to keep Clark Hewitt whole. You don't think we're going to let anything happen to him now, do you?'

I tried to look like I didn't have a clue as to what he was talking about, but I knew he was right. I also knew that if Clark was printing again these guys would lock him down without a second thought, and that the Markovs would like that just fine. If he was in prison, the Markovs would know exactly where to find him.

Jasper motioned me out onto the balcony. 'Let's talk out here, Cole. It'll be easier while these guys work.'

I went out with him, but I didn't like it much. The sky had filled with a deep white haze that masked the Channel Islands. You could barely see the ocean. I stared at the haze and breathed the sea air. 'Did you guys do my house?'

'Before we came here.'

'You find anything?'

Jasper smiled. 'You know we didn't, and you know we're not going to find anything here either, but we gotta cover the bases.'

'Great, Jasper. That makes me feel better.'

Jasper crossed his arms and leaned with his back to the balcony rail. He was wearing little round government sunglasses and a dull gray suit, fine for Seattle but hot down here. It would be hot, and it just screamed 'fed.' He said, 'I don't like doing this, but I think you're holding out.'

'Moi?'

'I asked people about you, and those people said if you were looking for a guy, then you probably found him. I just can't figure why you won't come clean.'

'Maybe they're wrong.'

He nodded. 'Could be.'

'But maybe I just don't like being muscled, so I'm being petulant.'

He laughed. 'They said that, too.' He let the laugh fade. 'I know that Clark Hewitt was in Seattle. I know from eyewitnesses that a man matching Hewitt's description was seen in contact with Wilson Brownell, a former close associate and master counterfeiter. I'll bet you know that, too.'

'I saw Brownell when I was in Seattle. He didn't know anything.'

'I hope for Clark's sake he didn't.' Jasper watched the men inside work for a while. The black agent discovered the Pinocchio clock and nudged the red-haired agent, then they both stared at it. Jasper said, 'Brownell was tortured to death with a steam iron. I brought down the pictures. You wanna see?'

I shook my head.

'Here's a safe bet, Cole. Whatever Brownell knew, the Markovs now know. If Brownell knew whatever name they're living under, or an address or a phone number, they've got it now. You understand what I'm saying?'

'I get it, Jasper.' I took a breath, and stared south toward Catalina. I tried to see through the haze, but I could only make out the island's outline without seeing what was really there. 'I don't know where Clark is.'

The pocked agent came to the French doors and said, 'Jasper.'

Jasper went in and the four of them gathered by my desk and mumbled in low whispers, the red-haired agent standing with his hand on the pocked agent's back. It wasn't enough that I was ducking Russians and had the weight of the U.S. government on my case, but now I was thinking that maybe Brownell had known exactly where Clark was, and what he was doing, and maybe Dobcek and Sautin were on their way now. Maybe they already had Clark, but if they did there was nothing that I or Jasper could do about it, and I told myself that thinking about it did no good. The kids were the important thing, and the kids were safe. Maybe Clark was still okay, and if I could find him I could save him. If I could find him, maybe I could even bring him to Jasper without having to worry about them nailing him for a counterfeit beef. If he was still alive.

The black agent shook Jasper's hand and walked out of my office. The red-haired agent pointed out the Pinocchio clock to the pocked agent, and the pocked agent shook his head. Jasper came back to the balcony. I said, 'Is the party over?'

Jasper said, 'You're not in the clear. You just get a pass

for today.' He gave me a card. 'I'm staying at the Marriott downtown. I wrote my room number here. You decide to do the right thing, gimme a call.'

'Sure.' The right thing.

He looked at the haze and shook his head. 'How do you people breathe this shit?'

'Makes us tough, Jasper. Angelinos have the toughest lungs in America.'

He nodded, probably more to himself than to me. 'Yeah, sure.' Then he took a deep breath of it and went back to the door. 'I've known Clark Hewitt since he came to us, begging us to save his ass from the Markovs, and I can tell you he isn't what he seems.'

I stared at him.

'He comes across like this doof, but he's more than that.' He smiled at me, but there was no joy in it. 'Whatever you think you know about him, I can promise you this: It ain't what it seems, and neither is he.'

Reed Jasper showed me his palms like he had given me the Rosetta stone and it was up to me what I did with it. Then he walked back through my office and out the door. The red-haired agent and the pocked agent walked with him, and they didn't bother to close the door.

I stayed on the balcony until they left the building and climbed into two dark blue G-rides and melted into the traffic on Santa Monica Boulevard. Then I went in, closed the outer door, and picked up my papers. It took most of an hour, but no more than that because there hadn't been a lot in my files. Nothing seemed to be missing, though a small ceramic statue of Jiminy Cricket had fallen and broken. I threw it away.

When the papers were in their folders and the folders back in their files and the files once more in the cabinet, I opened a longneck Budweiser, sat at my desk, and put my feet up. I said, 'Clark, you'd better be worth it.'

The phone rang then, and I scooped it up. Mr. Happy-go-lucky. Mr. Shirttail-out-and-nothing-on-my-mind, hanging around his office with a liplock on a longneck, the very image of the depressed detective contemplating the loss of his license and livelihood to the weight of the United States government. 'Elvis Cole Detective Agency, professional detection at going-out-of-business rates.'

Tracy Mannos said, 'Are you drunk?'

'Not yet.'

'Well, bag it. Can you come see me?'

I frowned at the Pinocchio. 'Now?' Thinking about Pike and those kids at the safe house. Thinking about following the Long Beach lead. 'You find out something about Lucy's negotiation?'

'I'd rather do this in person, here at KROK.' Ah.

'Why there?'

She sounded irritated. 'Stop being stupid and get over here.' Then she hung up.

I locked the office, then slowly drove to KROK to see Tracy Mannos. No one followed me.

No one that I could see.

163

CHAPTER 20

KROK Television, Power Channel 8 (*Personal News from Us to You – We take it personally!!*), was housed in a large brick and steel building off Western Avenue in the east side of Hollywood. I parked in the little security lot they have next to the building, and found Tracy waiting for me in the reception area. I hadn't expected her to be waiting, but she was, and she looked anxious. I said, 'Guess you found something.'

'Let's talk in my office.'

Tracy Mannos was a tall, attractive woman in her early fifties. Her hair was streaked with gray and cut close, and she carried herself with an erect, no-nonsense corporate manner, every inch the authoritative station manager. Lucy and I had met her when I was working on the Theodore Martin murder case, and she had been impressed enough with Lucy's bearing and legal analysis to suggest to her bosses that Lucy be offered the job of on-air legal analyst.

She led me through a heavy glass security door and along a sterile hall, near deserted because of the time of day. She said, 'Stu Greenberg's our head of business affairs. I asked him about Lucy's negotiation, and he said that there was nothing unusual about it. In fact, he told me not to worry.'

'Did you ask Mr. Greenberg if perhaps he's had some association with Mr. Chenier?' We went into a sleek white office with comfortable chairs and a cluttered desk. Photographs of a man and three children dotted the walls.

Tracy settled back in the chair and smiled at me. 'A television station is a very political environment, Elvis. People are easily offended, and more than one back around here sports multiple knife wounds.'

I nodded. 'You're saying you couldn't ask him straight out.'

'We have to be very careful that we don't step on something that bites us.'

I nodded again.

'Though I did manage to gain a bit of intelligence when I was in Stu's office.'

'Ah.' I knew that she had. You could see that in her eyes, too. A kind of ferocious twinkle.

'Stuart began his career in Houston, at the home office of Benton, Meyers and Dane.' Richard's firm.

'How about that.' The old-boy network rears its ugly head.

'Yes, but that doesn't prove anything. Greenberg is still the head of business affairs, and how he runs that department is his prerogative.' Then the twinkle became a hard glint. 'Until it becomes an issue that transcends acceptable business practices.'

'Such as an ex-husband pulling strings to limit his former wife's career options.'

'Yes. Then it becomes a larger issue, one to which this corporation would be sensitive.' She spread her hands. 'After all, if such were the case, Lucy might sue.'

'If she had proof.'

'Yes. But proof in such a case is elusive and hard to find. Maybe impossible to find.'

'Um.'

Tracy Mannos leaned toward me. Pointedly. 'Recognizing that, it could be something that simply appears to be proof. After all, if what we're talking about here is an issue of gender politics, the appearance of wrongdoing is something to which this station would be sensitive. When I was in Stu's office, I had the distinct impression that something might be there.'

'Like what?'

She spread her hands. 'You're the detective.'

She stayed with the lean, and I knew it meant something. I thought that she might have a very clear idea of what might constitute that kind of leverage, and where I might find it. I said, 'You got this impression while you were in his office?'

'More like when I was leaving his office and saying good-bye to his secretary.' Ah.

'And has Mr. Greenberg gone home for the day?'

She smiled, like maybe the slow kid in class was coming along after all. 'I'm not sure, Elvis. He usually leaves much earlier than this, but he might still be here.'

'I think I'll go speak with him.'

She settled back in her chair and nodded. 'You do that. I'm sure you'll find it enlightening.'

She told me how to get to Stuart Greenberg's office, and I found my way through the empty halls to the business affairs division. The lower floors of the station were bustling with activity as they mounted the evening broadcasts, but the upper business floors were deserted except for the cleaning crews. No one was around to ask who I was or what I was doing.

Stuart Greenberg had a nice corner office, replete with diplomas and family photographs and plants that were healthier than mine, but I didn't need to go there. I had listened to Tracy closely, and read between the lines, and figured that if anything was to be found it wouldn't be in Greenberg's office, but at his secretary's desk, and if anyone was going to find it, it was going to be me, and not Tracy Mannos. She would go only so far, and no farther. The risk would be mine.

The phone log of Greenberg's outgoing and incoming calls was there, next to the phone. I nodded at the cleaning crew, then sat at the desk and flipped backward through the pages, and found exactly what Tracy Mannos had suggested I would. Three days ago Richard Chenier had phoned Stuart Greenberg twice. There wasn't anything to indicate the content of the conversations, but, as Tracy had also suggested, there didn't have to be. I took the log to a copy machine, copied the page reflecting Richard's calls, then put the log back and drove home.

The cat was sitting in the mouth of my carport when I eased up to the house, one ear up, one down, and his head canted to the side. He looked surly and out-of-sorts, and he did not move even though I nosed the car toward him. I had to park on the street. I said, 'This last week has been hell, hasn't it?'

He ignored me. Snubbed by my cat.

I let myself in through the kitchen and walked through the house to see what the feds had done. Four drawers had been dumped, others left open, and three empty Falstaff cans were sitting on the dining room table. Most of the search seemed to have been in the kitchen and my bedroom, but the mess was not as bad as the office. I guess Jasper had told them to take it easy. Or maybe they were too busy drinking my beer.

I put out a fresh bowl of food for the cat, then called Joe at the safe house. The phone rang twice, and Charles answered. 'We don't want any.' Then he hung up.

I took a deep breath, let it out, and rubbed at my eyes. I dialed again. This time Joe answered on the first ring. I said, 'Can the kids overhear us?'

'No.'

I told him about Reed Jasper and the feds having searched my house and office, and Wilson Brownell turning up dead. Pike said, 'I guess these Russians mean it.'

'They mean it.' I told him about finding the money and catalogs in Clark's attic. 'We have to assume that they know what Brownell knew, where Clark was living and that Clark was using the name Haines. I think we're okay as long as we stay away from there.'

'Where are you now?'

I told him.

'What if Clark goes home?'

I had already thought it through and I didn't like where it led, but there weren't a lot of options. We could sit at the house and wait, but a proactive search seemed better. We could periodically check the house. I told Joe that I had other calls to make, and that I might not come by the safe house until morning 'Besides, my house has been searched by Richard's guy, and now by the feds. Maybe Dobcek and Sautin will come by next, and I can shoot them to death.'

Pike said, 'Take your fun where you find it.'

I hung up, then called Lucy at home. She answered as if she were perched by the phone. I said, 'It's me.'

'Let me change phones.' I waited. Ben was probably there.

When she came back on the line I told her about my conversation with Tracy Mannos, and what I had found in Stuart Greenberg's phone log. When I finished, she said, 'I'm coming out there.'

'Maybe you should talk to Tracy first. Tracy knows what you're up against, and I think she knows how to handle it, but this is pretty flimsy evidence.' In fact, it wasn't evidence at all, but I didn't want to be a defeatist.

She didn't say anything for a while, and then she said, 'I am not going to simply allow this to happen. Richard has no right to use his influence to affect my life. If I do nothing, and Tracy fails, then I'll feel all the worse.'

I didn't answer.

'I'm mad as hell, but I'm also a professional. Now that I know what I'm dealing with, I have no doubt that we can win. These are just two old-boy assholes trying to keep the little woman in her place.'

Pretty much what Tracy had said.

'Well, this is the wrong little woman.' She was quiet for a moment, but I guessed she was thinking. 'I don't care what Richard told you, it's not about Ben. Richard was a lousy father from day one, and he's still a lousy father. This is about me, and about power. That's why I divorced the sonofabitch.' She was mad, all right. 'He's an arrogant, self-involved prick, and if he thinks he can pull a stunt like this on me, I'll cut him a new asshole and stuff his head in it.' Whew.

I said, 'Luce?'

'What?' She almost shouted it.

'Please don't give yourself a stroke.'

She fell absolutely silent, and then she laughed. 'Wow. I'm really mad.'

'Glad I'm not on the receiving end.'

'Not you, Elvis. Not ever.' She laughed some more, and it was good to hear her laugh. Good to hear her sound so strong. 'I have to come out there and do this, even if it makes everything worse. Even if it costs me this job. You see that, don't you?'

'Sure.' I told her about the safe house, gave her the number there, and told her to call Joe with her flight information. After we hung up, I said, 'Richard, prepare to be sawed.'

It took me a little better than an hour to go through the house and put my things in order. I guess if I were a more accommodating person, I could find value in government agents doing such a thorough job.

After all, these were our tax dollars at work.

CHAPTER 21

I drove down the backside of Laurel Canyon into Studio City the next morning, going maybe fifteen miles out of my way to avoid detection. If I couldn't slip the Russians and the feds by slick driving, maybe I could wear them out with LA's morning rush-hour traffic.

The condo Pike had found for a safe house sat in the rear of a quiet, two-level garden building just off Coldwater Canyon near the Studio City Park. It was a classic ranch-style building of the kind constructed in the late fifties, all dark-stained wood and used brick, with mature pine trees lining the sidewalk and a parking lot for residents in the rear. Just the kind of place where unsuspecting inhabitants would never dream that the new people in the corner apartment were being stalked by homicidal maniacs from Seattle.

I parked at the curb, gathered the catalogs I'd taken from Clark's duffel bag, then wandered through the garden courtyard until I found the right door. I rang the bell at ten minutes after nine. Charles's muffled voice came from behind the door as if he'd been waiting there. 'Go away.'

I said, 'Charles.' What a way to start your morning.

The door opened and Pike was there, tall and expressionless. I gave the big grin. 'Well, Joseph, bet you had a fun evening.'

Charles eyed me from the safety of the kitchen. 'It was a joke.'

Pike's head swiveled toward him and Charles ducked out of the kitchen and into the living room. Fun evening, all right.

The entry led past the kitchen to a dining area and the living room beyond, stairs climbing one wall of the living room to open to the second floor. The condo was large and spacious and fully furnished, as if whoever owned the place was away on a short trip. Thriving green plants dotted the room, and the plants were healthy and firm and devoid of yellow. Maybe I should ask whoever owned them for lessons. I nodded at Pike. 'Nice. Better than the Airstream.'

Pike shrugged. Guess it didn't matter to him either way.

Teri and Winona were at the dining room table, and Charles had assumed a position in front of the television. Watching one of those morning exercise shows on ESPN. Kiana Tom doing ab work. Winona said, 'Did you find our daddy yet?' Everyone was dressed and clean and ready to start their day of waiting for the detective to find their father.

'Not yet, hon. But I'm hot on his trail.' Hope is everything.

Teri said, 'Would you like breakfast? Joe and I made cottage cheese pancakes.'

'No, thanks. I ate before I left home.'

She looked disappointed. 'There's fresh coffee.'

I let her pour a cup, sipped some, then nodded. 'Good.'

Teri smiled and seemed pleased.

Joe said, 'We can talk upstairs.'

I followed Pike up with the coffee into one of the three bedrooms. It had been made up as a home office with desk and telephone and fax machine, but there was nothing around to indicate the owner's identity. Maybe

Pike owned the place. For all I knew, Pike owned most of Los Angeles. He said, 'What'd you find?'

'Twenty thousand bucks in counterfeit hundreds and these.' I showed him the catalogs. Several pages were dog-eared, and quite a few items had been marked on the dog-eared pages, including two different grades of offset plate blanks from a firm in Finland, a high-end Hitachi digital scanner from a discount mail-order house in New York, a four-thousand-dollar Power Mac from a mail-order firm in Los Angeles with a commercial graphics software platform that cost almost as much as the computer, something called a dual-side regulator from a commercial printing firm in London, a high-volume paper shear from the same company, and sixty liters each of indigo #7 and canyon orange #9A oil-based ink, as well as lesser amounts of forest green #2, classic red #42, black, kiss blue #12, and yellow AB1, all of which came from three different ink manufacturers, two in Europe and one in Maryland. Pike said, 'He's printing, all right.'

'Yeah, but what?' Hundred-dollar bills are green and black. 'Why would he need indigo and orange?'

Pike took out his wallet and pulled out a hundred-dollar bill. Walking around money. 'Maybe you have to mix them to get the different shades of black. Maybe he uses them to reproduce the security fibers.'

'Maybe if we just took all this stuff to your pal Marsha Fields she could tell us.'

Pike put his hundred away. 'The new hundreds are too hard to copy. If he's making hundreds, he'll make the older series.'

'If?'

Pike flipped back through the catalogs. 'This is almost forty thousand dollars' worth of material. Wonder where he's getting the money to pay for it.'

I was wondering that, too. He almost certainly wasn't sending counterfeit cash through the mail, and he knew better than to try to buy money orders or certified checks at a bank or at American Express. I said, 'If he ordered this stuff, it had to be delivered. Maybe Clark's wherever that is.'

Most of the companies had an 800 number for phone orders, so I took a flyer and called the Los Angeles computer wholesaler first. A young woman with a Hispanic accent answered, 'Good morning from Cyber-World! What would you like to order?' Bright and cheery and wanting to help.

'I placed an order a couple of days ago and the machine hasn't arrived.' Just another customer on just another day.

'Why, let me track down that bad boy!' Wanting to make my phone shopping experience a happy one. 'Your name, please.'

'Clark Haines.' I waited a couple of seconds, then said, 'Oh, you know, my secretary placed the order and she might've used our company name, Clark Hewitt. Heh-heh.' Lame, but what can you do?

The young woman said, 'Gee, we're not showing an order to either of those names. Could she have made the order in another name?'

I thanked her and hung up.

I called three more companies, and none of them had or was processing an order for Haines or Hewitt either. When I put down the phone, I said, 'Hell.'

Pike said, 'Maybe he hasn't ordered yet. Maybe he's going to.'

'Maybe.'

I thought about Clark phoning Wilson Brownell, and how they had spoken often, and how Clark was willing to risk the Russians to go see Brownell. I called the

173

electronics wholesaler in New York and told him exactly what I had told the other four companies, only I told him that my name was Wilson Brownell. He came back on the line almost at once and said, 'Oh yes, Mr. Brownell, here it is.'

I gave Pike a thumbs-up.

The order clerk said, 'Mm, your scanner won't go out until tomorrow. Isn't that what you requested?'

'I wanted it today.'

'I'm sorry, sir. Whoever took the order must've made a mistake.'

'Well, as long as you're on the phone let's double-check the destination. I'd hate to think it was going to the wrong place.'

'Yes sir. We show the airbill addressed to *Pacific Rim Weekly Journal*, hold for airport pickup, on United flight five, direct to LAX.'

I wrote it down. 'And that's tomorrow?'

'Yes sir. It's right here on the form.'

I hung up, then dialed Los Angeles information and asked for the number of the *Pacific Rim Weekly Journal*. The information operator said, 'I'm sorry, sir. We have no listing in that name.'

'Try the valley.'

'Sorry, sir. Still no listing.'

I thought about Tre Michaels. 'Try Long Beach.'

She said, 'Here we go.' She gave me the address and phone, and I said, 'Touchdown.'

'Pardon me?'

'Nothing, Operator. Thanks.'

I dialed the number, and a woman answered with a heavy Asian accent. '*Journal*.'

'May I speak with Clark, please.'

She hung up without another word, and I looked at Pike. 'I think we may be onto something.'

Pike stayed with the Hewitt children, and I took the long drive south to Long Beach, following the Hollywood Freeway to the Harbor Freeway, then dropping straight south for almost an hour before picking up the San Diego Freeway east to the 710 and turning south again to parallel the Los Angeles River all the way to the ocean. Downtown Long Beach is a core of redeveloped modern high rises surrounded by an older landscape of two-story stucco bars and craftsman homes and traffic dividers dotted with palm trees that lend a small-town water-front feel. It would've been a fine place to bring Teri and Charles and Winona for ice-cream cones and a walk in the sun around Belmont Pier to watch the boats coming and going to Catalina Island, only sun walking and boat watching often lose their appeal when you're thinking that your father might've been tortured to death by a steam iron. Maybe another time.

I followed Ocean Boulevard east along the water, then turned north along Redondo Avenue, watching the landscape evolve from small-town waterfront to middle-class residential to lower-class urban, the signs gradually changing from English to Spanish and finally to Asian as the faces changed with them. The *Pacific Rim Weekly Journal* sat two blocks off Redondo in a small three-story commercial building between a tiny Vietnamese restaurant and a coin-operated laundry filled with tiny Asian women who were probably Vietnamese or Cambodian.

I cruised the building twice, then parked one block south and walked up past the *Journal* to the restaurant. I glimpsed two people in the *Journal* office, but neither was Clark Hewitt.

It was still before eleven, and the restaurant was empty except for an ancient Vietnamese woman wrapping forks and spoons in white cloth napkins. Preparing for the lunch-hour rush. I smiled at her. 'Do you have a take-out menu?'

She gave me a green take-out menu. 'You early.'

'Too early to order?'

She shook her head. 'Oh no. We serve.'

I ordered squid fried rice with honey, and told her that I would wait out front on the sidewalk. She said that would be fine.

I stood around out front with the little menu and tried to look as if I had nothing on my mind except food, and snuck glances in the *Journal* office next door. An Asian woman in her early sixties sat at a wooden desk, talking on the phone. Behind her, the walls were lined with corkboard and about a million little bits of paper and photographs and what looked like posters for community events had been pinned to the board. A couple of ratty chairs were at the front of the office, and another desk sat opposite the woman's, this one occupied by a young Asian guy who looked to be in his twenties. He wore a Cal Tech sweatshirt and tiger stripe field utilities and Top-Siders without socks. He was leaning back, the Top-Siders up on the desk, reading a paperback. A half wall split the space into a front and a back, only you couldn't see the back from here in the front. Maybe Clark was in the back. Maybe I could whip out my gun, charge through the front into the back, and shout, 'Gotcha!' Be impressive as hell if he was really there.

The young guy saw me looking. I smiled and took a copy of the *Journal* from a wire rack bolted to the front of the building, just another bored guy killing time while he waited for his food. It was a tabloid-sized Vietnamese-language newspaper filled with articles I couldn't read and pictures of Vietnamese people that I took to be from the local community. The printing was cheesy and smudged, and I wondered if maybe Clark had been hired to give them a more professional look. 'Do you read Vietnamese?'

The young guy was standing in the door. Inside, the woman was still on the phone, but now watching me.

I shook my head and put down the paper. 'No. I'm just waiting for some food next door. I was curious.'

He grinned. 'They're free. Help yourself, if you want. They make a great birdcage liner.' Mr. Friendly.

I strolled back past the restaurant and up a short alley, looking for the rear entrance. One of the wonderful things about being so close to the water is that the temperatures are so mild that you rarely have to use air-conditioning. It was in the low seventies, so the *Journal's* rear door was open for the air. I peeked inside. Furtive.

No Clark.

I listened at the door, then stepped in. An Apple laser printer was humming on a little desk beside another door that led to a bathroom. Industrial metal shelves were stacked with reams of paper and office supplies and a well-used Mr. Coffee, but nothing screamed *counterfeiter* and I didn't see any of the things that Clark had marked in his catalogs.

I slipped out, went around to the front again, and this time I walked into the *Journal* office. The young guy was back with his book and the older woman looked up from her word processor. The young guy smiled, but the older woman didn't. I said, 'My name is Elvis Cole, and I'm looking for Clark Hewitt.' I put one of my cards on the young guy's desk. 'His life is in danger and I'm trying to help him. I'm also trying to help his children.' Sometimes honesty is the best policy.

The young guy's smile vanished, and the woman said something in Vietnamese. The young guy answered, also in Vietnamese.

I said, 'Sorry?'

The young guy stared at me for a couple of seconds before he shook his head. 'I don't know what you're talking about.' You could tell that he did. You could tell that he knew exactly what I was talking about, and that he did not like it that I had asked, or that I knew.

I glanced at the woman, and she turned away. Fast.

I said, 'I'm driving a 1966 Corvette convertible parked down the block. It's yellow. I'll be sitting in it.'

I went to the restaurant, paid for my food, then walked back to my car, put the top up to cut the sun, and sat. The squid fried rice was excellent, but I didn't have much of an appetite for it.

Twenty minutes later the guy in the Cal Tech sweatshirt came out to the street, looked at me, then went back inside. Sixteen minutes after that, a black 500-series Mercedes sedan circled the block twice, two Asian men in their mid-sixties inside. I copied their license number. Maybe eight minutes after that, a bright red Ferrari Spyder appeared from the opposite direction and eased to a stop a car length away from me. Whoever these guys were, they had money. The Ferrari was driven by a very young Asian guy, but an older man was in the shotgun seat, and, like the people in the Mercedes, both of them were nicely dressed in Italian business suits. I copied the Ferrari's plate number, too. The two men in the Ferrari stared at me for a couple of minutes, talking to each other, and then the young guy rolled down his window and eased next to me to talk. I said, 'Clark Hewitt.'

The young guy shook his head. 'Got no idea who that is.' Flawless English without a trace of an accent. Local.

'I think you do.'

The young guy looked nervous, but the older guy seemed calm. The younger guy said, 'My mother works at the paper, and you're scaring her. I'm going to ask you to leave.' I guess the paper was a family business, but it probably didn't pay for his Ferrari.

'Do you own the paper?'

'I think you should leave.'

I settled back in my seat. 'Can't leave until I see Clark Hewitt.'

The older man said something, and the younger guy shook his head. 'We never heard of the guy.'

'Fine.' I crossed my arms and made like I was going to take a nap.

The older man mumbled something else, and the younger guy said, 'Are you the police?'

'Clark knows who I am. I gave your mother a card.'

The older man leaned past the younger guy. 'If you don't leave, we'll have to call the police.'

'Go ahead. We can talk about Clark and his association with your newspaper.'

The younger guy's jaw flexed, and now he said something to the older guy. 'You're not going away?'

'No.'

The younger guy nodded. 'Big mistake.'

He dropped the Ferrari into first gear and rocketed away, tires screaming and filling the air with smoke and burning rubber. Guess he'd seen someone do that in a movie.

The Mercedes left, too.

I waited. I had found the *Pacific Rim Weekly Journal*, and I had found some people who clearly knew Clark Hewitt. I was making gangbuster progress, and I was feeling proud of myself. Elvis Cole, Smug Detective.

Ninety seconds after the Ferrari roared away three men came out of the alley and approached me. They weren't in Italian business suits, and they didn't look as if they would've been any more impressed by a kid peeling out than I had been. They looked hard and lean and focused with flat, expressionless faces, and all three were wearing long coats. They walked with their hands in their coat pockets, and when they reached the car the one in the middle pulled back his coat enough to reveal a stubby black Benelli combat shotgun. He said, 'Guess what you're going to do?'

'Leave?'

He nodded.

'Tell Clark I'll be back.'

I started the car and drove away.

Honesty might be the best policy, but leaving is the better part of valor.

CHAPTER 22

I drove back to Belmont Pier, parked in front of a shop that sold whale-watching tickets, and used a pay phone there to call Lou Poitras. He said, 'Bubba, you really take advantage.'

'Funny. Your wife said the same thing.'

Poitras sighed. 'Just tell me what you want.' Humor. You break them down with humor, and victory is yours.

I gave him the two license numbers, asked for an ID, and waited while he brought it up on his computer. It took less than twenty seconds. 'The Mercedes is registered to a Nguyen Dak of Seal Beach.' Seal Beach is one of the wealthier communities along the south beach.

'What about the Ferrari?'

'Guy named Walter Tran. He's down in Newport Beach.' Another big-money community.

I said, 'These guys show a history?' Asking him if they'd ever been arrested.

'Couple of speeding tickets on the Ferrari, but that's it. You want to tell me what this is about?'

'Nope.' I hung up, bought an iced tea from a sausage grill, then stared at the bay. The water was clean and blue, and Catalina was in sharp relief twenty-six miles away. A young woman in short-shorts and a metallic blue bikini top Rollerbladed past on the bicycle path. I followed her motion but did not see her. The detective in thoughtful mode. I had never heard of Nguyen Dak or

Walter Tran, but that didn't mean anything. Multi-cultural crime was flourishing with the Southland's growing diversity, and it was impossible to keep up. I had also never heard of the *Pacific Rim Weekly Journal*, but I was pretty sure I knew someone who had.

I went back to the pay phone, and called this reporter I know named Eddie Ditko. Eddie is old and cranky and sour, but he is nothing if not a joy. 'Christ, I got gas. You get to be my age, even water makes you cut the cheese.' You see?

'You ever heard of the *Pacific Rim Weekly Journal*?'

He went into a coughing fit.

'Eddie?' He was coughing pretty bad.

'Jesus, I'm choking to death.'

'I'll hang up and call nine-one-one.' The coughing was getting worse.

'Screw nine-one-one. They'd probably just put you on hold.' He made a gakking sound, then got the coughing under control. 'Christ, I just popped up something looks like a hairball.'

'That's more than I needed to know.'

'Yeah, well, try living with it. Getting old is hell.'

'*Pacific Rim Weekly Journal*.' Sometimes you have to prompt him.

'Yeah, yeah, yeah. Hold your water and lemme see what we got.' He was probably scanning the *Examiner*'s computer database.

'Check out Nguyen Dak and Walter Tran while you're at it.'

'Christ, you're pushy.' He made a hawking sound, then he spit. Sweet. 'Here we go. It's a political soapbox for nationalist Vietnamese who want their country back. LAPD's Antiterrorist Task Force has them on the monitor list.'

The blader with the metallic top rolled past in the opposite direction. I said, 'Political terrorists?'

'You know how the Cubans in South Florida want to overthrow Castro? It's the same thing. The *Pacific Rim Weekly Journal* raises money and lobbies politicians to discourage normalization with the Commies.' Commies. 'They also advocate the overthrow of the Communist government over there, and under our statutes that qualifies as terrorism, so LAPD has to waste money watching them.'

'What do you mean, 'waste'?'

More coughing. Another hawking sound, and then the spitting. 'Christ, that one had legs.'

'Why a waste, Eddie?'

'We did a feature on these guys in the Orange County edition a couple of years back. Dak and Tran and some of their pals fund the paper, but it's not how they make their living. They're self-made millionaires. Dak washed dishes until he scraped together the money to open a noodle shop. That led to more noodle shops, and pretty soon he was building strip malls. Tran bought a goddamned carpet shampooer to wash rugs after the day shift, and now he's got six hundred employees.'

I thought about Tran in his Ferrari. 'Tran's a young guy.'

'You must be talkin' about his kid, Walter Junior. Walter Senior's gotta be in his sixties. These guys came here with nothing, and now they're living the American dream.'

'Except that they're listed as terrorists.'

'Yeah, well, they didn't come over here for the oranges. They fled Vietnam to escape the Communists, and they damn well want the Commies out so they can go home.'

'Thanks, Eddie.'

I put down the phone and stared at the Rollerbladers and thought about self-made men without criminal records who just want to go home. Good Republicans with a raggy little newspaper and a career counterfeiter on the payroll. Maybe they couldn't quite raise enough money for the cause through strip malls and carpet cleaning and political action committees, so now they were branching out into crime. Crime, after all, is America's largest growth industry.

I made one more call, this time to Joe Pike. 'You hear from Lucy?'

'Yes.' She had given him her flight information, and he passed it to me. She would be arriving on a Delta flight from New Orleans in a little less than two hours, and she would expect me to pick her up. She had made arrangements to stay with Tracy, and, if I couldn't make it, I was to call Tracy.

'Kids okay?'

Pike hung up. I guess too much time with Charles will do that to you.

I worked my way back onto the freeway and made the long drive north to LAX, periodically checking the mirror for Russians, federal agents, and Vietnamese thugs with Benelli autoloading shotguns. If I could bring these guys together, we could have quite a party.

The traffic was dense and sluggish, but I found myself smiling more often than not, and feeling pretty good about things. I was getting closer to Clark, and I was only minutes away from seeing Lucy. I had been neither shot nor beaten in almost three days. Happy is as happy does.

I was still happy when Lucy Chenier came out of the jetway, saw me, and opened her arms. She was wearing a charcoal suit and carrying an overnight bag. She wasn't smiling, but that was okay. I was smiling enough for both of us.

We hugged, and I could feel the tension in her back and shoulders, and the strength there. I whispered into her hair, 'It is so good to see you. Even for a rotten reason like this.' Her hair smelled of peaches.

She hugged harder, and an overweight man with no hair scowled because we were blocking his way.

'You want me to take you to Tracy's?'

'I want to spend some time with you first. There's something that we need to talk about.' Her face was composed and empty of emotion, and I thought it must be her game face. The same face she would use in court; the face she had used when she was working her way through college on a tennis scholarship.

'Okay. Do you have bags?'

'Only this.' She let me carry her bag, and as we walked to the car she said little. Focused, I guess. Sleek and stripped down and ready for war. Or maybe she was just scared.

Once we were on the freeway, she brought my hand into her lap, holding it tight with both of hers. I thought she might fear letting go. I said, 'Does Ben know what's going on?'

Her eyes were not quite on the creeping red lights ahead of us. 'No. I've always kept the bad things between me and Richard from him. I've thought that was best.'

I nodded.

'I didn't want him in the middle.'

'Of course.'

She glanced at me. 'I don't want you in the middle either.'

I looked at her. A woman in a black Jaguar cut in front of us and I had to brake. 'Luce, there is no middle here for me. I love you, and I'm with you. I'll help any way I can.'

A tiny smile worked at her lips. The smile was so

small that it was almost impossible to see. I almost didn't. She said, 'I know that you do, but I have to do this without you.'

I didn't say anything.

'It's important to me that you understand that I'm not being selfish. This isn't about Ben.'

'All right.'

'When we got divorced, I offered Richard open visitation rights. He never took advantage of it. When Ben would stay with Richard on weekends, or during the summer or on holidays, Richard was never there. He would hire a sitter, or drop Ben at his grandmother's. What's happening now isn't about Ben, it's about me, and Richard's need to control me, so please don't think that I'm this horrible woman who's stealing a man's child.' She looked at me then, and something in great pain was peeking through the composure. 'I am not the villain here.'

'Luce, you never could be.' She said it all as if she'd spent most of the flight thinking it through. I guess that she had. 'And you don't have to explain yourself or your former marriage to me.'

She looked at our hands, twined there in her lap. 'I know you want to help me through this. You already have, and I'm grateful, but you can't help me anymore.' She tugged at my hand, and when I looked over I think she was trying not to cry. 'I will not have my life defined by triangles. It's not fair to you, and it's not fair to me. Richard is my mistake, and I have to live with it.'

I didn't know what to say.

'What's going on now is between me and Richard, and only us. I need it to be that way. Do you understand?'

'No.'

She frowned. 'This is all about control, and he has to know that he can't control me, or intimidate me.' She frowned harder. 'I have to know that, too.'

I stared at her. Lucy Chenier seemed like the most uncontrollable woman I'd ever met, but maybe she hadn't always been so, and maybe she needed to remind herself.

'I could just shoot him. That would solve the problem.'

She smiled, and it was warm. 'I know, but then you would have saved me, and I wouldn't have saved myself. This is for me.'

'Okay.'

'I am the saver, and not just the savee.'

'You don't want me to be with you at KROK.'

She squeezed my hand again. 'No, you can't be there.'

I didn't like it, but I tried not to look sulky.

'Richard and I will be the only two players on the court, and when I kick his ass, and get his good-old-boy buddy up the proverbial creek, Richard will think twice about ever trying anything like this again.'

I looked at her, and thought that she was the most beautiful woman I had ever seen. 'Can I shoot him later?'

She smiled again, and this time patted my hand. 'We'll see.'

Something to live for.

'When are you going to see the KROK people?'

'Tracy arranged a meeting for tomorrow afternoon.'

Tomorrow was when the scanner arrived at LAX. Pike and I would be there waiting. We would be following the scanner, and hoping it brought us to Clark. 'I'll be working.'

She squeezed my hand again. 'Of course you will, my dove. That's as it should be.' She squeezed my hand another time. 'And I will be loving you.'

'Good.'

We continued up through the Sepulveda Pass into the Valley, and then on toward the safe house, riding in silence.

CHAPTER 23

The condo in Studio City smelled of rosemary and baked chicken. Joe and Teri were in the kitchen, and Winona and Charles were in the living room, but the TV wasn't on. Guess Pike had drawn the line. I said, 'That smells terrific.'

Winona bounced in from the living room. 'Teri and Joe made chicken. Hi, Lucy.'

'Hi, sweetie.'

Charles peered at Lucy from the dining room and grunted hello. Teri didn't say anything. She was behind a little forest of pots at the stove, frowning.

Lucy went into the kitchen and gave Teri a hug. 'How are you doing, dear?'

'Fine.' Tight and terse and futzing with the pots.

Lucy said, 'That smells wonderful. What is it, rosemary chicken?'

'Um.'

Lucy came back to me and took my hand. Teri frowned harder, then suddenly smiled brightly at me as if Lucy wasn't there. 'I saved some for you, Elvis.' The bright smile turned sad and she looked at Lucy. 'But I don't think there's enough for two.'

I stared at her.

Lucy said, 'Oh, that's all right. I should call Tracy and tell her how to get here.'

'I'll take you there.'

Lucy grinned, and you could tell she was trying to

188

keep the grin from growing wider still. 'No. We made plans to discuss strategy over dinner. She wants to take me out.'

I stared at Teri some more, then showed Lucy to the living room phone. She sat on the edge of the couch to make the call.

Teri beamed at me from the kitchen. 'Heating the chicken shouldn't take long. When would you like to eat?'

'Later.' What was with this kid?

Teri bustled away in the kitchen, the pots and pans rattling. 'I'll get started now. Then you can eat whenever you want.' Happy is the little homemaker, happy as a bee. 'Can I bring you a beer?'

'No.'

Winona said, 'Did you find our daddy yet?'

'Not yet.'

Charles eyed Lucy on the couch, then edged closer and craned his head. I watched all the craning, then figured it out. He was trying to see up Lucy's skirt. I said, 'Charles.'

He scuttled away. 'I didn't do anything.' Just another fun evening hiding out with the Cole posse.

Lucy spoke with Tracy, then asked me to give Tracy directions. I did, then they spoke a few more minutes, and Lucy hung up. 'Tracy says it should take her about a half hour to get here.'

Pike glanced up the stairs. 'We should talk.'

Charles said, 'Why ya gotta go upstairs? Why don't ya just say it here in front of us?'

Teri said, 'Elvis knows what he's doing. Leave him alone.' Teri turned back to the stove, and put cool eyes on Lucy. 'I'll call you the second your friend arrives.'

I looked from Lucy to Teri, then back to Lucy. Lucy's eyes glittered and she pulled me toward the stairs.

When we got upstairs and closed the door, I said, 'Do you have frostbite?'

Lucy smiled wider. 'You don't know?'

'Know what?' Mr. Idiot.

Lucy glanced at Pike, and Pike's mouth twitched. I said, 'What?'

'She's got a crush on you, dopey.'

I looked back at Pike. 'You think this is funny?'

Another twitch. Everyone was having a good time with this but me.

Lucy said, 'Think about it. She's always been the caregiver. She's never had a male authority figure take care of her before, and now you're doing that.'

'Great.'

'Also, you're cute.' Lucy bumped me, and her eyes said she was enjoying this, even if I wasn't. 'I can hardly blame her, can I?'

Pike said, 'Tell me about the newspaper.'

I told them, the three of us sitting there on the office floor, me holding Lucy's hand. I told them about the paper, and about the Ferrari and the men with the shotguns, and what I had learned from Eddie Ditko about Dak and Tran. Just having Lucy here made me feel better about things, and I wondered if this is what it would be like when she lived here full time. When I finished, Lucy said, 'They don't sound like terrorists to me.'

I shrugged. 'No, and they don't sound like criminals either, but they've hired a counterfeiter, and three of their people flashed me with shotguns.'

Pike nodded. You could tell he liked the part about shotguns.

Lucy said, 'What are you going to do?'

'The scanner arrives at LAX tomorrow. I'm thinking that Joe and I meet it, then follow whoever picks it up and see if they take it to Clark.'

Lucy's mouth tightened and she shook her head. 'This has grown far and above finding a missing father. I think you should turn this over to the police.'

'If I turn it over to the police, they'll arrest Clark.'

'Perhaps Clark deserves to be arrested.'

'I'm not doing it for Clark. I'm doing it for these kids. Clark isn't the world's greatest father, but if he's arrested, the Markovs will be able to get to him. If I can find him before he does anything stupid, I might be able to scare him into doing the right thing.'

She didn't seem convinced.

'Also, I promised Teri.'

Lucy sighed. 'Everyone else falls for a doctor or an engineer. I fall in love with Batman.'

Pike said, 'It's the cape. Women love the cape thing.'

Someone banged hard on the door, and Charles yelled, 'Some woman is here!' He said it so loud that half the apartment complex probably heard him.

Lucy said, 'That's Tracy.'

We looked at each other and I held her hand tight, feeling that if I let go she would go her way and I mine, and, having lost her, I might not find her again. 'I wish you could stay.'

'I know. Me, too.'

The three of us went down.

Tracy Mannos was standing in the entry, looking tired but determined. I hugged Lucy again, and so did Pike, and then they left. I said, 'Hell.'

Teri said, 'Your dinner's ready.' She said it with a broad bright smile.

I looked at her, then at Charles and Winona on the couch, watching television. 'I might have a line on your father, but to follow it I'm going to need Joe's help. Can you guys stay by yourselves tomorrow?'

Teri filled a plate with rice and chicken and something

that looked like stewed tomatoes. She brought it to the table and put it down at a place that had been carefully set. 'Of course, silly.' Silly? 'When we met we'd been alone for eleven days, hadn't we?'

I nodded. I sat.

Teri said, 'Can I bring you a beer now?'

'I'll get it.'

I started to rise but she pushed me down. Hard. 'I'm already on my feet.'

She got the beer, opened it, and set it on the table by my plate. I said, 'Thank you.'

She smiled and sat with me.

'You don't have to sit with me.'

'I want to.'

Pike went upstairs. Guess he couldn't stand it.

I looked at Teri. She looked back. 'Is it good?'

I nodded. 'Very.'

She fluttered her eyes and sighed.

Man.

CHAPTER 24

Pike and I left for LAX early the next morning, leaving the apartment as the sun was torching the eastern sky. That part of the morning, the air was still and cool, and we made good time; the southbound traffic moved easily, even though dense with commuters from the Simi and Antelope Valleys grinding toward the Los Angeles basin. I said, 'We're just another couple of guys on their way to work.'

Pike said, 'Uh-huh.'

The Beretta autoloader was on the floorboard behind our seats. I had the Dan Wesson, and Pike had his Python and maybe even an MX missile. Just another couple of guys.

We left the San Diego Freeway at Howard Hughes Parkway and dropped south through Westchester to LAX. The scanner was due in at nine that morning, and, according to the dispatcher in New York, was to be held at the airport for pickup at the Small Package Delivery office in the baggage claim area. Being a small package, it would come down the carousel with the luggage, where a United employee would pick it up, then take it to be held in the SPD office until it was claimed by someone from the *Journal*. That person might be Clark, but more probably it would be someone that we couldn't recognize, so we had to be in position to identify the package and follow its movements.

We left Pike's Jeep on the arriving flights level as close

to baggage claim as we could, then went into the SPD office. An attractive African-American woman was behind the counter there, stacking small packages for a guy in a gray express delivery uniform. I said, 'Excuse me. Could you tell me which carousel the luggage from United flight five will come down?'

'That would be carousel four. But that flight isn't due in until nine. You're awful early.'

I smiled at her. 'The wife's coming in and I miss her.' The wife.

'Oh, isn't that nice.'

The people in the terminal ebbed and flowed with the early morning flight schedule of the big cross-country flights to New York or Miami or Chicago, then grew steadily as the number of flights increased. At eight-thirty we separated and positioned ourselves with a view to all points of egress in case Clark showed. He didn't. A family of Hare Krishnas came through snapping finger chimes and offering pamphlets for money, moving from person to person until they reached Pike, and then they hurried past. Strong survival instinct.

At exactly nine a.m. the arrival monitor indicated that flight five had landed, and a few minutes later the carousel kicked on and luggage began sliding down its ramp. The fourth piece down was a white cardboard box taped with a bright yellow airbill. Pike drifted to the carousel, watched the package pass, then came back. '*Pacific Rim Weekly Journal.*'

Twenty minutes later, almost all of the crowd and luggage was gone. The attractive African-American woman appeared, and took the package into the SPD office. I said, 'Watch for the package, not the people.'

People carrying packages came and went through the SPD office, but none of them had the white box.

We waited some more.

Pike said, 'Maybe you scared them off.'

Nothing like support from the home team.

We were still waiting at sixteen minutes after ten when an Asian guy went into the office and claimed the white box with the yellow airbill. I looked at Pike. 'Ha.'

We followed him out to a plain white van, then out of the airport to the San Diego Freeway, then south. It took almost an hour and forty-five minutes to reach Long Beach, but the white van didn't seem to be in a hurry, and neither were we. Pike said, 'Paid by the hour.' Cynic.

The white van left the freeway at the Long Beach Municipal Airport, then cruised north along the west side of the airport into an area of warehouses where he turned into the parking lot between two enormous modern storage buildings. The buildings were painted a plain beige and bore no identifying signs. We cruised past to the next building, then turned back, slowing long enough to see our guy carrying the white box into the north building. I said, 'Want to bet Clark is in there?'

Pike shook his head. 'We could shoot our way in and grab him.'

You never know when he's kidding.

The street was lined with similar buildings, most of which were occupied by carpet wholesalers or appliance outlets or metalworking shops. We parked across the street and trotted back, Pike going around the north side of the building, me strolling across the parking lot. The building was divided into sections, with offices in the front and three big truck doors evenly spaced along the parking lot, and no windows. All the better in which to do crime. The people door at the front was heavy and industrial, and it was also closed. The guy from the van had entered a door on the side of the building, but that door was closed, too. In fact, all the doors were closed. Maybe the Roswell aliens were in there.

I had just reached a row of Dumpsters at the rear of the building when the people door kicked open and the guy from the white van came out with three other men, the four of them laughing and yucking it up. One of the men I had never seen before, but the other two had leaned on me outside the *Journal*. Pike drifted up beside me, and we watched as the four men climbed into the van and drove away. 'The middle two guys fronted me yesterday at the newspaper.'

Pike didn't respond. Like it didn't matter to him one way or another.

I said, 'Anything on the other side?'

'Two doors, both locked. No windows.'

'I'm thinking Clark's inside. There might be other people inside, too, but with four bodies out, now might be our best shot.'

Pike said, 'We could always just call the police.'

I frowned at him.

'Just kidding.' Then he looked at me. 'What if Clark won't come?'

I looked back at the door. 'Clark will come if I have to put a gun to his head. He will come and we'll sit down with those kids and we'll figure out what to do next.' I think I said it more for me than for Pike. 'But he will come.'

'Optimist.'

We drew our guns, and went through the side door into a long colorless hall that smelled of Clorox. The hall branched left and straight. Pike looked at me and I gestured straight.

We moved past a series of small empty offices to the door at the end of the hall, then stopped to listen. Still no sounds, but the Clorox smell was stronger. Pike whispered, 'Stinks.'

'Maybe they're dissolving bodies.'

Pike looked at me. 'Acid to cut litho plates.' I guess he just knows these things.

We eased open the door and stepped into a room that was wide and deep and two stories high, lit by fluorescent tubes that filled the space with silver light. A lithograph machine sat in the center of the floor, surrounded by long cafeteria tables that had been lined with boxes of indigo ink and acid wells and printers' supplies. A high-end Power Mac was up and running, anonymous screen-saver kittens slowly chasing each other. The scanner was still in its box, the box on the floor by the Macintosh. A color copier was set up on one side of the litho machine, and three front-loading dryers stood in a row against the far wall. The smell of oil-based ink was so strong it was like walking into a fog. I said, 'Clark's going to print, all right.'

'Yeah, but what?'

Pike nodded toward a row of wooden crates stacked on pallets near the door. The crates were labeled, but the printing wasn't Arabic. Pike said, 'Russian.'

The top crate had been opened and you could see blocks of paper wrapped in white plastic. One of the blocks had been slit open to reveal the paper inside. The sheets were something like eighteen inches by twenty-four, and appeared to be a high-grade linen embedded with bright orange security fibers. The sheets also looked watermarked, though I couldn't make out the images. I said, 'Our money doesn't have orange security fibers.'

Pike drifted to one of the long tables.

'You think they're going to counterfeit Russian money?'

Pike reached the table. 'Not Russian, and not ours.'

Pike held up what looked like a photo negative of a series of dollar bills, only when I got closer I could see that they weren't dollars. The denomination was 50,000, and the portrait wasn't of Washington or Franklin or even Lenin. It was Ho Chi Minh. Pike's mouth twitched. 'They're going to print Vietnamese money.'

I put down the negative. 'We still have to find Clark.'

We went back along the hall toward the front of the warehouse, passing more empty offices. The hall reached a kind of lobby, then turned right to more offices, and as I passed the first office I saw a small camp cot against one wall, covered by a rumpled sleeping bag. 'In here.'

We went in. 'Guess he's supposed to stay here until the job's done.'

Clark had been here, but he wasn't here now. An overnight bag sat on the floor beside the cot, and a cheap card table with a single folding chair stood against the opposite wall. A little radio sat on the table, along with a few toiletry items and a couple of printers' magazines. Diet Coke cans were on the floor, along with crumpled bags from Burger King and In-n-out Burger and a large bottle of Maalox and a mostly used tube of cherry-flavored Tums. The room smelled of sweat and body odor and maybe something worse. A candle and a box of matches and a simple rubber tube waited on the table. Drug paraphernalia. I said, 'Goddamn. The sonofabitch is probably out scoring more dope.'

Pike said, 'Elvis.'

Pike was standing by the overnight bag, holding a rumpled envelope. I was hoping that it might be something that would lead us to Clark, but it wasn't. The envelope was addressed to Clark Haines in Tucson, and its return address was from the Tucson Physicians Exchange. It was dated almost three months ago, just before the Hewitts had left Tucson for Los Angeles.

I felt cold when I opened it, and colder still when I read it.

The letter was from one Dr. Barbara Stevenson,

oncologist, to one Mr. Clark Haines, patient, confirming test results that showed Mr. Haines to be suffering from cancerous tumors spread throughout his large and small intestines. The letter outlined a course of treatment, and noted that Mr. Haines had not returned any of the doctor's phone calls about this matter. The doctor went on to state that she understood that people sometimes had trouble in dealing with news of this nature, but that it had been her experience that a properly supervised treatment program could enhance and maintain an acceptable quality of life, even in terminal cases such as Clark's.

The medical group had even been thoughtful enough to enclose a little pamphlet titled *Living with Your Cancer*.

I guess Jasper was right; Clark Hewitt was more than he seemed. I looked at Pike. 'Clark's dying.'

Pike said, 'Yes.'

That's when a hard-looking man with an AK-47 stepped through the door and said, 'He's not the only one.'

CHAPTER 25

He was an older guy with a hard face that looked as if it had been chipped from amber. He waved the AK. 'Hands on heads, fingers laced.' The accent was thick, but we could understand him.

I said, 'The building is surrounded by the United States Secret Service. Put down the gun and we won't have to kill you.'

'Lace your fingers.' I guess he didn't think it was funny.

He took a half-step backward into the hall, and when he did Pike shuffled one step to the right. When Pike moved, the older guy dropped into a half-crouch, bringing the AK smoothly to his shoulder, right elbow up above ninety degrees, left elbow crooked straight down beneath the AK's magazine, the rifle's comb snug against his cheek in a perfect offhand shooting stance. Perfect and practiced, as if he had grown up with a gun like this and knew exactly what to do with it. I said, 'Joe.'

Pike stopped.

The older guy yelled down the hall without taking his eyes from us. A door crashed and Walter Tran, Junior, came running up, excited and sweating, expensive shoes slipping on the vinyl tiles. When he saw me, his eyes got big and he barked, 'Holy shit!' He clawed at his clothes until he came up with a little silver .380 that he promptly dropped.

I said, 'Relax, Walter. We're not going anywhere.'

He scooped up the .380, fumbling to get the safety off and pointing it at the older guy who snapped at him in Vietnamese and slapped it out of his hands. The old man shifted to English. 'You're going to shoot yourself.'

I said, 'Walter, take a breath.'

Walter Junior pointed at me. 'This one was the guy at the paper. I've never seen the other one.' Pike, reduced to 'other' status.

The older guy narrowed his eyes again. 'He said they were with the Secret Service.'

Walter Junior said, 'Holy shit,' again, and ran back down the hall.

'I was kidding. We're private investigators.'

The older guy shrugged. 'Gives the boy something to do.'

The door crashed once more and Walter Junior was back, skidding to a stop just ahead of Nguyen Dak and two of the shotgunners who had fronted me at the *Journal*. I said, 'We could sell tickets.'

Nobody laughed at that one either.

Nguyen Dak was wearing a fine wool suit that had probably cost three grand. He looked at me. 'We told you to stay away.'

'Clark Hewitt has three children, and I have them. A bunch of Russians from Seattle are looking for Clark because they want to kill him. That means they're looking for his kids, too.'

'You should have listened.' Guess none of it mattered to him.

'We're here because we're working for Hewitt's children. We don't care about the printing.'

I guess that didn't matter to him either.

They made us lie face down with our fingers laced behind our heads, then searched us as if they were looking for a microphone or a transmitter. I guess maybe they were. Dak positioned the two shotgunners in the front corners of the room so they could cover us without shooting each other. The guy with the AK took our guns and our wallets, tossed them to Dak, then tied our hands behind our backs with electrical utility wire. Dak called him Mon. When our hands were tied, they lifted us into the two folding chairs. I said, 'It started out like a pretty good day.'

Dak made a gesture and one of the shotguns punched me on the side of the head. Seattle all over again.

Dak looked through my wallet first, then Pike's, then handed them to the guy with the AK. 'Private investigators.'

'I told you that.'

'You told this gentleman you are with the Secret Service.'

'Bad joke.'

Dak stared at me some more.

I said, 'We came here to find Clark Hewitt. We know he's working with you, and we know he's been here.'

Dak lit a Marlboro and looked at me through the smoke. The guy with the AK said something in Vietnamese, but Dak didn't respond. He said, 'We now have a problem.'

'I kinda guessed.'

'Who do you really work for?'

'Clark Hewitt's children.'

More cigarette, more smoke. 'I think maybe the FBI.'

I shrugged at him. 'If that's true, your problem's bigger than you think.' You could tell he knew that, and didn't like it. 'If we're feds, then other feds know where we are. If they know where we are, and we turn up dead, you're history.'

Dak clenched his jaw and waved the cigarette. 'I told you to stay away, and you did not. You came onto our property, and you have seen things that you should not have seen.'

I said, 'I don't give a damn what you're going to print, or why, or what you're going to do with it. I came here because Clark and his children are in danger.'

The AK spoke Vietnamese again, louder this time, and Dak shouted back at him, the other Viets looking from one to the other like some kind of tennis match was taking place, maybe yelling about killing us, maybe saying murder us clean right here in the room, then sweat it out with the cops and pretend they didn't know what happened or how or why. They were still going through it when Clark Hewitt came in with Walter Senior and another younger guy. Clark was wearing a cheap cotton shirt and baggy trousers over busted-out K-mart canvas shoes, and he had the vague, out-of-focus look of someone who'd just shot up.

Clark saw us and said, 'Oh, dear.'

Dak's eyes flashed angrily, and he jerked the cigarette. 'Get him out of here.'

The younger guy was pulling Clark back into the hall when I said, 'The Russians are in LA, Clark. I've got your kids stashed, but they're in danger.'

Clark jerked his arm away and came back into the room. 'Where are they?'

'At a friend's.'

Dak told the younger guy to get Clark out of there again, and when the younger guy grabbed his arm, Clark swatted at him. 'Get away from me!'

I looked back at Dak. 'I've got his children, goddamnit. Shooters from Seattle are down here looking for him, and he knows it's a fact.' I looked back at Clark. 'The Russians killed Wilson Brownell, and that means they know everything that he knows.'

Clark's face worked. 'They killed Wil?'

The AK screamed again, and this time he shoved past the others and leveled the gun at us. When he did, Clark shrieked, 'No!' and lurched forward, shoving him away. Both Walters and the other Viets swarmed around him, and Dak slapped him hard, twice. Clark didn't quit. He punched at Dak, throwing awkward punches with nothing on them, but he kept throwing them until a Walter hung onto each arm and a third man had him around the neck. Clark was just full of surprises.

Pike said, 'Payback's going to hurt.'

The three men pulled Clark out of the way, and Dak waved at us, saying, 'Kill them.'

Clark said, 'If you kill them I won't print your goddamned dong.' Vietnamese money is called dong.

Dak's face went dark, and he shook Clark's arm. 'You agreed to print for us and you will make the money!'

Clark said, 'Like hell I will.' When he said it a little bit of spit hit Dak on the shirt.

The AK had had enough with all the talk. He pushed past Dak and ran at us again, barking in Vietnamese. When he did, Dak yelled 'No!' and grabbed him from behind.

Dak and the AK and the other two older guys shoved and screamed at each other, and I knew what it was about. They were revolutionaries, but they were also businessmen with families and property and things they would lose if they were discovered. They were shouting about killing us, and it was clear that they wanted to. Pike tensed beside me, probably thinking that if the younger shotgunners looked at the older guys he would come out of the chair and risk the charge, maybe hit the near guy hard enough to knock free the gun, maybe get the gun and do some damage even with his hands tied behind his back.

Helluva morning. Drive down to Orange County to die.

I said, 'Clark, whatever Brownell knew, the Russians know. They'll have your address and phone number, and that gives them a place to start looking. If I can find you, they can find you, too.'

Clark was nodding, trying to hear me past all the yelling. A faint sheen of sweat covered his face, and he looked pale and more than a little nauseated. I thought that even with the dope whatever was eating him up must hurt like hell.

I said, 'I've got the kids stashed in a safe place, but you're going to have to do something. Either go back into the program or get out of town.'

Clark was looking from me to the Viets, me to the Viets, over and over again. 'I need this money.' Whatever they were paying him to do the job.

'Clark, what good's the money if they murder your children?'

All the screaming had peaked, and Dak jerked the AK away from the other guy and used it to shove Clark toward the door, screaming, 'We have the paper now, we have the machines! Go into the other room and print the dong!'

But Clark didn't go into the other room. He grabbed hold of the AK, and shouted, 'I'm not going anywhere! If you kill them I won't print your money.'

Dak was breathing so hard he sounded like a bellows.

One of the other guys ran up beside him and tried to wrestle the AK away but Dak shouted a single Vietnamese word and the man stopped. Now they were both breathing loud, and Clark was breathing loud, too. Clark grabbed Dak by the front of his jacket and shook him. Clark's face was so pale I thought he might keel over. He shouted, 'My children are in danger and these men are taking care of them.' He looked back at me. 'If they let you go, you won't tell, will you?'

'No.'

'You won't stop me from printing the dong?'

'Clark, if they let us go, we'll do everything we can to help.' I wanted Clark Hewitt to get his money.

The other man shouted and Dak raised the gun. Dak was shouting, too, and with all the shouting I thought that no one could understand anything and that the moment had taken on an inevitable life of its own. I thought that Dak would shoot right through Clark, the 7.62mm bullets ripping through Clark into me and Pike and ending us all, but then the shouting stopped and Dak muttered a single coarse Vietnamese curse, and he looked at me with an expression of infinite weariness. He said, 'All right.'

He told Dak to cut us loose.

My heart began to beat again.

CHAPTER 26

The one named Mon didn't like it. He stomped around, waving the AK and making a big scene until Nguyen Dak slapped him and took the gun away. The others started shouting and arguing, but when Dak finally had them quiet, he said, 'Make the dong and let's be done with this.'

I said, 'How long will it take to print the dong?'

Clark frowned. 'Well, after I make the plates, a couple of days.'

'How long start to finish?'

'Three days.'

'Okay. Your children can stay with you here while you print the dong, and you can decide what you want to do.' I wanted to get the kids out of LA, and I was hoping that I could work on getting Clark and his children back into the witness protection program while he was down here guarded by Dak's people. 'When you have the money you can leave from here without going back to Los Angeles. That way it's a clean miss for the Russians.'

Clark was liking it. 'That sounds good.' He turned to Dak. 'We'll have to go to Los Angeles to get my family.'

Dak shook his head. 'Absolutely not. Print the money first, then do what you want.'

I said, 'Forget it, Dak. His kids are in danger as long as they're in Los Angeles. So is he.'

Dak glared at Clark. 'You agreed to make the dong.

We've bought the press and the materials. We have an enormous investment.'

Clark frowned. 'I'm still going to do it. I'll make the dong when I get back.'

Dak shook his head again. Adamant. 'No dong, no money.'

'I'll make the dong. I just want to get my children.'

Dak waved at me and Pike. 'You stay and make the dong. They can go get the children.'

Clark pursed his lips and scowled, and suddenly I could see Charles in him. 'No, I'm their father and I'm going to get them.'

I said, 'They're just up in Studio City, for chrissake. It's not like they're on Mars.'

Dak put his hands on his hips.

'We're talking about three hours round-trip.'

'No.'

I spread my hands. 'Look, if you're that scared Clark won't come back, why don't you come with us.'

Pike stared at me.

Dak huddled with the other Viets. There was more handwaving, but this time no one was shouting or pointing a gun at us. I guess they were getting used to the idea. Finally Dak came back to us and said, 'All right. Let's go get them.'

Pike sighed. 'Now it's 'us.' '

Dak looked at Pike. 'We have a large investment here that's worthless if he doesn't come back. We're going to protect it.'

Pike shook his head and stared at the floor.

I said, 'Clark, are you up to this?' He looked pale and clammy, and I was wondering just how much longer he could stay on his feet. He looked like he should be in a hospital.

Clark Hewitt pulled away from me. 'I'm fine. Just let me get my bag.' His drugs were in the bag.

They made me draw a map detailing how we would get to the safe house, and then we left, Dak and the two Walters following in Dak's Mercedes, Mon riding with us. The other guys stayed to guard the warehouse. I wasn't sure from whom, but you never know. Mon seemed sullen and resentful, and made sure we all knew he had a pistol tucked in his pants. He must've been something when he was younger.

We drove in silence for the first twenty minutes or so. I glanced in the rearview mirror at Clark every few minutes, but all he did was stare at the passing scenery without really seeing it. 'Clark, why didn't you tell someone about the cancer?'

He still didn't look at me. 'How do you know about that?'

'We found the letter from your doctor.'

He nodded.

'Does Teri know?'

'How could I tell them something like that?'

Pike said, 'You shoot dope for the pain.'

Clark glanced at Pike. It was the first time he had turned from the window. 'I don't have health insurance, and I can't afford prescription painkillers. Dealers buy and sell their drugs with cash, and they rarely put anything in the bank, so I just use the funny money.'

I looked at him some more. Even in the mirror I could see the faint sheen of sweat that covered his face. He was pale and he looked nauseated. 'Does it help?'

'Not as much as it used to.'

Pike said, 'How long?'

Clark turned back to the window, almost as if he was embarrassed. 'A few months.' He shrugged. Like that was the way he'd found to deal with it. Shrug and keep going.

'That's why you're printing for these guys.'

'I don't have any savings. I don't have insurance. I had to do something to take care of my children, and this is it. Printing is all I know how to do.'

'Sure.'

'I print the dong, and Dak will pay me real money that I can put into a bank. Enough to get them grown and through school. Maybe even enough for college.' He nodded to himself as he said it, almost as if he was saying it because he needed to hear it to keep himself going, telling himself that it would all work out, that his kids would be fine. It made me want to cry.

'You don't have family who can take them?'

'My wife and I were both only children. Our parents are dead.' Another shrug. 'They don't have anyone but me.' He finally looked at me through the mirror. 'I want you to know how much I appreciate everything that you've done. You're a very nice man.'

I stared at the road.

'When I get paid I'll pay you for all this.'

I stared harder and nodded.

We made good time in the late afternoon traffic, and would've made even better time except that the Mercedes kept falling behind. After about the eighth time, I said, 'What's wrong with that guy?'

Mon said, 'Dak won't go over the speed limit.'

'He's willing to kill us to protect his revolution, but he won't break the speed limit.'

'Dak wants to be a good American.'

I could see Pike out the corner of my eye. Shaking his head.

Clark said, 'These people aren't criminals. They're revolutionaries.'

'Sure. Counterfeiting dong.'

'They have this idea that if they put a lot of counterfeit money into the Vietnamese economy, it will destabilize the Communist government and force Vietnam toward a democracy.'

Pike said, 'Patriots.'

Clark shrugged. 'It was their country. They want it back.' Same thing Eddie Ditko had said.

I asked Clark if he wanted to stop at their house first, but he said no. I asked if there was anything we could get for him at the drugstore, but he said no again. He just wanted to pick up his children and go back to Orange County and print the dong. He sounded tired when he said it.

'I've got a doctor friend, Clark.'

'It wouldn't do any good.' Like he wanted to lie down and go to sleep for a long time.

I drove harder, and kept waving Dak faster. Dak didn't like it much, but as long as I didn't go too fast he kept up.

The late afternoon rush caught us in Hollywood and traffic began to back up, but twenty minutes later we were through the Cahuenga Pass and dropping off the freeway into Studio City. When I exited the freeway at Coldwater Canyon in Studio City, Clark sat up and seemed more alert. I wondered at the dull ache he must live with, and what it must be like for him to keep it muted by shooting drugs. Jasper was right. There was a lot more to Clark than it seemed.

Clark said, 'Are we close?'

'Yes.'

Two minutes later I parked at the curb in a spot that left room for Dak's Mercedes, and then the four of us climbed out of Pike's Jeep. Dak jerked his thumb at the building, and Mon said, 'Let's go.'

Clark was walking fine, though every once in a while he made a little wince. The cancer.

We reached the condo, knocked twice, and waited for Teri to unlatch her door. It should have been a surprise homecoming, and it should've been nice, but it wasn't.

Teri opened the door the third time I knocked, and I knew something was wrong. 'Teri.'

Her eyes made little round O's when she saw Clark. 'Daddy!'

Clark said, 'Hi, sweetie.'

'Teri, what's wrong?'

Teri's eyes filled and she threw her arms around Clark and wailed. 'Charles ran away.'

CHAPTER 27

Mon ran back to the Mercedes, and the rest of us went inside, Clark with an arm around Teri. Winona jumped off the couch when she saw Clark and ran to him, shrieking and grabbing him around the waist. Guess she wasn't all that worried about Charles, or maybe she was just that much happier to see her father. I said, 'How long has Charles been gone?'

Teri wiped her nose. 'Since before lunch.' It was after three now.

'Do you know where he went?'

'Uh-uh.' She wiped her eyes again. 'He said he wanted to look around the building. He said he'd be back soon, but he never came back.'

I gave her a hug and tried to look confident. 'It's okay, kiddo. We'll find him.' Charles might be anywhere.

Mon came back with Dak and the two Walters, and nobody looked happy. They stood in a little clump in the front door, Dak angry and firm. 'Now what?'

'Clark's son is missing.'

Dak glared at me as if I had to be kidding.

'We can't just drive away. We have to find him.'

Dak looked angrier still. 'You said this wouldn't take long. You said we would pick them up and leave.'

Teri had stopped sniffling and was looking at Dak and his pals. She said, 'Who are these people?'

Clark said, 'These are the men I'm working for,

honey.' Like they were Sears, and had a great retirement plan.

I said, 'What can we do, just leave him?'

Dak stalked past me, slumped onto the living room couch, and shook his head. Walter Senior and Walter Junior sat next to him. Mon stood by the coffee table and gave Dak a smug smile, the look saying 'I told you so.' They talked among themselves, then Dak sighed and looked defeated. 'Describe the boy and we will help you look for him.'

Teri told us that Charles was wearing big shorts and the black Wolverine T-shirt, and after a bit the four Viets left, Dak telling them to meet back at the condo in thirty minutes. Revolutionary operation.

I said, 'Did Charles take anything with him?'

Teri said, 'No.'

'Winona?'

Winona shook her head without looking at me.

'Did he say anything about the park or a 7-Eleven or anything like that?' The Russians didn't know where we were and had no reason to be in Studio City, so I wasn't worried about them. The Studio City Park was a block away, and two convenience stores were within a couple of blocks. The convenience stores would have video games and magazines and comic books, any of which would be an ideal way to kill a few hours if Charles was bored.

Teri said no and Winona shook her head again.

Pike and I split up. I cruised the park, getting out of the car and walking around the community center they have there. Half a dozen moms with babies were in the sand pit, but none of them had seen a boy matching Charles's description. Eight guys were playing basketball, but they hadn't seen Charles either. I cruised the surrounding streets, then stopped at the little market and the two convenience stores, again describing Charles and again being told that no one matching that description had been around.

Thirty-eight minutes after I left the safe house, I was back, and so were the Viets and Joe Pike, and none of us had found Charles or anyone who had seen him. When I came in empty-handed, Nguyen Dak put his face in his hands. More delay. Teri said, 'Didn't you find him?'

'Not yet. But we will.' I was thinking that if Charles had met another kid here in the complex, he had probably gone home with that kid to hang out. Probably playing Sega right now. I told Clark what I was thinking. 'You and the girls could go down to Long Beach with Dak, and I can wait here. When Charles shows up, I'll join you.'

Dak stood. 'That's an excellent idea.' I think he smiled for the first time in hours.

Clark considered it, but didn't seem convinced. 'Well, maybe.'

Teri said, 'What's in Long Beach?' You could hear an edge in her voice. Tired of always moving. Tired of all the new places.

Clark said, 'That's where I work, honey.'

Winona looked uneasy. 'I want to go home.'

I shook my head. 'If you need anything there, Joe and I will pick it up for you. Best if you guys go straight to Long Beach.'

Winona looked even more uneasy, and picked at her shoe. 'I think we should go home first.'

I stared at her. Teri looked at her, too. 'Winona, you know something?'

'No.' Stubborn.

The muscles in my shoulders and neck tightened, and now I didn't like what I was thinking. Now what I was thinking scared me. 'Winona, did Charles say anything to you?'

She shook her head.

'Did Charles tell you that he was going home?'

She picked harder at the shoe and a little piece of rubber came away. 'Charles said he'd beat me up if I said.' Charles.

Joe said, 'Little girl.'

Winona snuck a glance at him. Joe was standing against the wall with his arms crossed, eyes dark and hidden behind the glasses. If you were Winona's size he probably looked twelve feet tall. He said, 'I'll protect you.'

Winona still wasn't happy about telling. 'He said he thought waiting around here was dumb because we all knew that Daddy would come home. He said he was going to go wait for him.'

Clark said, 'Oh, dear.'

Winona said, 'He made me give him my key.' The little troll key ring.

Walter Tran Senior looked at his son and nodded. 'Children are a source of great misery.'

I glanced at Pike, and neither of us were liking it. The Russians knew about their house. 'Home is pretty far away. Would Charles know how to get there?'

'Charles is good with directions.'

If Charles headed home, he'd probably use Laurel Canyon to get over the mountains to the basin side. If he was walking it would take a long time and he might still be on the road, but Charles didn't seem like the type who'd hesitate to put out his thumb. If he caught a ride, he might be there now. Of course, the Russians might be there also.

I dialed their number and let it ring fifteen times. No one answered.

Teri said, 'Maybe he's scared to answer.'

'Sure.' I didn't believe it, and that gave me hope. If Charles was there he'd have to answer just to say something smart. 'Okay. I'll drive over and see if he's there.'

Clark and Teri both said, 'I'm going, too.'

'No. Stay here and pack your things. If Charles is there, we'll leave as soon as we get back.'

Dak put his hands together like he was praying. Mon smirked, and rolled his eyes.

I left Pike with them, and drove along the route that I thought Charles would take, cruising slow enough to check out storefronts and lawns and the knots of people standing at pay phones and bus stops. I cruised the parking lot of every minimall I passed, looking in the 7-Eleven and the Subway and the game arcades, and Charles wasn't in any of them, and little by little, I worked my way over the mountain and down into the basin and along Melrose to the house that the Hewitt family called home.

It took me almost an hour and fifty minutes to reach their house, and when I got there I checked the street for Dobcek's tan Camaro. The Camaro wasn't around, and that made me feel better about things.

I parked behind the Saturn, went to the front door, and was just fitting the key into the lock when someone opened the door from the inside. I thought it was Charles, but it wasn't.

Alexei Dobcek stared at me with his bottomless Spetnaz eyes, then pointed a pistol at me. 'We knew one of you assholes would show up sooner or later.'

I guess they had parked the Camaro a couple of streets over.

CHAPTER 28

Dobcek stepped away from the door, and waved me inside. The house was warm and dark and close, and quiet the way empty houses are quiet. I called, 'Charles?'

Dobcek smiled. 'What? You think we'd tie him in the bathroom?' He dangled Winona's key ring, the one Clark had brought her from Seattle, and the one she had given to Charles. The little troll was matted and ugly, and looked pleased with events.

'The boy better be all right, Dobcek.'

Dobcek smiled, telling me that I could be as tough as I liked, but he still had the boy. Sautin was in the living room, sitting in Clark's chair, watching the Food Channel without sound. The Too Hot Tamales were goofing with each other, smiling and kidding around in total silence, and Sautin was smiling with them. His eye and the side of his face was swollen and purple where Joe had kicked him. Dobcek said, 'Don't you hate being found out a liar, you telling us you know nothing about these people?'

'Sure. I wake up sweating about it every night.'

The house had been turned inside out. Drawers had been emptied onto the floor and plates smashed and living room furniture upended and slit open. Even the dining room table was upside down, its legs pointing to heaven like some dead beast. I guess they'd been searching when Charles showed up. I wondered if he had tried to fight them. I wondered if they had hurt him, and, if they had, I thought that I might kill them. I said, 'Where's the boy?'

'Somewhere safe.'

'Where?'

Dobcek put his hand under my jacket to get the Dan Wesson, and when he did I caught his gun with my left hand and twisted it up and out at the same time that I drew the Wesson and pointed it at his nose. 'The boy.'

Dobcek made the shark smile. 'Dmitri, you should have seen what he did. That was pretty good.'

'Da.' Dmitri Sautin was still watching Susan and Mary Sue.

I thumbed back the hammer.

Dobcek made the shark smile harder. 'And then what happens to the boy?'

I stared at him past the gun. Sautin said, 'Da, the boy,' but still didn't move.

Dobcek said, 'What we have here is what you call a Mexican standoff.'

'I've got Clark, and you've got Clark's boy.'

'Da. Put away the gun and let's deal with this.'

I breathed deeply, and then I stepped back and lowered the gun. He held out his hand, and I gave back his gun. A nice new Sig P226. Nine millimeter. Easy to shoot. Since Pike and I had taken his other gun, I wondered where he'd gotten this one. 'I reach into my pocket, okay?'

'Sure.'

He took out a hotel card from the Sheraton-Universal. 'We're staying here. The boy isn't, but we are.' The boy was probably with Markov. 'You ask Clark if he wants to see his boy again, then you give me a call and we talk about it.'

'The boy for Clark.'

'That's right.' He said something in Russian to Sautin,

and Sautin came around the chair. The swelling was nasty, and I hoped it hurt.

Dobcek winked at me, and then they left.

I stood in the house without moving for maybe five minutes, watching the Too Hot Tamales, and thinking. The Hot Tamales were making something with ancho chiles and tequila, and laughing a lot. They looked like they were having fun, and I wished I was with them and laughing, too, but I wasn't. I was in a devastated house that had just been vacated by a couple of Russian hit men who were holding a little boy, and I was trying not to let panic overwhelm me. Panic kills. I felt like a juggler with too many balls in the air and more being added. Okay, Cole, take a breath. I said, 'Good-bye, ladies,' and turned off the Tamales.

The house had been turned upside down because Dobcek and Sautin were looking for a clue to find Clark. Then Charles had walked in, and Charles was better than a clue. He was a don't-pass-go E-ticket straight to the big money payoff.

I went into the hall and looked at the attic door and saw that it was undisturbed. I pulled down the door, and went up for the duffel. It was where I had left it, and I thought that maybe I could use it. I wasn't sure how yet, but maybe. I dropped it out of the attic, closed the hatch, then locked the house and drove back to Studio City. I drove slowly, and thought about Markov, and what he wanted, and Clark, and what he wanted, and little by little the bits and pieces of a plan emerged.

When I let myself into the safe house, Joe and Clark and Teri were at the dining room table, and the Viets were still clumped together in the living room. Winona and Walter Junior were watching *Animaniacs* on television. Everyone in the room looked at me, and Teri and Clark spoke at the same time. 'Did you find him?'

'Dobcek and Sautin were at the house. They have Charles.'

Clark drifted one step to the side, then caught himself on the back of a chair. Teri squinted. 'Who are Dobcek and Sautin?'

Pike said, 'They work for the man who wants your father.'

'What's that?' She was staring at the duffel.

I didn't answer. I looked at Clark instead. 'Charles is okay, but we need to talk about this.' Clark was staring at the duffel, too.

Teri said, 'That's what this is all about, isn't it? That's his counterfeit money.' Her voice getting strained.

Clark said, 'Teri, please take Winona upstairs.'

Teri didn't move.

'Teri, please.'

'Don't treat me like a child!' It was a sudden, abrupt shriek that caught Clark by surprise. 'I'm the one who takes care of him. I'm more his mother than you're his father! Why don't *you* take Winona upstairs?' She was shouting, and Winona was crying, and Clark was looking like he must've looked the day he found out he had cancer, as if a truth that he'd believed in with all his heart had now been proved a lie.

Dak turned away. Embarrassed.

I said, 'Teri.' Soft. 'Teri, it's not your fault.'

Teri came around the table and hugged me, mumbling something that I could not understand. I think she was saying, 'I will not cry. I will not cry.'

I stroked her hair, and held her, and after a time she took Winona and went upstairs.

Clark stared at the floor.

'Clark.'

He looked up at me. 'Yes?'

I told them what Dobcek had said. The father for the

221

boy. While I was saying it, Clark ran one hand over the other in a kind of endless wringing motion, and when I was done, he said, 'Well, I guess we have to call them.'

Pike said, 'They want you dead.'

'They have Charles.' Clark's face was tinged a kind of ochre green. 'I can't let them hurt Charles.'

Mon said something to Dak in Vietnamese. Probably seeing their revolutionary dream crumble.

I said, 'We don't want them to hurt Charles, but trading you isn't the answer. They won't let Charles go if they have you. They'll kill you both because that's the only way they can protect themselves.'

Clark shook his head. 'What do you mean, protect themselves?'

'Think about it, Clark. They want to kill you. If they do that, and anyone is left alive, what's to keep Charles or me or someone from going to the police?'

Clark pinched his lips together. 'But what do we do?'

Mon mumbled something again, and Nguyen Dak said, 'We make them want to keep you alive.'

I looked at Dak, and Dak seemed dark and enclosed and dangerous. I thought he must have looked this way many years ago. War is war.

Pike said, 'Yes.'

Dak said, 'The Russian wants vengeance, but he will trade his vengeance for greed. All criminals are this way.'

I watched him. 'Are you willing to help?'

'I want the dong. If I have to help you in order to get the dong, then I will help.' There was something hard in his eyes, and maybe a bit of a smile at the edges of his mouth.

Mon said, 'Russians.'

Pike's mouth twitched, and I knew Pike was seeing it, too. Old wars merging with new wars. The Russians had supported the North against Nguyen Dak, and the

Russians still supported the North's Communist regime today. It would all be the same to these guys. A war they needed to win to go home.

I touched the duffel with my toe. 'Is this Markov's money?'

Clark nodded. 'Uh-huh.'

'Will Markov know it, and will he know it's counterfeit?'

Clark dug a packet of the bills from the duffel and flipped through them. 'He won't know they're his, but he can tell they're counterfeit. He has people who know how to tell.'

Pike said, 'What are you thinking?'

'Markov knows what Brownell knew. That means he knows that Clark is printing again, but he may not know what. He knows Clark is good, but what if he thinks Clark is even better now?'

Clark shook his head. 'I don't understand.'

'What if we buy Charles back?'

'With what?'

'Funny money.'

Clark said, 'But he'll know it's counterfeit. He can get counterfeit money anywhere.'

'Not just any counterfeit. What if it's counterfeit that's so good that it looks exactly like the real thing, so good that Markov couldn't tell it was funny money, and neither could a bank inspector.'

Pike nodded. 'Like the super notes from Iran.' Iran was rumored to be counterfeiting U.S. hundred-dollar bills that were so good they were undetectable.

'Exactly.' I looked at Clark. 'Markov knows you're good. What if we tell him that you're as good as the Iranians?'

Clark was shaking his head. 'But I can't print anything

like that. The Iranians use intaglio presses from Switzerland just like our Treasury. They use a paper just like ours.' He kept shaking his head. 'I couldn't duplicate that paper. I can't get an intaglio press. They cost millions.'

Pike said, 'Real money.'

Clark opened his mouth, then closed it.

I said, 'We flash a few thousand bucks in real hundreds, only we tell them it's counterfeit. We let Markov examine them, whatever he wants, and we offer to buy back the boy. All the funny money he wants for Charles.'

Clark said, 'But when we give him the counterfeit dollars, he'll know. He'll be able to tell that they aren't the same.'

'I know, Clark. That's why we'll need the police.'

Clark simply said, 'Okay.'

Walter Tran, Jr., gasped, and Mon turned a dark, murky color. Dak said, 'Why the police?'

'We need the police to get Markov off the board. Markov takes possession of the funny money, we get Charles, and the feds make the bust, taking down Markov both for the funny money and the kidnapping.' I turned back to Clark. 'If we give Markov to the feds, they might be willing to let you print the dong.'

He stared at me.

'That way you still get your money from Dak.'

He nodded.

'For your kids.'

Clark looked past me at something far away. You could almost see an exit light come on a door at the far end of a hall in his mind.

Nguyen Dak crossed his arms, still looking dangerous, but now looking thoughtful, too. Maybe thinking about his own children. Or maybe just wondering how he could get out of this without losing everything he'd worked for.

I said, 'I can call Dobcek and set a meet, but we still need the flash money. A few thousand in hundreds that we may not get back. Markov might want it. We might even have to destroy it to convince him that it's fake.'

Clark rolled his eyes and made a deep sigh. 'Oh, that's great. Where can we get that?'

Nguyen Dak said, 'Me.'

I was staring at him when he said it, and he was staring back. 'All right,' I said. 'All right.'

Mon looked happy, liking the idea of getting back at the Ruskies.

CHAPTER 29

Dak made two phone calls to arrange for the money. After that, I called Dobcek and told him I thought we could work out a trade, but that we would have to talk about it. I didn't mention the money, but I made it sound like Clark was willing to exchange himself for the boy. It was a classic bait and switch, promise them one thing, give them something else. Whether they like it or not. Dobcek said, 'You will bring the father.'

'Right. And you'll bring the kid.' Classic.

Somebody said something behind Dobcek. Background noise. Then he said, 'We will not discuss the details now. Give me your phone number.'

'Why?'

'I will have to discuss this with our friend. I will call you tomorrow with the details.' Our friend. He meant Markov.

'Forget it, Dobcek. I'll call you.'

Dobcek snickered. 'You don't trust us. You think we find you with the phone number?'

'I'll call you.'

Someone spoke behind him again, then Dobcek's voice hardened. 'Call us exactly at nine tomorrow morning. Be ready to act immediately. Do you understand?'

'Dobcek, I am the master of understanding. Remember that.'

'Da.'

'I am also the master of vengeance. That boy better not be harmed.'

Dobcek gave a single raspy laugh, then hung up.

Clark, Joe, and the Viets were looking at me. 'We'll set the time and place tomorrow at nine. Will the money be here?'

Dak said, 'Twenty thousand dollars in one-hundred-dollar bills will be here in a few hours.'

Pike nodded. 'You're okay, Dak.'

I was climbing the stairs to see Teri when the phone rang. Pike answered, then held it out. 'Lucy.'

'What happened?' My heart began hammering. Worse than with the Russians. Worse than when Mon was holding the AK on me.

Pike held the phone.

I ran down, took it, and said, 'Luce?'

'We won.' Two words that cut through the adrenaline like a sharp edge. 'Elvis, it's over. We won.'

'You got the job.'

'Yes.'

Pike was staring at me. I nodded at him, and he gripped my shoulder and squeezed. 'We've got time. Go see her.'

I looked at Clark. I frowned toward the stairs.

Pike said, 'Jesus Christ. Go.'

Tracy Mannos lived in a small contemporary home on a lovely street off Roscomare Drive at the top of Bel Air. It was almost ten when I got there, but Lucy and Tracy were bright and excited and celebrating their victory with a bottle of Mumm's Cordon Rouge Brut. Tracy opened the door, but Lucy almost knocked her down getting to me. We hugged hard, the two of us beaming, and Tracy laughed. 'If you two start taking off your clothes, I'm calling the police.'

Lucy and I started laughing, too, as if someone or

something had pulled a plug and an ocean of tension was draining away. Lucy said, 'How long can you stay?'

I stepped back, and the laughter faded a bit. 'Not long.' I told her about the money. I told her what we were going to try to do. 'I don't know how long this is going to take. I might be busy the next couple of days.'

She had one of my hands in both of hers again, squeezing hard. 'I know. I'll have to get back to Ben tomorrow.' Two ships passing. The price of adulthood.

'Yes, but you'll be back.'

Her smile widened again. 'You bet your buns I will, Studly.'

'Tell me about it, Luce. Tell me everything that happened today.'

They did, some of which they now knew as fact, and some of which was supposition. It was neither complicated nor elaborate, because such things never are. It was merely ugly. Stuart Greenberg wasn't the evil, old-boy-crony that we'd suspected. When Richard had learned it was KROK that offered Lucy the job, he used his position at BM&D as an entrée to KROK's parent firm, then suggested to them that Lucy was erratic in the workplace. When the parent firm, concerned that KROK was in the process of hiring an uncertain (not to mention, untested) on-air personality, passed along their concerns to Stuart Greenberg, Greenberg questioned this information, and was told to contact the source, namely one Richard Chenier, a highly respected partner at the Baton Rouge office of Benton, Meyers & Dane. Greenberg had only been reacting to what Richard reported. Tracy said, 'When Stuart realized what had happened, he spent the rest of the meeting apologizing.'

Sometimes you just have to shake your head. 'And that was it? You've got the job?'

Lucy smiled. 'We agreed to agree. Stuart promised to

228

phone David Shapiro and wrap up the negotiation as quickly as possible.'

Tracy leaned toward me. 'She has the goddamned job.'

I said, 'What about Richard?'

Lucy's game face reappeared. 'I've phoned his office. I've also phoned his boss.'

Tracy said, 'I think she should sue the sonofabitch.'

Lucy's mouth formed a hard knot. Thinking of Ben, maybe. Thinking how far do you take a war like this when some of the fallout might rain on your child. She said, 'Yes. Well. We'll see.' Then she seemed to force the thoughts away, and took my hand again. 'I want to thank you.'

'I didn't do anything.'

'Of course you did. You supported my need to fight this without you.' She smiled and jiggled my hand. 'I know you. I know it couldn't have been easy.'

I shrugged. 'No big deal. You said I could shoot him later.'

'Well, yes. I guess I did.'

Lucy glanced at Tracy, and Tracy smiled. Voiceless female communication. Tracy kissed my cheek, and handed me the bottle of Brut. There wasn't much left. 'You take care of yourself, doll.' And then she walked away.

I said, 'Did you just send her away?'

'I did.'

'Good.'

Lucy and I sat in Tracy's living room, holding hands. It was late, and getting later, but I did not want to leave. Lucy said, 'I do wish I could stay, Elvis.'

'I know.'

She looked at me carefully, and then she touched my face. The bruise from Seattle had faded. 'I'll be out soon to find a place to live. As soon as Ben finishes school, we'll move.'

I nodded.

'You damn well better still be here.'

I nodded again.

'Please be careful tomorrow.'

'Careful is my middle name.'

'No, it isn't. But it should be.'

'I'll be here when you move out, Lucille. You have my word.'

She kissed my hand, and we sat like that, and not very long after, I drove back to Studio City.

CHAPTER 30

I let myself back into the safe house a few minutes after one that morning to find Mon hiding behind the door with his pistol. Mon shrugged when I looked at him, and said, 'Can't be too careful.'

Walter Junior was stretched out on the floor, sleeping. Dak and Walter Senior were at the dining room table, playing cards. Clark was sitting with them. 'Money come yet?'

Dak was concentrating on his cards. 'Soon.'

'Where's Pike?'

Mon said, 'He left, but he did not say anything.' His eyes narrowed. 'I no like that.'

'He never says anything. Forget it.'

Clark's skin seemed greasy, and if you looked close enough, you could see that his hands were trembling. 'Clark?'

Clark shook his head.

'How're the kids?'

'Sleeping.'

I joined them at the table and waited. No one spoke. The waiting is often the worst.

At twenty minutes after two that morning, someone knocked softly at the door and handed Dak an overnight bag containing twenty thousand dollars in nice neat hundreds. Real hundreds, printed by the U.S. Treasury on paper milled at the Crane Paper Mill in Dalton,

Massachusetts. Dak probably kept them under his mattress.

Clark pronounced them too clean, put the bills in a large Ziploc plastic bag with a half pound of ground coffee and one pound of dried kidney beans, and put the bag into the dryer. It wouldn't hurt the money, Clark said, but it would uniformly color the money as if it had been falsely aged.

Joe Pike returned at just after four. He gave Clark a small brown vial of prescription pills, and murmured something to Clark before moving to a dark corner of the living room. Clark looked at the vial, then stared at Pike for a long time before he went into the bathroom. A little while later he appeared to be feeling much better.

None of us formally went to bed; instead, we perched on the couch or in the big chair or on the floor, and drifted in and out of nervous uncertain catnaps, waiting for the dawn.

Sometime very early that morning, Teri came downstairs and moved between the napping men and cuddled against her father.

I phoned Dobcek at nine the next morning, exactly as I said I would. He said, 'We meet you on the Venice boardwalk in exactly one hour.'

'Let me speak with the boy.'

He put Charles on the line, and I told him that everything would be fine. I told him to stay calm, and to trust that Joe and I would bring him home. Dobcek came back on the line before I was finished. 'You know the bookstore they have there?'

'Yeah.' Small World Books.

'Wait on the grass across from that. We come to you.' Then he hung up.

I looked at Clark. 'You up to this?'

'Of course. Charles is my son.'

'Then let's go.'

Dak agreed to stay with Teri and Winona while Joe and Clark and I went to the meet. We used Joe's Jeep, with Joe driving. Two long cases were on the rear floor that hadn't been there yesterday. Guess he'd gotten them last night.

We used the freeways to get to Santa Monica, then turned south along Ocean Boulevard, riding in silence until we came to Venice. Pike turned onto a side street and stopped. He said, 'What's the deal?'

'They want Clark and me across from the bookstore on the grass. They'll come to us. They're supposed to have the boy, but I wouldn't bet on it.'

Clark leaned forward. He was holding the overnight bag on his lap like a school lunch. 'Why won't they have Charles?'

'They'll say that the boy is in a car nearby, and maybe he will be, but probably he won't. They're not coming here to trade, Clark. They're coming here to kill us. Keep that in mind.'

'Oh.'

'They'll say the boy is somewhere else to get us to go with them to a place they've picked out. It will be a private place, and that's where they'll do the murder. We in the trade call that the kill zone.'

Clark said, 'You say that so easily.'

Pike shrugged. 'It is what it is.'

'But how will we get Charles?'

'We'll show them the money. Your job is to stay calm and convince them that you printed this money and that you can print more. That's very important, Clark. Can you do that?'

Clark nodded. 'Oh, sure.' Oh, sure.

'Markov wants you dead, but if he thinks he can get

something from you before he kills you, he might go for it.'

'What if he doesn't?'

Pike said, 'Then we'll kill him.'

When we were two blocks north of the bookstore, Pike turned into an alley, got out, and slipped away without saying a word. He took one of the cases. Clark said, 'Where's he going?'

'He's going to make sure they don't kill us while we're waiting for them.'

'You think they'd do that?'

'Yes, Clark. They would do that.'

I climbed behind the wheel, and at nine forty-two, I left Pike's Jeep illegally parked in a red zone behind the Venice boardwalk. 'Let's go.'

I led Clark along the alley to the boardwalk, and then to the bookstore. It was a bright, hazy day, just on the right side of cool. Street people were already up and walking their endless laps of the boardwalk, and shop merchants were hawking tattoos and sunglasses to tourists come to see what all the excitement was about. Tall palms swayed in the breeze. Joggers and Roller-bladers and male and female bodybuilders with great tans moved through the streams of people with practiced indifference. Clark said, 'Where's Joe?'

'You won't see him, so don't look for him. The Russians will wonder what you're looking for.'

He locked his eyes forward, afraid now to look anyplace other than directly ahead. 'Do you see them?'

'No, but they're probably watching us.'

'Oh.'

The bookstore had just unlocked its doors, and a dark-haired woman with glasses was pulling a wire magazine rack onto the walk. I walked Clark into the store and told him to wait inside with the bag and watch me through the window. I told him not to come out until I waved for him. The dark-haired woman eyed us suspiciously. Probably thought we were shoplifters.

I walked back across to the grass and waited. Three homeless men were lying on the grass there, one of them holding a fat dog. The man with the dog looked at me, and said, 'Spare any change?'

'Sorry.'

'Don't be cheap. It's for the dog.'

I shook my head. 'No change.'

The man smirked at his friend. 'Cheap.'

I looked along the boardwalk first one way, then the other, then along the beach behind me, and into the parking lots and alleys, just another guy hanging around on the boardwalk wondering if he could get his gun out in time to save Clark Hewitt's life, not to mention his own. I eyed the fat dog. 'Looks like he could use a little exercise.'

The homeless man was affronted. 'Mind your own goddamned business.' So much for small talk.

Six minutes after ten o'clock, Alexei Dobcek walked out of the bookstore's parking lot and came directly toward me as if we were the only two guys on the beach. I said, 'Where's the boy?'

'Near. Let's get Clark and go see him.'

I lifted the bag. 'We had a different idea.'

Dobcek glanced at the bag, then past me and to both sides, like maybe someone might be coming up on him fast. He smiled like I should know better than to try anything like this. 'We know Clark is in the bookstore. Why you want to get stupid like this?'

I dropped the bag at his feet. 'Look in the bag.'

He glanced at the bag, but didn't pick it up. The homeless man was eyeing the bag, too. Dobcek said,

'Markov is near with the boy. We had an agreement, did we not?'

'Look in the bag. It won't bite you.'

The homeless man said, 'Can I look?'

Dobcek pasted the homeless man with dead eyes. 'Leave here before I crush your dog.'

The homeless man gathered up the dog and scurried away.

Dobcek said, 'Fucking trash.' All heart, these guys.

'Look in the bag, Dobcek.'

He glanced at me again, then squatted and opened the bag. He reached in, felt the paper, then closed the bag and stood. 'So?'

'It's Clark's new project. Bring it to Markov, have him look at it, and tell him we'd like to work out a different arrangement.'

Dobcek stared at me, then shook his head. 'What do you mean?'

'Bring it to Markov and have him look at it. I'll wait here.'

Dobcek leaned close to me. 'We'll kill the boy.'

'Have him look at the money, Dobcek. I'll wait and so will Clark. We're not going anywhere, and Markov will want to talk about it. Tell him this is a sample.'

Alexei Dobcek looked one hard long time at the bookstore, then walked away with the bag.

I watched couples share coffee and breakfast at the little restaurant next to the bookstore, and I thought I might bring Lucy down here. She'd like the bookstore, and we could sit at one of the little outdoor tables and watch the street performers and enjoy ourselves. Read a little, eat a little. Be nice to do if I survived the next ten minutes or so.

Dobcek reappeared between the street vendor tents, and this time Sautin and Andrei Markov and a fourth man were with him. The fourth man was wearing jeans and a green polo shirt, and he was carrying the bag. Markov was wearing a sharkskin jacket and gold chains, and looked like a second-rate Vegas lounge act. A young woman in a green bikini looked at him as she Bladed past and laughed. Probably wasn't the fashion reaction he was hoping for.

When they reached me, Markov made a little wave at the bag. 'I always worry when someone change the plan on me.'

'So why didn't you just kill the boy and drive away?'

'Maybe I still gonna do that. Maybe the boy and you and Clark, too.' Markov smiled toward the bookstore, then waved toward the bag again. 'Why you wanna show me this?'

'Clark printed it. He's going to print more, and we were thinking you might like some of it instead of killing Clark and his boy. We were thinking that you might like so much of it that you'll forgive Clark for the little problem in Seattle and let bygones be bygones.' They would either go for it or they wouldn't. We could either convince them it was counterfeit, or we couldn't.

The fourth guy put the bag on the ground, and took out one of the hundreds. He snapped the bill and sneered at me. 'You sayin' this is funny?' He snapped the bill again. 'My goddamned ass it is.'

The fourth guy wasn't Russian. He sounded like he was from Georgia or Florida, and I didn't like it that he was here. He sounded like he knew about printing, and he might be able to call Clark a liar and get away with it. Maybe he was Markov's current funny money specialist. I said, 'Who the hell are you?'

'The guy sayin' you're bullshit.'

I smiled at Markov. 'You're not interested, that's fine.' The homeless guy with the dog had set up shop ten yards down the boardwalk in front of a stand selling African robes. I called, 'Hey, dog man.' When he looked over, I closed the bag and tossed it to him. 'Have a party.' I turned back at Markov and spread my hands. 'Your loss, Andrei. We're sitting on a couple million more of this stuff.'

Ten yards away, the homeless guy looked in the bag and shouted, 'Yeow! Jesus has returned!'

Markov sighed and tilted his head. 'Dobcek.'

Dobcek trotted over and pulled the bag away from the old man. The old man didn't want to let go, so Dobcek punched him once in the forehead. Hard. I kept the smile on my face like it didn't matter to me. I kept the smile like I didn't want to take out my gun and shoot Dobcek to death. Like I didn't feel like a dog because I had brought it on the old man.

The fourth guy said, 'Hey, Mr. Markov, if those bills are righteous I'd like to know how.' Wounded and whiny, as if his feelings were hurt that Markov doubted him.

I said, 'Clark's in the bookstore. You give him a pass to come out here and talk about it?'

'Da.'

I waved Clark out. When Clark reached us he stood a little behind me, and kept his hands in his pockets. The sun made him squint so much that his eyes were little slits. Markov said, 'You look like shit.'

Clark said, 'Hi, Mr. Markov.'

The fourth guy toed the bag. 'This is intaglio, not offset. This is Crane paper.' He shook his head. 'My ass you printed this.'

Clark blinked at me, and I gave him an encouraging smile. 'Guy thinks you're bullshit. Guy wants to know how you did it.' I crossed my arms so that my hand was near the Dan Wesson and hoped that Pike was zeroed on

Dobcek because I was planning on shooting Sautin. I would shoot Sautin first, then Markov, and then the fourth man, and hope that I could do all that before someone shot me. We were maybe twenty seconds from all the shooting, and if we survived the boy would still be lost, all because some cracker who knew a little printing just happened to be with Markov.

Clark blinked at me again, and I said, 'Tell the man, Clark.'

Clark blinked once more, then took a bill from the bag, snapped it just as the cracker had, and smiled at Andrei Markov. 'Of course it's Crane paper. You can't fake that wonderful sound.' He snapped it again, then held up the bill. 'They used to be one-dollar bills.'

The cracker frowned.

Clark said, 'Real U.S. money printed on real Crane paper.' He held the bill to Markov. Markov took it. 'But they were ones. I washed them, Andrei. Bleached the original ink, then washed them and pressed them and reprinted them as hundreds.' Clark's smile widened. 'You wouldn't believe the wonderful technology we have now, Andrei.'

The cracker took a bill from the bag and frowned harder at it.

Clark said, 'I bleached eight hundred pounds of paper, and I've got an intaglio press. It's older, but it's one of the Swiss originals that a printing firm in France had until they went out of business last year.' Clark let the smile turn shy. 'Well, it's not mine, really, but these people I know have it. I'm printing for them just the way I was printing for you.' I was staring at Clark. Staring, and impressed as hell.

Markov said, 'You gonna steal from them, too?'

'If I have to.' He said it directly to Markov and he said it well.

The cracker said, 'Where'd you get the plates?'

'Scanned them off a series of mint collector notes, all perfect hundreds printed between 1980 and 1985. I used a high-density digitizer to get a pretty clean line, then created a photoneg off the digital image and used the photoneg to acid-etch the plates.' Clark pointed at the hundred the cracker was holding. 'You can see the inks are a little off, but I think I got pretty close.'

The cracker squinted at the bill and nodded. 'Yeah, a little too dark.' Afraid that Clark was showing him up in front of Markov.

Markov watched them talk with no more understanding of what they were saying than any of the rest of us, but he seemed to be buying it and that was all I cared about. I said, 'It doesn't matter that the inks are a little off. What we're talking here is bank-quality notes, counterfeit bills that will fool a bank or a cop or a Secret Service agent. Clark can print some extra for you. You get the money, and he gets his boy and you let them walk.'

Markov stared at me. Probably thinking about his older brother sitting in prison.

I rested a hand on Clark's shoulder. 'And when he finishes this job, maybe you guys can go into business again.'

Markov's eyes shifted to Clark, then back to me. They went to Clark again. 'How much of this paper you have?'

'Eight hundred pounds, like I said.'

'When it's gone, can you make more, da?'

Clark shrugged. 'Maybe, maybe not. The chemicals were very hard to get. I won't lie to you about that.'

Markov nodded, thinking, then looked at the cracker. The cracker shrugged. 'It's good, Andrei. It's the best I've ever seen.'

I picked up the bag and held it out to Markov. 'Here.

You keep it. You got any doubts, go see how it spends and think about getting more of it.'

Andrei Markov took the bag but didn't look into it or think anymore. He said, 'Five million.'

I looked at Clark. 'Can you print five million extra?'

Clark said, 'Oh, sure. No problem.'

I smiled at Markov. 'How about letting the boy go as a sign of good faith?'

'Don't be stupid. You'll get the boy when I get the money.'

I nodded. 'And after that Clark and his family are done with it. You give them a pass?'

'Sure.'

'I'll call Dobcek at the same number when we've got the money.'

Andrei Markov nodded again, and then the four of them walked away. I took Clark by the arm and we walked away in the other direction. I said, 'You did fine, Clark. We're going to get your son.'

Clark didn't say anything. Just past the bookstore he collapsed to one knee and threw up. I waited until he was done, then helped him to his feet.

Now all we needed were the cops.

CHAPTER 31

Joe Pike reappeared at his Jeep five minutes after us, the long gun in its case. I said, 'Anyone follow us?'

Pike shook his head. 'How'd it go?'

I helped Clark into the backseat and patted his leg. 'Fine. Clark, you did fine.'

Clark smiled, but it was tired and weak, and two blocks later he hung his head out the window and threw up again.

We drove directly to my office to make the calls. I wasn't worried that the feds had tapped the phone because that's who I was calling. We left Pike's Jeep in my parking spot, then took the elevator up to the fourth floor. Normally, I would walk, but not with Clark.

I let us in, then opened the French doors for the air. 'You want anything to drink?'

'Uhn-uhn.'

'You need the bathroom, it's down the hall.'

'Thank you.' He sat on the couch and stared at the Pinocchio clock. I took a breath, organized what I wanted to say, then called Marsha Fields. When she came on the line, I said, 'Are you familiar with a Seattle mobster named Andrei Markov?'

'No. Should I be?'

'Markov and his organization are in your system. A U.S. Marshal named Jasper is down here now because of him. I'd like to call you back in five after you've checked this out.'

She seemed impatient. 'Does this have anything to do with your counterfeit money?'

'Yes.'

I hung up and leaned back. Pike was standing in the French doors, watching the city. Clark was on the couch, hands in his lap, breathing gently. He was smiling at the Pinocchio clock and the little figurines. He said, 'Your office isn't what I would've expected.'

'Neither are you.'

He looked at me and nodded, and I nodded back. 'Thanks again for doing all this.' He wet his lips like he was going to say more, but then he said nothing.

I gave Marsha Fields ten minutes, then called. She said, 'Okay, your boy Markov is a real sweet piece.'

'That's one way of saying it.'

'I understand Jasper's down here looking for a printer who turned state's against Markov's brother.' Marsha Fields had done a lot in ten minutes.

'I can give you Markov for possession of counterfeit currency and for kidnapping.'

'Kidnapping who?'

'Markov is holding Hewitt's twelve-year-old son.'

'Well, good Lord.' She didn't say anything for maybe ten seconds. 'Is Clark Hewitt printing?' She had done more than a lot.

'Markov's people murdered a guy named Wilson Brownell four days ago in Seattle. They're using the boy to try to get to Hewitt, and then they'll kill the whole goddamned family. Do you want Markov or not?'

'You want something for Hewitt, don't you?'

'Hewitt will testify for you, just as he did in Seattle, and he will participate to such a degree as will allow you to bust Markov, but his other activities are not to be investigated and must not be questioned.'

Marsha Fields said, 'No one can agree to that.'

'That's the deal.'

I could hear her breathing on the other end.

'I will tell you this much: Clark Hewitt is not printing U.S. currency, and his activities involve no other crime, either civil or criminal. It's a one-shot deal, and you'll never have to worry about Clark Hewitt again.'

'How do I know that?'

'He's dying of stomach cancer.' When I said that, Clark Hewitt did not react in any way. I guess he was used to it.

She took a single breath, then let it out. 'How do I know that's true?'

'Your own doctor can examine him if you want.'

She hesitated.

'Come on, Marsha. You'll get Markov and half a dozen of his people, and maybe his whole operation. It's either worth it to you, or it isn't, and all I want you to do is let Clark Hewitt walk away when it's over.'

'Where are you?'

I gave her the number, and she told me that she would call back within the hour. It only took forty minutes. She said, 'No one is agreeing to anything at this time, but we're willing to talk about it. Will Hewitt come in?'

'No.'

'You're really being a prick.'

'He'll come in after you agree to the deal, but not before.'

'My office at noon.'

We phoned Dak and told him we were on our way in. Pike dropped me at my car, then he and Clark went back to the safe house while I made my way downtown to the Roybal Building. I got there at three minutes after noon. Reed Jasper was there with his red-haired pal from the LA office of the U.S. Marshals, along with a muscular balding guy with little square glasses named Lance

Minelli. Minelli was Marsha Fields's boss at Treasury. The last person there was a chunky African-American woman with gray-flecked hair from the U.S. Attorney's Office. She was wearing a dark green linen business suit, introduced herself as Emily Thornton, and from the way everyone kept glancing at her you could tell she was the one with the juice. I said, 'Man, Jasper, you get around.'

Jasper didn't offer to shake my hand, and neither did the other marshal. 'I knew you had something going with Hewitt. I could smell it on you like stink.'

Emily Thornton cleared her throat. As soon as she sat, the others sat, too. She said, 'Special Agent Fields indicates that you have information regarding a man named Andrei Markov.'

'Did the special agent describe that information?'

Jasper said, 'Describe. Can you believe this guy?'

Thornton's eyes flicked to him and her eyebrows went up maybe an eighth of an inch. 'You're here by invitation, I believe, aren't you, Mr. Jasper?'

Jasper frowned but said nothing. I was liking Emily Thornton just fine. She came back to me. 'Ms. Fields did tell me the situation, but I'd like to hear it from you.'

I went through it again, telling her that I could offer them Andrei Markov on a count of possessing counterfeit U.S. currency with intent to distribute and defraud, and for the more serious charge of kidnapping a minor. I told them that I could offer Clark Hewitt as a witness to both counts. Thornton listened without speaking until I was done, and then she said, 'Who is this minor?'

'Hewitt's twelve-year-old son.'

She wrote something on a pad. 'Is Hewitt now printing this money?'

'Hewitt is in the Los Angeles area.'

Jasper's pal said, 'Oh, to hell with this guy!' He put his

forearms on the table and made a face at Minelli. 'Christ, Lance. Fuck this guy.'

Thornton's eyes went to him. 'Would you get us coffee, please?'

He blinked at her.

Emily Thornton repeated herself. 'Coffee for everyone, with sweeteners and a creamer of some kind.'

Jasper's pal's face went dark red, and he forced out an angry smile, like she was confused about something and he was going to set her straight. 'You want coffee, lady, I think you oughta ask someone in the hall.'

Emily Thornton didn't move, but Lance Minelli said, 'Step out of the room, please.' His voice was quiet and his face said absolutely nothing.

The red-haired man opened his mouth, closed it, then abruptly walked out and closed the door. He closed the door so softly that you could barely hear it. I guess he was the one confused.

When he was gone Thornton pursed her lips, and tapped one immaculately enameled nail on the table. 'I would think your Mr. Hewitt would come to us anyway, with his son in danger.'

'We're going to get his son back with or without your help, Ms. Thornton. Your help will make it easier.'

A microscopic smile touched the corners of her mouth. She said, 'You were involved with Ida Leigh Washington, weren't you?'

'Yes, ma'am.' Ida Leigh Washington was a woman I'd helped a few years ago. I'd proven that a small group of corrupt police officers had murdered her son, and then I'd helped her recover damages from the city.

The smile broadened for just a moment, then vanished. 'Yes, well, I imagine you could get the boy back.' She tapped the nail again. 'What is it you want?'

'Clark Hewitt is dying of stomach cancer. He is

246

currently engaged in an activity to earn money to care for his children after he dies. I want him to be able to complete that activity free of investigation or prosecution.'

Emily Thornton shook her head. 'I couldn't possibly agree to that.'

'Then we have no deal.'

Jasper said, 'How about we just throw your ass in the tank?'

I spread my hands. 'On what charges?'

Jasper frowned and Minelli shrugged. 'We could probably think of something.'

'So play it that way if you want.'

Marsha Fields said, 'What is Hewitt doing?'

I looked at Emily Thornton when I answered. 'He is not printing U.S. currency, or any other paper negotiable in the United States. He is not committing fraud, nor is he engaged in any other crime for which he could be charged.' I spread my hands. 'Should you agree to this arrangement, you don't want to ask any more or know any more.'

Emily Thornton was nodding. 'If we knew more, and approved it, we'd be stepping over the line into entrapment.'

'Yes. We want Markov off the board, and you can do that for us. That's why I'm here. I can get the boy back, but there's less risk if you're involved. That's also why I'm here. But everything that I want to happen is going to happen whether you're a party to it or not. If you're a party to it, you get Markov and you'll bring down his entire operation.' I leaned back and waited.

Lance Minelli said, 'How do you see the scam?'

'Markov is going to receive a large amount of counterfeit U.S. currency as ransom for the boy. When I learn the time and place of that transfer, I'll let you know so your people can be there. You get to arrest Markov in possession of the counterfeit money, and Hewitt will testify against him in the kidnapping.'

Marsha Fields was gently rocking in her chair. She was staring at me, and I could see that she was liking it. She said, 'You know, the more funny money Markov has on him, the more we could charge him with.' Everyone looked at her. 'He had about a million bucks, say, we could hit him with a manufacturing count, as well as possession with intent to sell. A million dollars would do just fine.'

Emily Thornton said, 'That's dangerously close to plotting an entrapment, Special Agent.'

Marsha Fields blinked at her. 'Oh, I wasn't suggesting anything. I was just thinking out loud.'

'Mm-hm.'

Lance Minelli smiled.

Reed Jasper said, 'Markov is responsible for the death of a U.S. Marshal. His organization is suspected in at least fourteen unsolved homicides in the Seattle area.' He shook his head. 'I don't give a damn what we have to do to get Markov as long as we get him.' Way to go, Jasper. But then Jasper leaned forward, and jerked a thumb at me. 'But my interest is in keeping Hewitt safe, and I wouldn't trust this sonofabitch any farther than I can spit. If we go along with this, we should have someone on the site to make sure things don't get out of hand, and I'm here to volunteer.'

I frowned at him. 'What do you mean, on site?'

Lance Minelli looked at Thornton. 'I go along with having someone there, Emily. I'd want to make sure Hewitt doesn't cut and run as soon as he gets his kid.' He shook his head and looked back at me. 'I don't believe this cancer thing for a minute.'

Marsha Fields nodded. 'Agreed. I could see my way

clear to buy into this, but I'd like to know what's going on even if we're not going to follow up.'

Emily Thornton said, 'That's it, then.'

I said, 'Wait a minute. I've got other people involved, and they may not go along.'

Emily Thornton stood. 'They don't have any choice. I think we can do business here, but only if we have one of our people on the inside to maintain a level of control.' She offered her hand. 'That's our final offer, and now you can take it or leave it.'

I stared at her for maybe a thousand years, and then I took her hand and we shook. 'I guess we'll take it, Ms. Thornton.'

She smiled nicely. 'I knew you would.'

Juice.

CHAPTER 32

Thornton and Minelli left first. I thanked Marsha Fields, and told Jasper that I would call him as soon as I had talked with Clark and the other principals.

Jasper said, 'I'll wait here until I hear from you.'

'It might be late.'

He shrugged. 'I don't have anything else to do.'

I drove back to Studio City, and reached the safe house at six minutes before three o'clock. Joe Pike was standing beneath a pine tree on the front sidewalk. He said, 'We on?'

'We're on. They went for it, but a fed has to come along. Jasper.'

'Dak won't like it.'

'We didn't have a choice, and neither does he. They agreed not to investigate.'

Pike's jaw moved imperceptibly. 'But they'll still know.'

'Yes. They'll know. You ready to go?'

'Always.'

We went inside and explained the setup to Clark and the others. When I got to the part about Jasper coming along, Dak made a hissing sound, and both Mon and Walter Senior said, 'No, no, no, no. They will know everything about us.' Like they'd rehearsed it. Walter Junior was asleep on the floor.

'Stop saying no and listen. The feds have given you guys a pass. Jasper is just going to be there to make sure we're not scamming them. They've agreed not to investigate you, or interfere with Clark in any way.'

Mon said, 'I can't believe this is happening.' He was running his fingers through his hair, and fistfuls of gray hair was coming out. 'We'll be ruined.' So much for revolutionary fervor.

I said, 'Look, their only interest here is Clark and Markov. If you're worried about it, go down to the warehouse and remove anything that could connect you or your people to that location. Just leave whatever Clark will need to print the money.'

Mon was still pulling his hair, but Dak nodded. 'What about the dong?'

'When the business with Markov is finished, we'll come back with Clark and print the dong.'

Dak said, 'We could all end up in jail.'

'You knew that when you conspired to break the law, but you're safer now than you were before. Before, they might've gotten wind and investigated and thrown your asses in jail. Now, they're going to look the other way and not even ask your name.'

Walter Senior said, 'Can we trust these people?'

'Yes.'

Mon started to say something else, but Dak shook his head and spoke in Vietnamese. Twenty seconds later they were gone. I looked at Clark. 'Can you set up to print U.S. currency?'

'Oh, sure.' Like it was nothing.

'How long will it take you to run off a million dollars?'

He frowned. 'Markov said five million.'

'That's what he wants, but it's not what he's going to get. All we need to do is make sure he's busted with a million in his possession. One million is the magic number.'

Clark nodded. 'Three or four days.'

'You're printing for Charles, damnit. You have to do it faster than that.'

Clark frowned again. 'Well, I don't have the right kind of paper. I don't have the right inks.'

'It doesn't have to be good, Clark. All it has to be is phony and add up to a million.'

'But Markov will take one look at it and know right away that it isn't like the money you showed him.'

'He won't have a chance to look at it. He'll be listening to Marsha Fields reading his rights.'

Clark thought some more, then looked at his watch. 'Well, I know where we can get some paper that might be good enough. And we'll need something to carry the money after it's printed.'

Pike said, 'How big is a million bucks?'

'About five suitcases worth. We'll need five regular Samsonite suitcases. That should do it.' The voice of experience.

'Okay. I can get the suitcases.'

'How long, Clark?'

More thinking. 'Tomorrow by noon.'

I looked at him. 'You can print a million dollars by tomorrow at noon.'

He frowned. 'Well, it won't be my best work.'

I used the kitchen phone to call Dobcek at the Sheraton. 'Da?'

'We can have the money for you by mid-afternoon tomorrow.'

'Five million dollars.'

'Sure. Five million. How about we meet at Griffith Park?'

Dobcek laughed. 'Call us again when you have the money. I will tell you when and where.'

'Whatever you want.'

I hung up. 'We're on. Everything will happen tomorrow afternoon. We should leave as soon as possible.'

Clark took his vial of pills into the bathroom, but this time he brought his bag, too. The pain was getting worse. I went upstairs to the second-floor office to Teri and Winona. Winona was coloring and Teri was helping her, but she looked up when I stepped in. I said, 'How're you guys doing?'

Teri's face was flat. 'Fine.'

'We need to leave you and Winona here again. Will you be okay?'

'Of course.' Angry about being excluded. And maybe about something else.

'There's plenty of food in the fridge, and there's a market on the corner.' I took forty dollars from my wallet and put it on the desk. 'Here's some money.'

Teri didn't look at the money. 'How'd it go for your friend?' Lucy.

I sat on the floor beside her. Winona was drawing a picture of the troll. It looked sad. 'It went okay. She got things worked out.'

'How nice for you both.' She said it so cold that we might as well have been sitting in a Subzero, but then she realized that and turned red. She adjusted her glasses and looked away. 'I'm sorry. That was so bush.'

I put my arm around her and squeezed. Fifteen going on thirty, and feeling all the pain at once. 'Been tough on you.'

'You like her a lot.'

'Yes, I do.'

'You'd rather be with her, right now, wouldn't you?'

'That's right. But my obligation is to see this through for you and your father and Charles.'

Pike rapped softly at the doorjamb. 'Clark's ready.'

Teri's eyes were wet and she reached under the glasses to wipe them. She said, 'I really like you, too.'

Winona said, 'Oh, yuck.'

I smiled at Teresa Hewitt. 'I like you, too. But Lucy's my girlfriend.'

'Can I hug you, please?'

She hugged me hard, and then she said, 'Please take care of my daddy. Please save my little brother.'

'That's what this is all about, Teresa.'

I went downstairs to Clark and Joe. We decided that Clark and I would get the paper, and Pike would pick up Jasper and the suitcases. I called Reed Jasper in Marsha Fields's office. Marsha Fields answered. 'We're on. Is Jasper there?'

She gave him the phone without a word, and he said, 'We ready to rock?'

'Joe will pick you up in forty minutes.'

'I've got a car. Just tell me where to meet you.'

'Joe will pick you up. If you're happier driving, follow him.'

I hung up before he could say anything else, and we went to print the money.

CHAPTER 33

Clark phoned paper suppliers until he found one that had the kind of paper he wanted. 'It's a nice cotton blend, but it should look okay.' Like he was talking about sheets.

'Remember, Clark, it doesn't have to be perfect. It doesn't even have to be pretty good.'

'Well, you want it to look like a legitimate attempt to counterfeit money, don't you?'

'Yes.'

He looked sulky. 'Believe me, no one will confuse this stuff with Crane paper, but at least it won't look like Monopoly money.' I guess he had an artist's temperament about these things.

The paper supply house was in a little red-brick building on Yucca Street in Hollywood, a block north of Hollywood Boulevard. The clerk had two boxes of the paper waiting for us, each box about the size of a standard moving box. It didn't seem like much, but the boxes were heavy. I went inside with Clark because I had to pay for the paper. On my Visa.

When we had stowed the boxes in the little bay behind my car's seats, I said, 'Doesn't seem like very much paper.' Clark had said that the million dollars would fill five Samsonite suitcases, but this paper only filled two boxes.

'Air. Factory bundles are packed tight. When the

255

sheets have been printed and cut and stacked, they'll take up more room.'

'Ah.'

The drive to the warehouse in Long Beach was in the worst of the evening rush-hour crush, and took almost three hours. For most of that time, Clark seemed in a kind of peaceful half-sleep. The eastern sky purpled, slowly fading to black as the sun settled on our right and, around us in the heavy traffic, people ended their day in a slow, frustrating march toward home.

We turned into the parking lot next to the warehouse just before eight that night as a huge Air Korea 747 thundered into the sky. The lot was empty except for a single white Pontiac that probably belonged to someone who worked at the adjoining building or across the street. Dak and his people were gone, but the parking lot was lit and a single light burned at the warehouse front door. 'Clark.'

Clark opened his eyes.

'We're here.'

He nodded. 'We have a lot to do.'

I used Dak's key to open the side door. They had left some of the inside lights on, but not all, and the still space of the empty building made me feel creepy and afraid. I took out the Dan Wesson, but no one was waiting behind the door or in the long hall or in the big room with the printing equipment. I hadn't expected anyone, but I felt better with the gun all the same. Thirty-eight-caliber pacifier.

Clark turned on the banks of fluorescent lights and filled the printing room with a cold blue light. He looked over what Dak's people had left on the tables, then powered up the litho printer and the plate maker and the Macintosh. I said, 'Is there anything I can do?'

'Turn on the radio.'

I turned on the radio and tried to stay out of his way. Help at its finest.

The crates of Russian paper were gone, as were the dong plates and most of the boxes of inks. I said, 'They took damn near all the ink.'

Clark didn't bother to look. 'All we need is black and green. I told Dak what to leave.' He checked something on the litho machine. 'You could bring in the paper.'

I went out and got the two boxes of paper. Didn't trip even once.

Pike and Jasper arrived forty-five minutes after us, first knocking at the door, then coming through with the suitcases. A black guy with short hair was with them. Clark stopped connecting the scanner to the Macintosh when Jasper walked in. 'Hello, Mr. Jasper.'

Reed Jasper smiled. 'Damn, Clark, you're a hard man to find.'

I was looking at the black guy. He was wearing a navy suit, and he was trying to see everything at once. 'Who are you?'

'Claude Billings, Secret Service.' He was chewing gum.

'I thought it was just Jasper.'

Billings blew a bubble the size of a grapefruit and walked over to the litho press. 'Guess they wanted the first team in the game.' Secret Service, all right. Cocky.

Jasper and Pike put down the suitcases by the long tables, then Jasper came over and shook Clark's hand. Clark seemed embarrassed.

Jasper put his hands on his hips and looked at the lithograph press and the plate maker and the computer. 'Well, I don't blame you for being scared after what happened that night, but you should've stayed in the program. After that night, you would've been fine.'

Clark said, 'I'm sorry about your friend.' Peterson.

'Yeah, well.' Jasper walked over to the big press and

ran his fingers along it. Billings took off his jacket, folded it, then put it on one of the long tables. Jasper said, 'I understand there's a problem with your boy. I'm sorry about that.'

Clark stopped futzing.

'We'll try to do a little bit better by you this time.' Jasper offered a friendly smile when he said it.

Clark turned back to the Macintosh and scanned a one-hundred-dollar bill. I watched him, and Billings came over and watched with me. Clark scanned the Franklin side, then turned the bill and scanned Independence Hall. When the images were scanned, he brought them up on the Macintosh, enlarged them, and began isolating sections of the bills. I said, 'What are you doing?'

'I have to make plates, and to make the plates I need a clean image. We're making Federal Reserve notes, and that means we need three plates. A back plate because the back of the bill is printed in a uniform green, and two front plates because the face of the bill is printed in black, but the serial numbers and Treasury seal are printed in green, so those images have to be separated.'

'Oh.'

Clark stopped what he was doing and looked at me and Billings. 'Do you have to watch me?'

'Sorry.'

Billings and I went to the table. There were five people and only two chairs, so I sat cross-legged on the table. Billings took one of the chairs.

The time oozed past like cold molasses. Clark worked steadily and hard, but the rest of us could only watch. Pike went into the far corner and stood on his head. I did a little yoga and felt myself getting sleepy. Jasper paced. Billings blew bubbles. Crime fighting at its most exciting.

Jasper said, 'I'm starving. Is anyone else hungry?'

Pike and Billings and I said, 'Yes.'

'Saw an In-n-out Burger on the way.'

I said, 'Joe doesn't eat meat.'

Jasper frowned, like that was the world's biggest problem.

Clark said, 'There's a Chinese place close by.'

Billings said, 'I could go for that.'

Pike and Jasper went for Chinese, got back just before ten, and we ate. Clark never stopped working, and didn't eat. Maybe the dope killed his appetite, or maybe he was thinking about Charles.

When Clark had perfect separate images, he had the computer reverse them and build perfect photonegatives, then copied the negatives in a pattern that would let him print twenty bills at a time. One million dollars was ten thousand hundreds, but if you could print twenty bills per every sheet, that meant only five hundred sheets. Of course, you had to run each sheet through the press three times, but it still meant that the press only had to run for three or four hours. All the time was in getting ready.

When Clark had the three master negatives, he mounted them in a plate maker and burned a positive image on a thin aluminum sheet, then, one by one, washed the sheets in a chemical bath to ready the plates for the ink. It took Clark about six hours to make the plates, and it was time that passed ever more slowly, with nothing for me or Pike or Jasper or Billings to do except offer the occasional word of encouragement. The In-n-out Burger was open twenty-four hours, and once Jasper went for drinks, and once I went, but most of our time was spent doing nothing. Clark grew pale again, and his skin seemed clammy, and twice he sat down, but neither time for very long. I said, 'Clark, why don't you take a break. Let's get some air.'

'It won't be very much longer.' He said it even when I didn't ask. He said it maybe a hundred times.

Jasper would watch Clark, then walk away, then watch some more, then walk away, like he was nervous about all of this and losing his patience. Finally, he said, 'It doesn't have to be perfect, for chrissake.'

Clark stopped working and stared at him. Jasper walked away.

At ten minutes after six that morning I went out into the parking lot and breathed the cool night air and watched the first traces of pink freshen the eastern sky. Moths swarmed around the parking lot lamps, banging into the glass with a steady tap-tap-tap, and I wondered if they welcomed the dawn. At dawn, they could stop slamming their heads into the thing that forever kept them from the light. People don't have a dawn. We just keep slamming away until it kills us.

Clark had worked steadily through the night, and I thought that his pain must be terrible, but, unlike the moths, he was doing it because he loved his son. I guess I would do it, too, and I hoped that the love helped with his pain.

When I went back inside, Clark Hewitt was still working. Billings had fallen asleep.

At eight minutes after seven that morning, Clark brought the plates to the lithograph machine, fitted the portrait plate to the printing cylinder, then filled the inkwell with black ink. He looked at me and said, 'I think we're ready.'

Jasper said, 'About goddamned time.'

Pike was still in his corner. I don't think he had moved for hours. Billings sat up, blew another bubble, then stared at Pike. I think he found Pike odd.

Clark said, 'We'll run some test sheets through, first. Just to see.'

I brought over a bundle of the paper. It made me feel useful.

Clark fitted a stack of the paper into the paper feeder, then ran through two sheets. The big machine made a whirring, snapping sound as the paper went through, and the paper went through faster than I'd expected. It came out smudged and dark. Clark said, 'Sucks.'

He made some adjustments with a little screwdriver, then ran through two more sheets. These looked fine to me, but Clark frowned again. Jasper rolled his eyes. Clark made another adjustment, printed two more sheets that I thought were identical to the last two, but this time he seemed pleased. 'This should do. I think we're ready to print.'

That's when Joe Pike said, 'Listen.'

Billings said, 'What?' He blew an enormous pink bubble.

Jasper said, 'For chrissakes, let's just print the money and get going.'

Pike moved to the lithograph and slapped the shut-off switch. The drum whined down and the humming stopped. Clark said, 'It's going to take a while to reheat.'

Jasper said, 'What are you people talking about?'

Pike held up a finger, his head cocked to the side, and then he took out his gun. 'Listen.'

There might have been the faint squeal of a door hinge, and there might've been the faraway thump of something hard bumping into a doorjamb or a wall. My first thought was that it was Dak and his people, coming to check on us, but it wasn't, and I didn't have time for another thought.

Claude Billings trotted to the door, stepped into the hall, and that's when Alexei Dobcek shot him once through the great pink bubble and blew out the back of his head.

CHAPTER 34

Pike pushed Clark down behind the litho press. I ran for the door, shooting three times into the darkness and once into the wall. Dobcek yelled something in Russian, and he and another guy fell back along the hall into the parking lot. I fired twice more, then pulled Billings back into the big room, but he was already dead. I said, 'The Russians. We're outta here now.'

I saw a flash of men moving in the parking lot, and I heard crashing at the front of the building.

Jasper checked Billings. 'Jesus Christ, how in hell did they find us? How many you see?'

'Five. Maybe more. They were running toward the front, so they'll probably enter that way.'

Clark said, 'But what about the money?'

Pike pulled him to his feet. 'That's over now.'

'What about Charles?'

'If they get you they won't need Charles.'

Jasper snuck a fast look out the door and down the hall that led to the parking lot. That door was closed, and there was probably a man with a gun waiting for whoever opened the door. All the noise was coming from the other hall, which led to the front. Jasper said, 'Shit, man, they've got us boxed.'

Pike said, 'Up.'

I pushed Clark toward the metal stairs and told him to climb. 'There's a stair at the front door and offices on the second floor. If we move through the offices and they stay on the ground, we can come down behind them and get out of here.'

Clark and Jasper and I clattered up the stairs to the catwalk and into the offices as Pike went back to the hall, fired four fast shots in the blind, then followed.

The upstairs offices were dark and hot, and we could hear the Russians moving beneath us, faint and faraway. I thought we were going to make it just fine until a squat guy with a thick mustache turned a corner, saw us, then ducked back behind the corner, shouting. I pushed backward into Jasper and Clark, yelling for them to get back, when the mustache popped out again, snapping off two shots that hit the ceiling above us. I shot back, then Alexei Dobcek darted across my field of fire into an adjoining doorway, firing as he ran. Jasper said, 'This really bites.'

We fell back along the hall, retracing our route onto the catwalk and down the stairs into the warehouse, reaching the bottom just as Dmitri Sautin and the guy with the mustache blew through the catwalk door, firing as they came. Dmitri Sautin was wearing a HAPPIEST PLACE ON EARTH T-shirt from Disneyland.

I yelled, 'Joe,' and pushed Clark down behind the plate maker as Joe Pike spun around and shot Sautin once with his .357.

The guy with the mustache dove back into the upstairs hall, but Sautin didn't. Sautin weighed three hundred pounds, but the .357 pushed him into the wall and knocked the gun from his hand. He looked down at his chest as red soaked through the HAPPIEST PLACE shirt. He said, 'Alexei?' Then he fell head first over the rail and hit the cement floor like a bag of damp flour.

A blond guy appeared in the hall door, fired twice, then disappeared.

The shooting stopped and no one was shouting and the

only sounds in the place were my own heart and a bubbly wheeze from Dmitri Sautin. He coughed twice, and then he started to cry. Jasper was under the stairs.

Dobcek said, 'I think we got you trapped. What do you think?' He said it from behind the catwalk door.

'I thought we had a deal, Dobcek.'

'Da. An' I think you were going to set us up.'

I was looking at the truck door. It was big and electric with a red open-close switch next to it on the wall about twenty feet away from me. All I had to do was run over there, hit the switch, then run back and hope that no one shot me.

Dmitri Sautin managed to roll onto his side, but that was as far as it went. He was crying the way a small child cries, with little gasping whimpers. He said, 'Oo, it hurts, Alexei. I need help.'

Dobcek called back, 'Shut up, fool.'

The sobbing became a wet, phlegmy cough.

Dobcek said, 'You give us Hewitt, maybe we let you live, yah?'

Pike snapped his fingers and pointed at the truck door.

I nodded. Somebody was probably waiting out there to shoot us, but if the door was up at least we could see. If we could see, maybe we could lay down a suppressing fire so that we could get out.

Pike reloaded the Python, and I reloaded the Dan Wesson. I said, 'Jasper, are you in?'

'Sure.'

'Joe.'

Joe Pike swung out from behind the plate maker, popping off two shots at the hall door, then three shots at the catwalk. I moved when he moved, sprinting hard to the door and slapping the big red button. The door started up with a lurch, and Dobcek yelled something and suddenly the Russians upstairs and the Russians in the hall were shooting as hot and as heavy as they could and I knew that they were coming.

Bullets slammed into the big door like hammers. The noise from the firing hurt my ears and made me squint, and I tried to stay low and close to the floor as I fired back. The closed space filled with smoke and the stink of gunfire and the shouts of men in a foreign tongue. I heard Jasper shout, 'I'm out,' and then his magazine hit the floor. Pike was reloading the Python and I was futzing with the Dan Wesson and the Russians in the hall door opened up again, pouring out rounds. One of them came through low and fast and made it to the base of the stairs to set up a cover position so that another could follow and then there came the surprising *boom-boom-boom* of a combat shotgun. Men in the parking lot screamed, and the big door was finally up enough for us to see Mon and two other guys running hard from the warehouses across the street as a black BMW with more Vietnamese guys screeched into the parking lot.

The three men running across the street had the shotguns, and all three of them stopped at the front of the warehouse and cut loose at two Russians in the parking lot, kicking one of them up and onto the Pontiac. The other Russian scrambled for cover behind it.

The Russians in the hall were shouting and running and shooting. One of them must've run to the parking lot door and seen the Viets. Dobcek was shouting more Russian, and shooting down through the doorway at us, but then the shooting stopped and there was a crashing noise from the second floor and Pike said, 'They're pulling back.'

'Stay down. Clark, you okay?'

'Uh-huh.'

'Jasper?'

'What the fuck just happened here?!'

Mon and another guy ran in through the big door with their shotguns, and I pointed upstairs. Mon and the other guy went up the stairs with practiced moves.

'Dak must've wanted his people to keep an eye on us. His people were across the street, and when they heard the shooting, they came.'

There was more shooting at the front of the building, and then from the street, and then a couple of cars roared to life and screeched away and the shooting was done.

Pike said, 'Charles.'

I ran to Sautin, kicked the gun away from his hand, and grabbed him by the shirt. 'Where's the little boy, Dmitri?'

Dmitri Sautin was making gasping noises. Mon and another guy ran back into the room, looked around, then high-fived each other like they'd just won the big game.

I shook Dmitri by his shirt. 'Damnit, where's the little boy?'

'With Markov.' You could barely hear him.

I shook him again. 'Where's Markov?!'

Dmitri Sautin made a soft gurgling sound, his eyes rolled back in his head, and all three hundred pounds of him died.

I pounded on his chest, and started CPR, yelling at him about Charles, demanding that he tell me where Markov had the boy, but Dmitri was beyond that now, and finally Jasper said, 'Jesus Christ, Cole, he's over. Lay off.'

I kneeled there, the points of my knees hurting from the cement floor. I said, 'Mon!'

Mon stopped all the high-fiving and looked at me with a big smile just as Dak walked in through the big door. He looked scared.

'They leave any cars?'

Mon shook his head. 'Two cars come, two go. We got three of the bastards!'

Pike said, 'I'm on it,' and trotted out through the big door.

I shoved between Mon and his pal. 'Get on the phone and describe their cars to the police.'

Mon's eyes went wide and he pointed the shotgun at me and when he did I rolled it away from him and hit him in the face with the barrel. 'You're safe from the cops, goddamnit. Now get on the phone and maybe we can find those people before they kill the kid.'

Mon looked like he wanted to kill me, but Dak said something in Vietnamese and Mon hurried away.

Sautin's shirt was wet with blood and the wet was spreading to his pants and along the cement floor. I didn't think about it. I rolled his body over and tore out his shirt pocket, and then his front pants pockets, hoping to find something that would point toward Markov. There was nothing. I felt something gritty in my eyes and I wanted to kick his dead body. Instead, I pushed up out of the warehouse and ran out into the parking lot to help Pike, but Pike had already found it.

Pike stepped away from the guy on the Pontiac with a hotel key card and said, 'I know where they are.'

It was a key card from the Disneyland Hotel.

CHAPTER 35

Disneyland was fifteen minutes away.

I used Dak's cell phone to call Marsha Fields, who said that she would contact the Orange County Sheriff's Department, as well as dispatch both Secret Service and FBI agents from the Orange County field office to the Disneyland hotel. She told me not to leave the crime scene. I said, 'Sure, Marsha.'

When I broke the connection, Pike said, 'If Dobcek tells Markov that it's over, Markov will kill the boy just so he can't testify in a kidnapping beef.'

'I know. You drive.'

Jasper didn't like it, but he came, too, the four of us piling into Pike's Jeep. We cranked hard onto the Garden Grove Freeway, then east to Anaheim. The Garden Grove was a nice straight shoot, but it was heavy with morning traffic, and Pike spent more time on the shoulder than on the freeway, blowing his horn and pegging his brakes, then jumping hard on the accelerator to shoot through gaps in the flow. Reed Jasper said, 'Do you have a death wish?'

Pike said, 'Pretend it's fun.'

We careened off the freeway at the Harbor Boulevard exit, then turned north toward the park and pretty soon we could see the peak of Matterhorn Mountain and then we were at the hotel. An Orange County sheriff's highway car was waiting beneath the monorail station, both deps sitting in the front seat with the doors open.

One of the deps was a tall ropy guy with a mustache, the other a slender African-American woman. Jasper flashed his marshal's badge, and the mustache said, 'They told us to wait here for the FBI.'

'You do that.'

We went inside. Jasper badged the desk clerk, then gave her the key card and asked for a room identification. Markov had four rooms blocked together on the ninth floor, one of them a suite. Jasper said, 'Okay. We'll wait for the others.'

I said, 'Come on, Jasper. If he's already taken off with the boy we're wasting time.'

Jasper looked worried. 'But if he's up there, we should go in with as many people as possible.'

Pike pushed past him. 'Forget it, Jasper.'

Jasper said, 'Ah, hell,' and followed.

The four of us walked fast across the back grounds past the swimming pool and into the rear building, and took the elevator to the ninth floor. Housekeeping carts were parked along the hall, and Andrei Markov's suite was open, the sound of a vacuum cleaner coming from inside. Markov was gone. We went through all four of Markov's rooms, trying to figure out what to do next when one of the housekeepers smiled at us. 'You looking for the man and the boy?'

All four of us stared at her. She was short and squat, and had probably come up from Ecuador. I said, 'That's right.'

She pursed her lips. 'They only go a few minutes ago. They said they were going into the park. The big man, he say he want to ride the mountain.' The big man. Markov.

Clark frowned. 'Matterhorn Mountain?'

She described how they were dressed as well as she could remember, then we thanked her and went back to the lobby. Clark was making little huffing sounds as we walked back past the pool, and I said, 'You okay?'

He didn't look at me. 'Fine.'

Two more Orange County deps had arrived, along with an FBI agent named Hendricks. They were standing with the manager and a tall blond guy named Bates who introduced himself as an executive with park security. When I introduced Clark, I said, 'This is the boy's father.'

Both Hendricks and Bates nodded, and Hendricks said, 'Maybe you should wait outside, sir.'

'But he's my son.'

Hendricks said, 'Please.' Polite.

Clark went outside. Jasper and I told them what we knew, and what the housekeeper had told us. More feds and Orange County cops were on the way, along with representatives from the Secret Service. Bates was calm and competent, and after we told him what the house-keeper said, he nodded. 'If they've gone into the park, we own them. We can put people at every egress, then just wait until they walk out.' He nodded, but maybe the nod was meant to bolster himself as much as us. 'We've worked with the authorities before. We know how it's done.'

It sounded workable. Markov wasn't likely to harm the boy inside the park, even if Dobcek found them. There was too great a possibility of being seen, and if he hurt the boy inside the park, what would he do with the body? So all we had to do was wait, and then we could recover Charles with a minimum of risk.

Pike and I left them to work out the details, and went back to the car to tell Clark, only Clark wasn't in the car. He wasn't standing around outside the hotel or in the lobby rest room, either. Pike said, 'He's on the monorail. He's going to get his son.' The monorail was pulling away from its station.

I yelled inside for Hendricks, and Pike and I were climbing the stairs to the monorail station when they ran out of the lobby. Jasper said, 'Hey, where are you guys going? Where's Clark?'

I told them, and I told them we were going in after him.

Hendricks said, 'Goddamnit, we said we'd wait. We got more people coming in.'

'He's going after them, Hendricks. If he gets to Markov or Dobcek, those guys are going to kill him. Then they might kill the boy, too, and the whole damn thing will blow up.'

Hendricks ran up the stairs after us, Jasper and Bates and three of the Orange County deps behind him. Bates talked us past the gate guard, and then we stood on the platform, waiting for the next monorail. We waited for two minutes that seemed like forever, and then the monorail came and Bates asked the people in the front car to please get off. He was polite and professional, but you could tell he was nervous about doing it. I guess things like this just don't happen at the happiest place on earth. When the car was clear we hustled aboard like an airborne assault team piling into an attack chopper, Bates talking into a Handie-Talkie. He said, 'I'm really not sure about this.'

Hendricks said, 'It'll be fine.'

'The shift supervisor's going to meet us at the station with some of our people.'

'It's going to be fine, goddamnit.' Hendricks's jaw was working and he looked like he wanted to hit someone. Probably me.

We glided silently over the parking lot, me describing Markov and Dobcek and Clark and Charles to the cops. Hendricks told them that our first goal was to find Clark, and remove him from the park before he stumbled into the Russians. After that, we would locate Markov and the boy, but he didn't want any move to be made against them until they had exited the park. When he said that part Bates looked relieved. Hendricks said, 'We'll hang back and watch them until they're in a safe place, then we can neutralize them with no danger to the boy.' Neutralize. There's a good word.

A small army of park security officers with hand radios met us at the Tomorrowland monorail station, and nobody looked like Mouseketeers. They looked like hard-core professional men and woman who would be more than happy to quell a small rebellion. Hendricks went through it again for them, and I once more described Markov and Charles and Clark. The park security people didn't want me or Pike involved, but we were the only ones besides Jasper who had actually seen the people we were looking for. Hendricks said, 'Just give 'em the radios, for chrissakes. They're for real.'

So they gave us little Handie-Talkies even though they weren't happy about it, and told us to take no action if we spotted Markov. They said hang back and call. I said, 'Fine.'

When Bates found out we had guns, he got red in the face and demanded we hand them over.

Pike said, 'Screw that.'

Jasper said, 'Look, it's private property and they're being damned cooperative. We don't want another goddamned war.'

Hendricks rolled his eyes, sighed, and looked at me. 'Please give 'em your guns and let's get this show on the road.'

Pike looked at me and I shrugged. I gave them the Dan Wesson and Pike gave them the Python. The security guy looked mollified, but not a whole lot. I guess he was thinking about lawsuits.

They gave us the radios, told us to check in, and then Pike and I went down the escalator and into the park. The security people broke into teams, and they moved out also, everyone going in a different direction.

We were walking past a cotton candy cart when Pike said, 'Over here,' and moved behind the cart like he was going to tie his shoe. He took a little Sig .380 from his left ankle and palmed it to me.

I smiled. 'What about you?'

'I've got something for me.' Always prepared.

We worked our way up past the Submarine grotto toward Matterhorn Mountain, doing our best to search the twenty or thirty thousand people we passed, with the grim and depressing awareness that we couldn't see everything and everyone, and that we might've passed Markov and Charles and Clark a dozen times without seeing them. Maybe they were in a rest room. Maybe they were standing in line for a hot dog or riding one of the submarines.

We split up at the Matterhorn, Pike circling to the left and me to the right, but we met again on the other side without having seen them. Pike said, 'The housekeeper said the mountain.'

'Yeah, but maybe they already took the ride, or they're on it. Maybe they're going to do something else and ride the mountain later.' Maybe a million things.

Pike's dark glasses were empty.

I said, 'You stay with the mountain, I'll follow the flow to Fantasy Castle. I'll go as far as the bridge, then circle back.'

Pike disappeared into the crowd as I continued along the walk. I moved past a pretty young woman selling frozen bananas, then between a small group of British sailors when Markov, Charles, and a hard-looking guy with leathery skin stepped out from behind a Kodak film kiosk and turned away from me. The hard-looking guy had a hand on Charles's shoulder. Charles was wearing a Mickey Mouse hat, but he didn't look happy about it. Markov was eating an ice-cream cone and wearing a set of Mickey Mouse ears, also. His name had been embroidered on the back of the cap in red. *Andrei*. I guess it's a magic kingdom even for mobsters from Seattle.

I stepped behind an overweight couple and keyed the Handie-Talkie. 'It's Cole. I've got 'em.'

Hendricks's voice came back. 'Where?'

I was telling him when Dobcek pushed through a tour group of elderly people from Florida, shouted something in Russian, then shot at me three times fast.

Around me, forty thousand people jerked as if hit by an electric current.

The shots went high and wide into a monorail support, and then Dobcek was running toward Markov. Markov dropped to the ground at the shots, but now he was up, grabbing for the boy as he listened to Dobcek. Markov pulled the boy close, using him for a shield as he scuttled backward through the panicked crowd and I gave Hendricks our location. Hendricks said, 'Stay the hell away from them.'

'Just get your people over here, Hendricks, but tell them to come in soft. Markov's using the boy as a shield.'

They ran toward Fantasyland, and I followed them, giving Hendricks a play-by-play, and trying to keep Markov in sight without getting too close. When they crossed the bridge into Fantasy Castle, I lost them. I told Hendricks, and ran faster, pumping across the bridge into the castle, and there was Markov and Charles, Markov's arm locked around Charles's neck, a small black pistol in his free hand, standing by Mr. Toad's Wild Ride like they were waiting for me. Dobcek was maybe ten yards behind him, but I couldn't see the leathery guy. Markov said, 'You lying prick. You tried to set me up.'

I wanted to stall him. I wanted the security people and cops to get here and cut him off and clear the crowds. 'Let him go, Andrei. The park's tied up. You can't get out.'

Markov said, 'You be surprised.' That's when the leathery guy stepped out from behind a juice bar cart, put his gun into my back, and said, 'Kiss your ass good-bye.'

When he said it, Clark Hewitt lurched past the line waiting to board Mr. Toad's Wild Ride, and shouted, 'You let him go!'

No one was expecting Clark.

Markov jerked sideways and so did Dobcek, and when they moved I spun into the leathery guy's gun side, forcing his gun away and bringing the little Sig up into his ribs. I pulled the trigger one time and its *pop* sounded hollow and faraway. A deep, larger *bam* sounded in almost the same instant, and Andrei Markov was slammed down onto the ground, the crowd of people in the small place suddenly surging in a panic, unsure where to go, moving in every direction like flake in a human blizzard.

Joe Pike was standing above us on the castle's parapet with a foot-long stockless shotgun. Dobcek fired five fast shots – *powpowpowpowpow* – to drive Pike down, then ran to Markov. I rode Charles and Clark to the ground, yelling for them to stay down. I thought Pike would shoot again, but he didn't.

I listened to my heart beat, and I took careful breaths, and felt the sobbing father and son beneath me as the herd of people ran around and over us with all the thought and caring of Cape buffalo. All the while I was on them, Clark said, 'We got you, Charlie. We got you.'

Over and over. I had never thought of Charles as a Charlie before.

I looked around until I spotted Pike, still high overhead on the parapet like some kind of avenging angel. I mouthed, 'Markov?'

Pike shook his head.

Markov and Dobcek were gone.

CHAPTER 36

Hendricks and Jasper came running up, and the Orange County cops set about securing the area. Hendricks said, 'Is everyone okay?'

Clark nodded. Charles made little breathy sounds, and squirmed around in his father's lap to see the leathery man. 'Is that guy dead?'

'They're okay, Hendricks. Markov's hit.'

Hendricks pumped his fist once and made a wide grin. 'Then we got the bastard.'

Jasper took out a cell phone. 'How bad?'

Pike said, 'Took a load of number four high in the right shoulder. Here.' Pike touched his shoulder to show them.

Jasper punched a number into his cell phone. 'Okay. Which way they go?'

Pike told him, and Jasper waved over Bates. While Bates was on his way, Jasper said, 'I gotta to be in on this, Cole, but I wanted to thank you.' He put out his hand, and helped me up. 'You did okay.'

'Thanks.'

'Where you gonna be? I wanna give you a call later, talk a little more.'

I gave him the number at the safe house, then he and Bates trotted away, Jasper talking into the phone as Bates deployed his security people. The clock was ticking, and it wouldn't be long before Markov was had.

Hendricks was frowning at me and Pike. 'I thought we took your guns.'

Neither of us answered.

Hendricks shrugged. 'Yeah, well, I guess it worked out.'

I took Hendricks aside. 'You understand the situation from Marsha Fields?'

Hendricks nodded. 'We're going to need to talk to the father to make the kidnap case. We'll need the boy, too.'

'I know that.'

He looked past me at Clark and Charles. They were still on the ground, Charles sitting in Clark's lap, Clark holding on tight. Clark looked shaken and scared, but Charles didn't. He was flipping off the dead man, and making faces at the body. 'Hang around a little while longer till we get this wrapped up. It shouldn't take long.'

'Sure.'

'You can wait at the hotel, you want. Get the kid something to eat.'

'Sure.'

'I'll get back there soon as we find this clown.'

Two more FBI agents, another half dozen Orange County deputies, and the representative from the Secret Service arrived. Everyone was smiling and patting each other on the back because they figured Markov was in the bag. Only so many ways out, they kept saying, and all points of egress were covered.

One of the cops took us back to the hotel, but Charles didn't like it much. He said, 'I wanna go on Space Mountain. I wanna ride the submarines. I wanna climb the Matterhorn.'

Some things don't change.

I called Teri from the hotel lobby and told her that we had Charles and that everything was fine. Teri passed word to Winona, and they both shrieked and clapped their hands. It made me smile.

We had hamburgers at the hotel cafe, then hung around the lobby and the monorail station for another two hours, but when Hendricks finally showed up they still hadn't found Markov or Dobcek. Pike said, 'You want me to come back in and find them?'

Hendricks scowled. 'I think we can manage, but thanks.'

Pike shrugged.

I said, 'I want to get these people home, Hendricks. You can talk to them later and arrange the statements.'

Hendricks said, 'Okay,' but you could tell he didn't like it.

Charles coughed. 'A-hole.'

Hendricks glared at him, then stalked away shaking his head.

Pike took us back to the warehouse for my car. The FBI and Long Beach cops were still standing around the place, but Dak and his people were gone, and so were the bodies. The big truck door was open, revealing the litho press and the computer and plate maker, but no one seemed to be paying attention. Marsha Fields was there, as was a representative of the U.S. Attorney's Office, both of them talking to a couple of Long Beach PD detective-supervisors. When Marsha Fields saw me, she came over, introduced herself to Clark and Charles, then smiled at Joe. 'Hi, Joe.'

Pike's mouth twitched. I guess they knew each other, all right.

She smiled at him a little longer, then put the smile on Charles. 'You're a good-looking little devil.'

Charles turned a nice plum red.

She said, 'Mr. Hewitt, we're very anxious to speak with you.'

Clark was still in the Jeep. Too tired to get out. 'Of course. Anytime you want.'

I took Marsha Fields aside and said, 'So where do we stand with this?'

She watched three Long Beach cops laugh about something at the far end of the parking lot. Nothing had gone as we had planned. Markov hadn't been arrested as a counterfeiter, and instead we'd managed to shoot up both Long Beach and Disneyland. A small army of cops had seen the printing equipment, and each and every one of them knew what it was. The bodies had to be explained, and I still wanted Clark to get his money, and that meant he still had to print for Dak. I told her what I was thinking.

Marsha watched the cops laughing, and nodded. 'We made the deal in good faith, and so did you. We'll still want Clark's testimony on the kidnapping count.' She looked back at me. 'A deal's a deal. Just have Clark get this finished, and tell whoever is behind this operation that if they break the law again, I'll make them my hobby. Are we clear on that?'

'Clear.' I offered my hand, and she took it. I gave her the safe house number, and she said that she would call as soon as she heard anything. I thanked her.

Marsha Fields took three steps away, then stopped, looked back, and raised an eyebrow. 'Dong?'

I spread my hands. I wondered how she knew.

When I rejoined Pike and Clark, and told them that we were free to go, Charles said he wanted to ride home with me. He liked riding in the Corvette with the top down, he said. He thought it was cool. It took an hour and thirty-five minutes to drive up to Studio City, and Charles talked constantly about Marsha Fields, and never once mentioned Markov. I didn't mind. He seemed fine, and I guess he had fallen in love.

We arrived at the safe house maybe a dozen minutes after Joe and Clark. Charles was disappointed. He said, 'What a gyp! They beat us.'

This kid is something, isn't he?

When we went in, Teri and Winona scooped up Charles in a big hug, everyone crying, but this time they were happy tears. I got hugs, too, and then I asked Pike if Hendricks had called. He hadn't, and that worried me. If Markov and Dobcek slipped through their net, we were back where we started. I didn't think they had, but you never know. I went up to the office and phoned Dak. He wasn't happy to hear from me, but at least he was cordial. He said, 'The boy is all right?'

'Yes. And so is Clark. I spoke with Marsha Fields about this, and the deal still stands.'

'The police have been asking questions.'

'Those questions will go away. The paper will not be investigated about the printing equipment found on its premises, nor will you.'

Dak said, 'How will we explain the bodies?'

'It's already been explained. Employees of the *Journal* discovered a robbery in progress and the bad guys drew guns. Your employees acted in self-defense.'

Dak didn't say anything for a moment. 'She can do this?'

'It's the government, Dak. She can do anything.'

Nguyen Dak said, 'You're a man of your word, Mr. Cole. I have much respect for that.'

'Not me, Dak. Her.'

I told him that Clark would call tomorrow and arrange for the printing, then I hung up, and stared at the phone in the quiet of the room. I could hear the others down below, but up here was peaceful and the peace was soothing. I didn't feel particularly noble, and I didn't feel like I'd won anything. I felt lucky. I had come very close to being shot. Charles and Clark could have died, and I had killed men whose faces I could not recall. I looked at my hands. Dmitri Sautin's blood was still crusted around my fingernails. I felt myself start to shake, and I closed my eyes and waited for the shaking to pass, and when it did I went into the bathroom and washed my hands and arms. I had to wash twice, and then I showered.

When I went downstairs, Teri said, 'We've decided to have a party. We're going to get pizza.'

'Great.'

The phone rang then, and I thought it might be Marsha Fields, but it wasn't. Reed Jasper said, 'Have you heard yet?'

'Heard what?'

'We got 'em. Snagged Dobcek and Markov trying to sneak out of a maintenance exit on the north side of the park.'

I cupped the phone, told everyone that Markov had been captured, and Jasper laughed at the shouts and applause. He said, 'You guys going to be around?'

'Sure. We're going to have a little party, then I guess I'll take them home.'

'I want to swing by and talk to Clark. I'll probably head back to Seattle in the morning.'

'Sure, Jasper. That'd be fine.' I gave him directions.

We ordered the pizza, and Joe and Winona walked to the little minimart for soft drinks and beer. I volunteered to make a salad. The Hewitts wanted to go home after the pizza, and I thought that would be a good idea. Let them be a family again. Let them fall asleep under the same roof without wondering if someone would come through the door and shoot them. Teri and Charles went upstairs to pack. Clark hovered at the pass-through, watching me mince garlic. I said, 'You're going to have to tell them.'

'I don't know how.' He fidgeted like he was nervous. 'I've thought about it a lot, but nothing I come up with sounds good.'

'You just tell them, Clark. You sit them down and tell

them you're sick and that you're going to die. Let them cry, and you cry with them.'

'They're so young.'

'They're older than you think.' I took tomatoes and a cucumber from the fridge. 'You feel bad, why don't you rest over there on the couch?'

He frowned at the couch.

'Would you rather help?'

'Huh?' He looked surprised.

'Would you like to help make the salad?'

Clark Hewitt stared at me. 'Sure.' He came around into the kitchen. I told him to wash the tomatoes and cucumbers, then slice them. As he did it, he nodded. 'I get it.'

'What?'

'I could sit on the couch over there and feel bad, or I can help make the salad.'

I put the garlic in a little jar and added some olive oil. 'Yep.'

'Either way I'm going to die.'

I nodded. It wasn't anything he didn't already know. The deal with Dak proved that.

'Maybe I should tell them tonight.'

'That would be good. If you want, I could sit with you.'

He thought about it, then shook his head. 'Thanks, but that's okay. I can do it.'

Good for you, Clark.

We were tossing the salad when someone knocked at the door, and Clark said, 'That's the pizza.'

I opened the door, but it wasn't the pizza. Reed Jasper came in, and Dobcek and Markov pushed in behind him. Dobcek pointed his gun at me, then backhanded me with it two hard times, knocking me into the wall. Clark said, 'Ohmigod,' and then Dobcek pointed the gun at him and touched his lips, going, 'Sh,' as he pushed us back into the living room.

Markov came in behind him. Markov was pale and shaky and standing hunched to the side with a wind-breaker draped over his shoulders to hide the blood. He looked at me with the kind of look that said he wanted to eat me while I was still alive, while the blood still pumped and he could feel it warm and hot in his mouth. I looked from the hungry eyes to Jasper, and I said, 'You sonofabitch.'

Jasper shrugged. He was holding his service gun loose along his leg. 'Hey, it's a living.'

Markov smiled when he saw Clark. His tongue raked dry lips. I guess you dry out when you're bleeding to death. 'I'm going to do you myself, you termite.'

Clark turned white and trembled. 'Please don't hurt my children.'

I said, 'Pike's upstairs. He's got a machine gun.'

Jasper pointed with his gun. 'Shut up and sit down.'

Markov slumped heavily on the couch, and Dobcek moved to the stairs.

I stared at Jasper. 'How'd you get them out of the park?'

Jasper looked in the salad bowl, nibbled at a piece of cucumber. 'It was touch-and-go there for a bit, but I managed. Dressed 'em up in a couple of maintenance uniforms.'

Markov shifted on the couch; you could tell he was hurting. 'Don't say a goddamned word.'

Jasper shrugged. 'What's it matter? He ain't going anywhere.'

'How long has Markov owned you, Jasper?'

Jasper ate more cucumber.

'That's why your buddy was killed the night Clark went under. You sold out three years ago, and it got a marshal killed.'

Jasper made a big-deal shrug. 'If he hadn't tried to play hero it wouldn't've been a problem.'

I stared at him, and then I looked at Markov. I was thinking that Pike and Winona should have been back. It was only two blocks to the market, and two blocks back. I was trying to remember if Pike still had his gun. I had left mine in my trunk. 'You've lost a lot of blood, Markov. You might not make it.'

'I'll make it. I'm gonna kill this bastard first, and then I'll get fixed up just fine.'

I looked at Markov, and then Jasper. 'You going to let him kill these children, too?'

Jasper nodded. 'Sure. Why not?' Like it was nothing.

Something thumped upstairs, and Charles said, 'Quit shovin', ya frig!' Charles and Teri came down the stairs with Dobcek behind them. Dobcek was holding Charles by the back of the neck, and Teri looked angry.

Dobcek said, 'Where's the other one?' I didn't know if he meant Pike or Winona.

Jasper looked irritated. 'Who gives a shit? Let's just do it and get out of here.'

Markov said, 'Da.'

When he said it, someone knocked on the door and Dobcek clamped a hand over Charles's mouth and aimed his gun at Clark. 'Sh.'

Jasper went to the door, raising his gun, and Markov pushed to his feet, holding his own gun loosely at his side. Pike and Winona had a key, but maybe Pike had seen Markov and Dobcek coming in. Maybe he'd seen Markov's blood trail leading to the door. Or maybe it was just the pizza man.

Jasper peered through the peephole, then frowned and stepped away from the door. 'I can't see shit.'

If it was Pike, he would make a move.

If it was Pike, the knocking would have been to focus our attention there while he came in from another place.

I looked at Teri and Charles and Dobcek. Dobcek was breathing hard and staring at the door with the kids in front of him and the muzzle of his gun maybe three centimeters from Charles's head. I stood. 'I'd give up, if I were you. It's the cops.' I said it in a normal speaking voice.

Dobcek pointed his gun at me. 'Shut up.'

Markov waved his gun at Dobcek and hissed, 'Make him shut up.'

Something creaked above us, and Dobcek glanced up the stairs, like maybe he'd heard it but wasn't sure. A drop of sweat worked down from his hairline and along his temple.

I spoke even louder. 'What's that smell, Dobcek? You so scared you messed your pants?'

Dobcek took a single step toward me, but he was still between the kids. I wanted him away from them, and thought maybe I could bait him to me. Of course, he might decide to shoot me instead.

I spoke louder still. 'Why don't you chickenshits just open the door and see who it is?' I took a step toward Markov. 'Christ, you want me to do it?'

Markov hissed angrily at Dobcek, 'Make him be silent, goddamn you.'

Dobcek surged past Charles and Teri, and put his gun to my head. He clamped his hand over my mouth and kept the gun there and smiled horribly. His face was red, and his snow-blond buzz cut stood sharp and spike-like up from his head. 'When this is done I will kill you slow.'

I caught Teri's eye and snapped a glance at the floor. She grabbed Charles and pushed him down.

Everything in the room was focused on the door when Markov wet his lips and told Jasper, 'Open it.'

Jasper threw open the door, but no one was there

except Winona's little troll, hanging over the peephole. It looked angry.

Jasper blinked. 'What the hell?'

A shadow flicked at the top of the stairs and Alexei Dobcek must've caught the move because I felt him tense a tenth of a second before Joe Pike shot him once through the temple and Dobcek collapsed away from me as the pressure wave and burnt powder residue blew past me like a hot rain.

Jasper jerked at the blast, but I was already moving. I put my shoulder into Markov, twisted the gun out of his hand, then shot Jasper three times, knocking him through the open door and out into the breezeway, shooting until he was over and out and gone.

When I turned back to Markov, Joe Pike was on him. Markov was still on the floor, confused and blinking up at us, profoundly surprised at how fast his life had taken a downward turn. I said, 'Close.'

Pike shrugged with an absolute lack of expression. 'Not even.'

That Pike is something.

The Hewitts were fine. I said, 'Clark, why don't you make a citizen's arrest, and we'll call the police.'

Pike said, 'Already called them. They're on the way.'

Charles ran over to Markov and kicked him. 'A-hole!' Pike had to lift Charles away to get him to stop.

The police didn't get there in time.

Little by little the angry wolf hunger drained from Andrei Markov's eyes and he was gone. Bled to death before the police arrived.

Pike went out and brought in Winona. He'd put her in his Jeep after he called the cops.

I put my arms around the Hewitt family, and I told them that it was over, and this time it was.

CHAPTER 37

The courtyard and the sidewalk by the street filled with police and gawkers, and pretty soon a news crew from the local ABC affiliate showed up.

The cops on the scene got pretty tense about finding three bodies, especially when one of the bodies was identified as a U.S. Marshal. I called Marsha Fields, but she was still in Long Beach. I finally reached Emily Thornton, and after she spoke to the lead cop, he was only too happy to accept my version of events. It pays to have friends in high places. When the pizza arrived, Charles ate some and the cops ate the rest. No one else wanted it.

When the lead detective told Clark that he could go, Clark came over and asked if he could speak with me. He looked embarrassed.

I took him aside, and he said, 'What about Dak?'

'Call him tonight and set it up for tomorrow. He'll probably send a limo, he wants the dong so badly.'

He looked at his children. The three of them were standing in a little group under a pine tree by the street. He said, 'Well, I might be down there a couple of days. I don't want to just leave them alone.'

I had to smile when he said it. 'Call me, Clark. They can stay with me.'

Clark looked uncertain, and then he went back to his family and the four of them walked away. Joe drove them home.

I left not long after, stopping at Gelson's for a nice salmon steak and a couple of fresh baking potatoes and a six-pack of Budweiser. I would've preferred Falstaff, but they didn't have it. As in all things, you do what you can.

When I got home I set the coals in my Weber, popped the potatoes in the oven, then took a shower while they cooked. After the shower I called Lucy. It was after eight in Baton Rouge by the time I called, and she answered on the second ring. I said, 'It's done.'

She asked me about it, of course, and I told her, speaking for most of a half hour as I watched the coals redden, their heat visibly rising in the cooling evening air. Stuart Greenberg had been good at his word, and now, one day after her meeting with him, he had finalized her deal with David Shapiro, the deal that would bring her to Los Angeles and, I hoped, make her a part of my daily life.

When the coals were ripe for the salmon, I told her so, and promised to send her Sunday's real estate section. She said, 'I love you, Elvis.'

'I love you, too, Lucy.'

Just talking to her made me smile.

I doused the salmon with soy sauce, placed it on the grill, and then the phone rang. I thought it might be Lucy calling back, or Joe, or Clark to tell me when he needed me for the kids, but it wasn't. A man's voice said, 'You didn't win anything.'

It was Richard Chenier.

He said, 'You think it's over, but it's not.'

Then he hung up.

I took a deep breath, then went back to the grill and turned the salmon. It dries quickly if you don't watch out.

I could have called Lucy, I suppose, but, as before, I did not. Before, it would have felt like tattling; now, to call her would have given him more weight in our lives than either of us wanted him to have.

I drank the Budweiser and ate the salmon, sitting on my deck in the liquid night, listening to the coyotes singing against the stars and the black cutout shapes of the mountain. Late that night I fell asleep there, thinking how very lucky I was that she loved me and no one else.

As Pike said, we could always kill him later.

CHAPTER 38

That same night, Clark Hewitt told his children of his cancer, and of his limited time on this earth. He later told me that Teri and Charles had taken it the hardest, but that Winona had borne up the best. I hurt for Teri, but I was glad to hear that she had not denied her pain. I thought of it as progress.

By Tuesday of the following week, Clark had printed one hundred million dong for Nguyen Dak and his fellow revolutionaries. His fee was $250,000 in U.S. currency. He was paid with hundred-dollar bills, none of which were counterfeit. Clark checked each bill to make sure. I guess he's sensitive to such things.

The federal government requires you to pay taxes on all income, even income derived from illegal activities like counterfeiting, but Clark had no intention of splitting his money with the feds. His children needed it more than the national debt, the welfare state, or the military-industrial complex. I agreed. I called a friend of mine who is a bank manager, and asked for her assistance. Normally, banks are required to report any cash transaction greater than ten thousand dollars, but I had once helped my friend's husband out of a very bad jam, and now my friend was only too happy to return the favor. She set up a trust account for Clark's children with me as executor, and together we distributed the money in a variety of conservative equity and bond fund vehicles. No report to the government was filed.

Clark offered to pay me, but I refused.

Clark had less than four months to live, and, after carefully weighing the few options available, decided that his children should attend a resident boarding school. Clark asked if I knew about such places, and I said, 'Why don't you have Teri look into it?'

He did, and, after some initial reluctance, Teri researched boarding schools with the same zeal with which she had researched private investigators. She already had her GED, but there's more to learn in school than books.

The following Sunday the five of us drove to a place called the Rutgers Boarding Academy in Ojai, California, an hour and a half northwest of Los Angeles. We took their Saturn. Clark sat in the front with me, and Teri, Charles, and Winona sat in the back. Charles said, 'Can I drive on the way back?'

Teri said, 'Don't be stupid.'

Teri appeared somber on the way out.

It was a beautiful, clear day, and the ranches and farms we passed were green from the spring rains. The Rutgers Academy was in the foothills, and as we turned through the gate and made the long drive toward a cluster of modern buildings, Clark said, 'This is very pretty.'

Winona said, 'Yeah.'

Charles said, 'Do we get to shoot guns?'

Teri leaned forward between the front seats and stared at the approaching buildings. Maybe she knew more deeply than the others that, if they agreed, this would be her home for the next few years. I said, 'Well?'

'They have stables and horses.'

'Uh-huh.' Three girls about Teri's age were walking roan horses along a bridle path.

'There's supposed to be tennis courts and a pool.'

'I'm sure they'll show us.'

The headmaster was a soft-spoken man in his fifties

named Adamson. I had phoned ahead, and he was waiting to show us around. He wasn't waiting alone. An attractive plump woman he introduced as Mrs. Kennedy was with him, along with a couple of sixteen-year-old students, Todd and Kimberly.

We introduced ourselves, and Mrs. Kennedy said, 'Why don't I show Winona the horses? Would you like that, Winona?'

'Yes!'

Kimberly was there to show Charles around, and Todd was there for Teri. Todd said, 'I can tell you anything you want to know about this place. I've been here since I was ten.' Todd looked like Robert Redford, young.

All three Hewitt children went in different directions, and Mr. Adamson said, 'We have a strong peer support program here. They're in good hands.'

Clark said, 'I have a lot of questions.'

'That's why I'm here, Mr. Hewitt. Why don't you and I go inside and discuss your situation.'

Clark went inside with Adamson, and I did, too, but I didn't stay long. I had already discussed Clark's situation with Adamson, as I had discussed fees and contracts. When Teri had first suggested the place I checked it out thoroughly both through the state and on my own. I am not the World's Greatest Detective for nothing.

The Rutgers Boarding Academy had a fine academic reputation, and was known as a safe and nurturing environment. Adamson had a doctorate in education, was married with three children, and had been elected Colorado Teacher of the Year twice before assuming headmaster duties at Rutgers. His record was impeccable. There had never been a charge of any adverse nature filed against the school, or against any of its teachers or employees.

I left Clark to ask his questions and went out into the courtyard and breathed the clean mountain air. A group of kids were sitting in a circle beneath an oak tree that looked five hundred years old, talking and laughing. Parents walked with other kids around the grounds, going to or coming from cars. They probably thought I was a parent, too. I liked this place, but what I liked didn't matter a lot. What mattered was whether or not it was right for Teri and Charles and Winona.

I couldn't see Winona or Charles, but I saw Teri. She and Todd walked out of the stables toward the three girls with the horses. Todd introduced them. The three girls smiled at Teri, and Teri smiled back. They talked for a few minutes, and then the three girls continued on, and Todd and Teri turned toward a group of buildings I figured were classrooms. Todd said something, and Teri laughed. Todd laughed, too, and Teri pushed him. Then they both laughed.

They disappeared into the buildings. A little while later they reappeared and joined me at the car. Todd said, 'Anything else you want to know?'

Teri told him that she didn't think so, and thanked him for showing her around.

'Anytime.' When Todd grinned, he flashed deep dimples.

Teri and I stood together by the car, waiting for the others. I said, 'How do you like it?'

She chewed at her lip. 'It's okay.'

'That guy's kinda cute, huh?'

She turned red and adjusted her glasses.

'Will you come visit us?' She was scared. If I was her, I would probably be scared, too.

'You bet I will. As often as you want.'

She chewed the lip some more, and then she slipped her hand into mine. I gave it a squeeze. 'You're going to be okay, Teri. You're going to be just fine.'

'I know.'

If you have enjoyed
INDIGO SLAM

Don't miss the new thrilling
novel from Robert Crais
THE SENTRY

Available in Orion paperback
Price: £6.99

New Orleans
2005

MONDAY, 4:28 A.M., the narrow French Quarter room was smoky with cheap candles that smelled of honey. Daniel stared through broken shutters and shivering glass up the length of the alley, catching a thin slice of Jackson Square through curtains of gale-force rain that swirled through New Orleans like mad bats riding the storm. Daniel had never seen rain fall up before.

Daniel loved these damned hurricanes. He folded back the shutters, then opened the window. Rain hit him good. It tasted of salt and smelled of dead fish and weeds. The cat-five wind clawed through New Orleans at better than a hundred miles an hour, but back here in the alley—in a cheap one-room apartment over a po'boy shop—the wind was no stronger than an arrogant breeze.

The power in this part of the Quarter had gone out almost an hour ago; hence, the candles Daniel found in the manager's office. Emergency lighting fed by battery packs lit a few nearby buildings, giving a creepy blue glow to the shimmering walls. Most everyone in the surrounding buildings had gone. Not everyone, but most. The stubborn, the helpless, and the stupid had stayed.

3

Like Daniel's friend, Tolley.

Tolley had stayed.

Stupid.

And now here they were in an empty building surrounded by empty buildings in an outrageous storm that had forced more than a million people out of the city, but Daniel kinda dug it. All this noise and all this emptiness, no one to hear Tolley scream.

Daniel turned from the window, arching his eyebrows.

"You smell that? That's what zombies smell like, brought up from the dead with an unnatural life. You get to see a zombie?"

Tolley was between answers right now, being tied to the bed with thirty feet of nylon cord. His head just kinda hung there, all swollen and broken, though he was still breathing. Every once in a while he would lurch and shiver. Daniel didn't let Tolley's lack of responsiveness stop him.

Daniel sauntered over to the bed. Cleo and Tobey shuffled out of the way, letting him pass.

Daniel had a syringe pack in his bag, along with some poppers, meth, and other choice pharmaceuticals. He took out the kit, shot up Tolley with some crystal, then waited for it to take effect. Outside, something exploded with a muffled *whump* that wasn't quite lost in the wind. Power transformer, probably, giving up the ghost, or maybe a wall falling over.

Tolley's eyes flickered amid a sudden fury of blinks, then dialed into focus. He tried to pull away when he saw Daniel, but, really, where could he go?

Daniel said, all serious, "I asked you, you seen a zombie? They got'm here in this place, I know for a fact."

Tolley shook his head, which kinda pissed Daniel off. On his way to New Orleans six days earlier, having been sent to find Tolley based upon an absolutely

4

spot-on lead, Daniel decided this was his one pure and good chance to see a zombie. Daniel could not abide a zombie, and found their existence offensive. The dead should stay dead, and not rise to walk again, all shamblin' and vile and slack. He didn't care for vampires, either, but zombies just rubbed him the wrong way. Daniel had it on good authority that New Orleans held quite a few zombies, and maybe a vampire or two.

"Don't be like that, Tolliver. New Orleans is supposed to have zombies, don't it, what with all this hoodoo and shit you got here, them zombies from Haiti? You musta seen something?"

Tolley's eyes were bright with meth, the one eye, the left, a glossy red ball what with the burst veins.

Daniel wiped the rain from his face, and felt all tired.

"Where is she?"

"I swear I doan know."

"You kill her? That what you been tryin' to say?"

"No!"

"She tell you where they goin'?"

"I don't know nuthin' about—"

Daniel hammered his fist straight down on Tolley's chest, and scooped up the Asp. The Asp was a collapsible steel rod almost two feet long. Daniel brought it down hard, lashing Tolley's chest, belly, thighs, and shins with a furious beating. Tolley screamed and jerked at his binds, but no one was left to hear. Daniel let him have it for a long time, then tossed aside the Asp and returned to the window. Tobey and Cleo scrambled out of his way.

"I wanna see a goddamned zombie. A zombie, vampire, *something* to make this fuckin' trip worthwhile."

The rain blew in hard, hot and salty as blood. Daniel didn't care. Here he was, come all this way, and not a zombie to be found. Anything was good, Daniel missed out. A life of miserable disappointments.

He looked at Tobey and Cleo. They were difficult to see in the flickery light, all blurry and smudged, but he could make them out well enough.

"Bet I could kill me a zombie, one on one, straight up, and I'd like to try. You think I could kill me a zombie?"

Neither Tobey nor Cleo answered.

"I ain't shittin', I could take me a zombie. Take me a vampire, too, only here we are and I gotta waste my time with this lame shit. I'd rather be huntin' zombies."

He pointed at Tolley.

"Hey, boy."

Daniel returned to the bed and shook Tolley awake.

"You think I could take me a zombie, head up, one on one?"

The red eye rolled, and blood leaked from the shattered mouth. A mushy hiss escaped, so Daniel leaned closer. Sounded like the fucker was finally openin' up.

"Say what?"

Tolley's mouth worked as he tried to speak.

Daniel smiled encouragingly.

"You hear that wind? I was a bat, I'd spread my wings and ride that sumbitch for all she was worth. Where'd they go, boy? I know she tol' ya. You tell me where they went so I can get outta here. Just say it. You're almost there. Give me a hand, and I'm out your hair."

Tolley's lips worked, and Daniel knew he was about to give it, but then what little air he had left hissed out.

"You say west? They was headed west? Over to Texas?"

Tolley was dead.

Daniel stared at the body for a moment, then drew his gun and put five bullets into Tolliver James's chest. Nasty explosions that anyone staying behind would have heard even with the lion wind. Daniel didn't give a damn. If someone came running, Daniel figured to shoot them, too, but nobody came—no police, no neighbors, no nobody. Everyone with two squirts of brain juice was hunkered down tight, trying to survive.

Daniel reloaded, tucked away his gun, then took out the satellite phone. The cell stations were out all over the city, but the sat phone worked great. He checked the time, hit the speed dial, then waited for a link. It always took a few seconds.

In that time, he stood taller, straightened himself, and resumed his normal manner.

When the connection was made, Daniel reported.

"Tolliver James is dead. He didn't provide anything useful."

Daniel listened for a moment before responding.

"No, sir, they're gone. That much is confirmed. James was a good bet, but I don't believe she told him anything."

He listened again, this time for quite a while.

"No, sir, that is not altogether true. There are three or four people here I'd still like to talk to, but the storm has turned this place to shit. They've almost certainly evacuated. I just don't know. It will take me a while to locate them."

More chatter from the other side, but then they were finished.

"Yes, sir, I understand. You get yours, I get mine. I won't let you down."

A last word from the master.

"Yes, sir. Thank you. I'll keep you informed."

Daniel shut the phone and put it away.

"Asshole."

He returned to the window, and let the rain lash him. Everything was wet now: shirt, pants, shoes, hair, all the way down to his bones. He leaned out, better to see the Square. A fifty-five-gallon oil drum tumbled past the alley's mouth, end over end, followed by a bicycle, swept along on its side, and then a shattered sheet of plywood flipping and soaring like a playing card tossed out like trash.

Daniel shouted into the wind as loud as he could.

"C'mon and get me, you fuckin' zombies! Show your true and unnatural colors."

Daniel threw back his head and howled. He barked like a dog, then howled again before turning back to the room to pack up his gear. Tobey and Cleo were gone.

Tolliver had hidden eight thousand dollars under the mattress, still vacu-packed in plastic, which Daniel found when he first searched the room. Probably a gift from the girl. Daniel stashed the money in his bag, checked to make sure Tolliver had no pulse, then went to the little bathroom where he'd left Tolliver's lady friend after he strangled her, nice and neat in the tub. A little black stream of ants had already found her, not even a day.

Cleo said, "Gotta get going, Daniel. Stop fuckin' around."

Tobey said, "Go where, a storm like this? Makes sense to stay."

Daniel decided Tobey was right. Tobey was the smart one, and usually right, even if Daniel couldn't always see him.

"Okay, I guess I should wait till the worst is over."

Tobey said, "Wait."

Cleo said, "Wait, wait."

Like echoes fading away.

Daniel returned to the window. He leaned out into the rain again, watching the mouth of the alley in case a zombie rattled past.

"C'mon, goddamnit, lemme see one. One freaky-ass zombie is all I ask."

If a zombie appeared, Daniel planned to jump out

the window after it and rip its putrid, unnatural flesh to pieces with his teeth. He was, after all, a werewolf, which was why he was such a good hunter and killer. Werewolves feared nothing.

Daniel tipped back his head and howled to match the wind, then doused the candles and sat with the bodies, waiting for the storm to pass.

When it ended, Daniel would find their trail, and track them, and he would not quit until they were his. No matter how long it took or how far they ran. This was why the men down south used him for these jobs and paid him so well.

Werewolves caught their prey.

Los Angeles
Now

THE WIND DID NOT WAKE HIM. It was the dream. He heard the buffeting wind before he opened his eyes, but the dream was what woke him on that dark early morning. A cat was his witness. Hunkered at the end of the bed, ears down, a low growl in its chest, a ragged black cat was staring at him when Elvis Cole opened his eyes. Its warrior face was angry, and, in that moment, Cole knew they had shared the nightmare.

Cole woke on the bed in his loft bathed in soft moonlight, feeling his A-frame shudder as the wind tried to push it from its perch high in the Hollywood Hills. A freak weather system in the Midwest was pulling fifty- to seventy-knot winds from the sea that had hammered Los Angeles for days.

Cole sat up, awake now and wanting to shake off the dream—an ugly nightmare that left him feeling unsettled and depressed. The cat's ears stayed down. Cole held out his hand, but the cat poured off the bed like a pool of black ink.

Cole said, "Me, too."

He checked the time. Habit. Three-twelve in the A.M. He reached toward the nightstand to check his gun—habit—but stopped himself when he realized what he was doing.

"C'mon, what's the point?"

The gun was there because it was always there, sometimes needed but most times not. Living alone with only an angry cat for company, there seemed no reason to move it. Now, at three-twelve in the middle of a wind-torched night, it was a reminder of what he had lost.

Cole realized he was trembling, and pushed out of bed. The dream scared him. Muzzle flash so bright it sparkled his eyes; the charcoal smell of smokeless powder; a glittery red mist that dappled his skin; shattered sunglasses that arced through the air—images so vivid they shocked him awake.

Now he shook as his body burned off the fear.

The back of Cole's house was an A-shaped glass steeple, giving him a view of the canyon behind his house and a diamond-dust glimpse of the city beyond. Now, the canyon was blue with bright moonlight. The sleeping houses below were surrounded by blue-and-gray trees that shivered and danced in the St. Vitus wind. Cole wondered if someone down there had awakened like him. He wondered if they had suffered a similar nightmare—seeing their best friend shot to death in the dark.

Violence was part of him.

Elvis Cole did not want it, seek it, or enjoy it, but maybe these were only things he told himself in cold moments like now. The nature of his life had cost him the woman he loved and the little boy he had grown to love, and left him alone in this house with nothing but an angry cat for company and a pistol that did not need to be put away.

Now here was this dream that left his skin crawling—so real it felt like a premonition. He looked at the phone and told himself no—no, that's silly, it's stupid, it's three in the morning.

Cole made the call.

One ring, and his call was answered. At three in the morning.

"Pike."

"Hey, man."

Cole didn't know what to say after that, feeling so stupid.

"You good?"

Pike said, "Good. You?"

"Yeah. Sorry, man, it's late."

"You okay?"

"Yeah. Just a bad feeling is all."

They lapsed into a silence Cole found embarrassing, but it was Pike who spoke first.

"You need me, I'm there."

"It's the wind. This wind is crazy."

"Uh-huh."

"Watch yourself."

He told Pike he would call again soon, then put down the phone.

Cole felt no relief after the call. He told himself he should, but he didn't. The dream should have faded, but it did not. Talking to Pike now made it feel even more real.

You need me, I'm there.

How many times had Joe Pike placed himself in harm's way to save him?

They had fought the good fight together, and won, and sometimes lost. They had shot people who had harmed or were doing harm, and been shot, and Joe Pike had saved Cole's life more than a few times like an archangel from Heaven.

Yet here was the dream and the dream did not fade—

Muzzle flashes in a dingy room. A woman's shadow

cast on the wall. Dark glasses spinning into space. Joe Pike falling through a terrible red mist.

Cole crept downstairs through the dark house and stepped out onto his deck. Leaves and debris stung his face like sand on a windswept beach. Lights from the houses below glittered like fallen stars.

In low moments on nights like this when Elvis Cole thought of the woman and the boy, he told himself the violence in his life had cost him everything, but he knew that was not true. As lonely as he sometimes felt, he still had more to lose.

He could lose his best friend.

Or himself.